Here's what critics [say about]
Gemma Halliday's Wine & Dine Mysteries:

"I rank *A Sip Before Dying* as one of my favorite fun reads.
I say to Gemma Halliday, well done. She wrote a mystery
that encompassed suspense flavored with romantic notions,
while giving us a heroine to make us smile."
—*The Book Breeze Magazine*

"Gemma Halliday's signature well-written story filled with
wonderful characters is just what I expected. All in all, this
is the beginning of a great cozy series no one should miss!"
—*Kings River Life Magazine*

"I've always enjoyed the writing style and comfortable tone
of Gemma novels and this one fits in perfectly. From the
first page, the author pulled me in...when all was said and
done, I enjoyed this delightfully engaging tale and I can't
wait to spend more time with Emmy, Ava and their
friends."
—*Dru's Book Musings*

"This is a great cozy mystery, and I highly recommend it!"
—*Book Review Crew*

"I could not put *A Sip Before Dying* by Gemma Halliday
down. Once I started reading it, I was hooked!!"
—*Cozy Mystery Book Reviews*

BOOKS BY GEMMA HALLIDAY

High Heels Mysteries
Spying in High Heels
Killer in High Heels
Undercover in High Heels
Christmas in High Heels
(short story)
Alibi in High Heels
Mayhem in High Heels
Honeymoon in High Heels
(short story)
Sweetheart in High Heels
(short story)
Fearless in High Heels
Danger in High Heels
Homicide in High Heels
Deadly in High Heels
Suspect in High Heels
Peril in High Heels
Jeopardy in High Heels

Wine & Dine Mysteries
A Sip Before Dying
Chocolate Covered Death
Victim in the Vineyard
Marriage, Merlot & Murder
Death in Wine Country
Fashion, Rosé & Foul Play
Witness at the Winery

Hollywood Headlines Mysteries
Hollywood Scandals
Hollywood Secrets
Hollywood Confessions
Hollywood Holiday
(short story)
Hollywood Deception

Marty Hudson Mysteries
Sherlock Holmes and the Case
of the Brash Blonde
Sherlock Holmes and the Case
of the Disappearing Diva
Sherlock Holmes and the Case
of the Wealthy Widow

Tahoe Tessie Mysteries
Luck Be A Lady
Hey Big Spender
Baby It's Cold Outside
(holiday short story)

Jamie Bond Mysteries
Unbreakable Bond
Secret Bond
Bond Bombshell
(short story)
Lethal Bond
Dangerous Bond
Bond Ambition
(short story)
Fatal Bond
Deadly Bond

Hartley Grace Featherstone Mysteries
Deadly Cool
Social Suicide
Wicked Games

Other Works
Play Dead
Viva Las Vegas
A High Heels Haunting
Watching You (short story)
Confessions of a Bombshell
Bandit (short story)

VICTIM
IN THE
VINEYARD

a Wine & Dine mystery

GEMMA HALLIDAY

Dedicated to Tom, who will one day appreciate my cooking.

CHAPTER ONE

I pulled my soufflé from the oven and groaned. Its sides were burnt, and the middle had collapsed, leaving it flat, dense, and looking more like a flopped pancake than a light, airy French delicacy.

"What's cookin', good lookin'?" my best friend, Ava Barnett, asked, coming into the kitchen on a cloud of peachy lotion and subtle jasmine incense. She had on a flowy off-the-shoulder top in a pale blue chiffon that matched her eyes, and her blonde hair was braided and twirled onto her head like some sort of halo. She peeked over my shoulder. "Pancakes?"

"It was supposed to be a soufflé."

"Ouch." She scrunched up her nose. "Bummer."

"I must have had the temperature wrong," I mused, more to myself than her as I checked the oven. Warm...but not necessarily as warm as it should have been. Great—my oven was on the fritz. Which matched my dishwasher that was on the fritz, my stand mixer that was on the fritz, and my oversized refrigerator that was currently barely working but I was sure was fritz-imminent. My mother had converted the old storeroom into a modern commercial kitchen fifteen years ago, with the hopes that having the ability to prepare gourmet meals on-site would make our little family run Oak Valley Vineyards a more enticing place to hold weddings and corporate events. And it had, for a short time, until my mother had become sick and everything at Oak Valley—including our kitchen appliances—had started to fall into decline.

But those memories were as sad as my soufflé, and I quickly shut them down. Today of all days, I needed to remain optimistic.

"Well, at least the brownies turned out okay," I said, trying to focus on the positive. I shot Ava my best try at an optimistic smile.

"What on earth was that grimace for?" she asked.

"Optimism?"

Ava laughed, a light tinkling thing that floated through the air. "Oh Emmy, if that's optimism, I'd hate to see you on a pessimistic day."

I didn't have time to make a snappy comeback, as the kitchen doors flew open again, my winery manager, Eddie, swinging through them.

"Good morning, my beautiful sunshines!" he sang as he practically danced across the worn tiles. "The birds are singing, the grapes are ripening, and the breeze through the trees is warm and fresh as a daisy!"

"Now *that's* how you do optimism," Ava said, grinning as she slipped onto a kitchen stool and stole one of my well turned out brownies.

"Good morning, Eddie," I said, ignoring Ava's playful jab. "How does the tasting room look?"

"Stocked to the gills with our finest wines!" He grinned, his entire pudgy face lighting up. Eddie Bliss had come to work for me a few months ago when I'd been desperate to fill the position. After years of living as a househusband, Eddie had acquired zero skills as a winery operator, but he'd been friendly, eager to learn, and, most importantly, willing to work for what I could afford to pay. Which was admittedly not much. Eddie was just a shade taller than my own 5'6", had ears that were made for a man twice his size, and was one of the snappiest dressers I'd ever seen, even if his partner, Curtis, did try to tone him down a bit. Today, though, it appeared Eddie had won the war of the wardrobe, opting for a pair of pressed checked pants, a matching blazer, and a bright blue shirt, topped off with a red bow tie. I wasn't sure if he was ready to sell wine or sing in a barbershop quartet, but I forced my optimism theme front and center.

"Very nice tie," I told him.

Eddie beamed. "Why thank you. Curtis gave it to me for Father's Day."

I stifled a laugh. I knew the only "child" Curtis and Eddie had was a Pomeranian named Winky. "How are things outside? Vendors still setting up?"

"Yes, but just putting on the finishing touches. Conchita is arranging the tasting plates in the dining pavilion, Jean Luc has glasses of Pinot Blanc at the ready, and Hector is prepping the stage for our cooking demonstration with Tyler." Eddie ticked off each of my staff's locations as he spoke, easing my tense mood a bit.

We were gearing up to host the Sonoma Fall Food and Wine Festival, featuring booths from local restaurants, up-and-coming chefs, and even a few tables from local artists, like Ava's Silver Girl display featuring handmade jewelry from her shop. And of course alongside it all we'd be serving the wines my family had been making at the vineyard for years: Chardonnay, Zinfandel, Pinot Noir, Pinot Blanc, and small runs of Petite Sirah. My vineyard manager, Hector, had diligently been preparing for the event for weeks, transforming our large meadow into a small village of culinary delights and local artisans.

And thanks to my sommelier, Jean Luc, being six degrees of separation from the TV celebrity chef Tyler Daniels, we'd been able to convince Daniels to act as MC for the four-day festival. Tyler was a wine country native who'd made good, becoming the star of several Cooking Network shows, including his latest, *Eat Up*. While his flagship restaurant was here in his hometown of Sonoma, he now owned a chain of Tyler's Place restaurants, including locations in Chicago, Los Angeles, and Atlanta. On his fame alone, we'd been able to sell out tickets for the event, and we were looking to draw a small crowd. One that I hoped enjoyed the wine enough to tell a friend about us and bring our revenue into the black so I could fix our fritzy appliances.

"Sounds like all the festival is missing is the host," Ava said, nodding toward me as she nibbled on her brownie. "Time to go get dressed for your public, Miss Oak."

I glanced down at the jeans and navy blouse I was wearing. "I am dressed."

Both Ava and Eddie stared at me as if I'd suggested we pair our Petite Sirah with fish tacos.

"What?" I asked. "This is a designer silk blouse." Which was met with more stares of disbelief. Okay, so the designer was Target, and it had been on sale. But it *was* silk.

"I'm doing casual chic," I informed them.

Eddie clucked his tongue and shook his head.

"Honey, do you think Gabby will be doing casual anything?" Ava asked.

She was referring to Tyler Daniels' sidekick on the television show *Eat Up* and our co-MC for the event, Gabriela Genova. She was known for her delectable Italian cooking, her warm Italian personality, and her sultry Italian looks that were usually encased in something tight and cleavage enhancing. I'd never seen the woman without a three-inch pair of heels on, and I'm pretty sure she was born wearing false eyelashes and cherry red lipstick.

"No," I admitted. "I don't think Gabby does casual."

"So, do you want to stand next to *her* for press photos wearing *that*?" Ava reasoned.

I sighed. "Fine. I'll go change."

Eddie shot my jeans—which may or may not have had a small hole in the left knee—a nervous glance before turning to Ava. "Maybe you'd better supervise."

* * *

Under Ava's watchful eye, I swapped my jeans for a flattering fit and flare lavender dress and a pair of low-heeled Grecian sandals. I added a little extra mascara and blush just for good measure before adorning my ears with a pair of silver hoops of Ava's creation. While her style might be a bit more boho than mine in the clothing department, she knew my taste in jewelry to a tee. In fact, Ava knew most everything about me to a tee, having been my bestie since childhood. Some people even thought we looked alike, though my blonde hair tended a bit more toward the frizzy side than Ava's smooth locks, and my hips might betray the fact that I liked soufflé a bit more than my lithe, athletic looking friend. But by the time the first guests started arriving, we both looked ready to face the hordes of wine enthusiasts (still working that optimism thing) who would soon descend upon our little winery.

As the tourists and weekenders started perusing our stalls, Ava and I did the same, walking among them to make sure all was running smoothly. Hector had set the booths up like a small village, two wide aisles of wares winding toward the center of the meadow, where he'd constructed a low stage that would house the twice daily cooking demonstrations by our celebrity guests. A variety of tempting scents wafted through the warm, morning air—sweet confections mingling with the savory tang of onions and garlic sautéing on portable cooktops. I heard several murmurs of approval and even a few groans of pleasure as foodies began sampling the chefs' creations, giving kudos on seasoning and spice. Everyone seemed to be enjoying themselves, and my nerves ticked down a notch.

Until I heard a shrill female voice carrying over the din of the crowd.

"I cannot work like this. This air is too dry. I can feel it zapping the moisture from my skin!"

"Is that Gabby?" Ava gently tugged on my arm, pointing toward the center stage where several pots, pans, and utensils sat atop of a long, low counter, ready for the first demo of the day.

Riffling through them was the female half of our celebrity chef duo, waving her arms at the young man standing next to her wearing a harried expression. As suspected, Gabby was dressed to the nines in a bright red, body hugging dress that ended well above her knee and dipped far below the modesty level in the front. Her perfectly tanned legs ended in spiky red stilettos that looked in danger of sinking into the dirt the second she stepped down from the stage.

"Why didn't anyone tell me we'd be outside?" she complained. "There are *bugs*!"

"This should be fun," I mumbled to Ava before pasting a bright smile on my face. "Hi. Gabriela Genova?" I asked, approaching the woman.

She gave me a blank look. "Sorry, no autographs."

I cleared my throat and thought I heard Ava snicker behind me.

"Uh, actually my name is Emmy Oak. We spoke on the phone. I'm the owner of the winery." Technically my family owned it, but with Dad gone and Mom losing more of herself day by day, I was the only Oak left to pull it up from its sinking bottom line. But I figured Gabby didn't need details. "Do you have everything you need for the demonstration?" I asked her.

"Well, finally someone comes to check on us. And no, I don't have everything I need, thank you very much."

"Is there something I can get for you?"

"I'm sorry, but this weather doesn't work for me."

"Th-the weather?" I looked up at the thankfully cloudless blue sky above us. While it was warm still, not yet having hit the chill of autumn, the majestic oak trees surrounding the meadow gave enough shade that it felt pleasantly sunny rather than sweltering as our summer had been.

"Yes," Gabby said, repeating herself. "The weather. My skin is dry, and my hair is lifeless. Look at it. Flat!" She ran a hand through her long dark hair that many women would kill for.

"I told you, you look great, babe," the young man beside her piped up. While he was several inches over six feet, he appeared at least a few years younger than Gabby, maybe in his midtwenties at the latest. He had a smooth baby face, a hard gym-dedicated body, and a shock of blond hair that fell over his forehead in a stylish cut. He shot me a wide smile, showing off a lot of white teeth and a cute little dimple in his right cheek. "I'm the boyfriend. Alec Post," he said, offering his hand.

The name clicked immediately. "You have that cooking webcast, right?" I asked as I shook his hand. "The Digest?"

If it was possible his smile widened. "Yes. You've seen it?"

I nodded. "Several times in fact. It's a fun show." While it was aimed more at the millennial audience with things like liquid nitrogen ice cream and pizza inspired ramen bowls, Alec's fresh take on food was actually quite entertaining.

"Well, unless someone can do something about the weather, *this* is not going to be a fun show today," Gabby whined, pulling my attention back to her.

"Babe, no one can control the weather," Alec reasoned.

"But no one told me it would be bone dry here!" Gabby shot back.

I'd had to wage a battle against my own frizz, just barely winning with the help of an army of hair products, so I'd hardly call it bone dry. But I was happy to report I kept the smile pasted on my face as I responded. "I'm so sorry. Can I get you a bottle of water perhaps?"

She blinked at me as if I were stupid. "I need a humidifier."

"A…" I trailed off, wondering where we'd get one of those.

"Hi, I'm Ava," my best friend jumped in, sticking her slim hand out toward Gabby. "You are amazing. I'm a huge fan!" she gushed.

Gabby acknowledged my friend for the first time, flashing her a sunny smile. Apparently playing to her ego was all you needed to get one.

"Thank you," Gabby answered. "You watch *Eat Up*?"

"Every morning at 8 a.m.," Ava replied. "Your banter with Tyler is almost as delish as the recipes you two cook."

Gabby smiled again. "I appreciate that. But, as you know, Tyler does most of the cooking."

"Oh, but my favorites are the recipes you bring from your family's life in the Italian countryside. You're so talented at weaving a story with the food."

"Tell that to my network." Gabriela laughed sarcastically.

"What are you planning to make today?" Ava asked. I could have kissed her for seemingly defusing the diva.

"Easy Mediterranean Chicken." She paused, the smile dropping. "*If* Tyler ever decides to make an appearance."

"Wait—Tyler's not here yet?" I asked, a small surge of panic hitting my belly. He was the main draw of the event, and I knew I'd have a mob of angry foodies on my hands if he was a no-show.

Gabby shrugged. "He hasn't graced me with his presence. Now about that humidifier…?"

"I'll see if I can find one," Ava promised her.

I mouthed a silent *thank you* in her direction before leaving Gabby and Alec to search for our star.

As I wove through the stalls again, I noticed the crowd had grown, including not only tourists but also several Sonoma locals and a few food critics and bloggers. I spied Bradley Wu, a syndicated food columnist who often covered the wine country scene, and I prayed that he enjoyed our Chardonnay pairings as he tipped his wineglass back, only spilling a slight dribble down the front of his tweed jacket.

What I did not spy was Tyler Daniels. Having searched the entire festival grounds, I left the meadow and made for the collections of low, Spanish style buildings that made up Oak Valley Vineyards. I walked into what I was delighted to see was a packed tasting room. Our sommelier, Jean Luc, was pouring with flourish, laying his French accent on as thick as the wax he used in his mustache. If Hercules Poirot had a slimmer, fussier, cousin from Paris, Jean Luc would be it. He was currently putting on a show for a woman in a tasteful little black dress and dark hair cut short in a stylish bob. As he slid the glass along the bar to her, I caught his attention.

"You haven't seen Tyler Daniels, have you?" I asked.

He shook his head, his slick black mustache twitching. "No, *mon amie*. Why do you ask?"

"He's…" I paused, hating to admit our star was missing. "…late," I decided on.

The woman at the bar must have overheard, as she snorted loudly. "Typical Tyler."

"Uh, Emmy, zees eez Ashley Daniels," Jean Luc said, making introductions.

"Charmed," the woman said, holding her drink up in a greeting that jangled the gold bracelets at her wrists.

"Pleased to meet you," I told her. "You said Daniels? Any relation to Tyler?"

"I have the unfortunate distinction of being his first wife. *Ex*, that is," she added with emphasis.

"I see," I said, not sure if I should congratulate her or sympathize with her.

"Ashley eez also a food critic," Jean Luc told me, sending me a meaningful look. "For zee *LA Times*."

"Oh, I *see*," I told him.

"Yes, I heard about your little shindig here, and I thought, why not treat myself to a weekend in wine country?" she said. Then she winked at me. "On the paper's dime, of course."

"Well, I hope you're enjoying our Pinot Blanc."

"It's delightful. Like drinking sunshine," she said, her words slurring slightly, as if perhaps she'd been in the sun just a bit *too* long. Which I took as a good sign, as long as the words "light" and "fresh" ended up in her review in the *LA Times*.

"You haven't heard from Tyler today, have you?" I asked them both again.

Jean Luc shook his head.

"Sorry," Ashley told me, "but I try to hear from my ex-husband as little as possible." She sent me another wink.

"Understandable," I agreed. "We're set to start the demo in half an hour, and I'm just getting a little nervous."

"Don't be," Ashley assured me. "Trust me, if there is any chance of attention, Tyler will be here. He never misses an opportunity to preen for an adoring crowd." She ended the comment with sarcastic *ha* at her own joke.

"I hope so," I said, excusing myself to continue my search.

I stepped out the main entrance to the front of the winery, where large, centuries old oak trees created a canopy of shade over a small gravel parking lot and long, winding driveway. Our spot on a small hill overlooking the valley was tucked away enough from the main road to feel like a hidden oasis yet was still a short, pleasant drive from downtown Sonoma, which I hoped many foodies and enthusiasts were willing to make today.

I spotted Eddie standing next to the carved wooden sign touting our winery's name, adjusting his bowtie as he played greeter to guests as they trekked from our parking lot to the festival site.

"We're getting a fair crowd," he told me, smiling and waving at a young couple with a baby in a carrier.

"That's good news," I told him. "But the bad news is we're missing our star."

Eddie turned to me. "I thought I saw Gabby arrive earlier. She was with this delish little boy toy with dimples." He paused, quickly covering his mouth with a pudgy hand. "Oh, don't tell Curtis I said that. He's got a wicked jealous streak ever since I made the mistake of saying I thought Derek Hough looked hot on *Dancing with the Stars*."

Despite my worried mood, I couldn't help a grin. "Your secret's safe with me. But I don't suppose you've seen our *other* star, Tyler Daniels?"

Eddie nodded. "As a matter of fact, I believe that's him arriving now."

I followed the line of his well manicured finger to see a man in his midforties stepping out of a Ferrari and running a hand through his trademark shock of red hair styled in an old fashioned pompadour. He wore jeans and a white T-shirt in a deceptively casual style and took a moment to survey the crowded lot before taking his mirrored aviator glasses off.

I felt relief flood me as I rushed forward to greet him.

"Mr. Daniels," I called.

His gaze turned my way, his blue eyes even brighter in person than they sparkled on TV.

"Emmy Oak," I introduced myself, approaching. "I'm the owner and coordinator of the festival. Thank you so much for being here."

"Let's make this quick, huh, doll," Tyler said, gaze going somewhere beyond me as if completely disinterested. "I'm not here to chitchat."

I cleared my throat, glossing over the whole "doll" thing. "Uh, right. Well, we're setting up for the first demo now, and it's about to start, so let me show you—"

"Yeah, we'll be postponing that."

"Excuse me?"

He shot me an annoyed look. "Do I look ready for a demo right now? Huh? Do I?"

"I-I'm not sure," I stammered. While I knew Tyler Daniels was known for his hotheaded persona on TV, I hadn't expected to bear the wrath of it before even making it out of the parking lot.

"Where can I put my trailer?" he demanded, crossing his arms over his chest as he barked at me.

"T-trailer?" I asked. "I'm not sure I—"

But I didn't get to finish as he gestured to the tree lined driveway where a large RV was pulling up. Along the side of the trailer was a huge image of Tyler's face—white veneers grinning for the camera in a much more charming fashion than the scowl I was currently encountering—along with his famous catchphrase, *Now we're cookin' with heat!*

I blinked. "Oh. I didn't realize you planned to stay here."

Tyler threw his head back and laughed, though the tone was more mocking than humor. "Honey, you couldn't pay me to stay *here*."

I tried really hard to keep a placid look on my face at the insult. Not that Tyler seemed to care what effect he had on little ol' me as he rambled on.

"I have a condo in town. Overlooking the *river*," he added for emphasis, lest I should think he lived among the peasants who couldn't afford a water view. "This," he said, gesturing to the monument to his ego, "is just to give me somewhere to escape my fans."

I sighed. His own trailer. Of course.

"So," he continued. "Where can my crew set up?"

"Crew? You brought a camera crew too?"

Tyler shook his head, frowning at me. "No, this is my *hair and makeup* crew." He paused. "You didn't expect me to go on without my stylists?" He did a smirk that said I was so naïve in the ways of the televised and famous.

"No. Of course not," I covered. I quickly surveyed the packed lot for anywhere to put the fifty-foot monstrosity. "Um, why don't you have them pull it around the back? We have some space where deliveries unload behind the kitchen."

For a moment I thought he was going to protest the back door placement, the frown deepening, but finally he must have realized space was at a premium, as he just barked out a quick, "Fine." Then he spun and stalked to the RV.

I let out a breath, having diffused the second diva of the day, and asked Eddie to direct the RV around the back of the building as I took over his greeter duties.

* * *

It took Tyler at least half an hour to have hair and makeup release him in the same white T-shirt and jeans, looking almost exactly the way he went into the trailer. Then he required an extra half hour to go over the recipe they'd be demonstrating with Gabby, who complained the entire time about how her makeup was melting in the moisture from the humidifier that Ava had miraculously found. By the time the cooking demo started, we were a good hour behind, but Tyler pulled on a welcoming smile, loud and booming voice, and jovial, humorous banter that had the crowd applauding and *oohing* and *ahhing* at his culinary creations. Gabby's warm laughter floated down to us as she seared the chicken on the grill, and as Tyler tossed a handful of red pepper flakes at the dish and yelled his catchphrase, the audience cheered with delight. For all the headaches, the two stars were consummate professionals on the stage, doing exactly what I had hoped they would to entertain and entice the crowd. I felt my nerves dissipating as the murmurs of approval rang all around me.

Once the demo was over, the crowd applauded heartily before dispersing to enjoy more tasty bites and sip the afternoon away. Tyler retired to his trailer, and Alec was able to convince Gabby to step inside the tasting room to get out of the "wretched outdoors."

The rest of the afternoon went off without a hitch, a couple of local bands taking the stage to play mellow country and then soft jazz as the crowd continued to grow. Tyler emerged from his trailer and camped out in our tasting room, drinking Pinot Noir like it was going out of style. Which I didn't mind in the least—if I was lucky, he'd order a couple of cases. If I was *really* lucky, he might start serving it in his restaurant chain. Ava sold several silver pieces to patrons, a couple of booths were so popular they ran out of food, and even Gabby seemed to enjoy herself, dancing with Alec as the jazz band encouraged amorous couples to gather in front of the stage.

By the time the sun was starting to set, we were ready for our second demo of the night—a final dessert dish to pair with our Zinfandel before the guests made their way home.

The sky was turning a dusky pink, the moon appearing just above the horizon in a pale crescent glow, as I spied Gabby taking the stage. I could see her gesturing her arms wildly at Alec, a frown on her beautiful features. I steeled myself against whatever she had to complain about this time as I approached.

"Gabby," I said, pasting a smile on my face. "The last demo was absolutely fabulous. The crowd loved it."

She blinked at me a moment as if trying to remember who I was before recognition set in. "Well, it should be. Tyler made us rehearse it enough. As if I don't know how to cook chicken breast." She snorted.

"Uh, where is Tyler?" I hated to ask.

Gabby put both hands on her ample hips. "*That* is just what I'd like to know. I swear if that man makes me stand out in the elements waiting again while he preens for an hour, I'll—"

"Maybe you could check his trailer?" Alec cut in, addressing me before Gabby could finish that threat.

"Thanks. On my way," I told him, quickly exiting the stage and leaving him to soothe the savage ego.

I crossed the meadow, coming around the back of the main winery buildings, and spotted the trailer parked under a large tree that just skimmed the roof. A couple of guys with spiky, bleached hair and lots of piercings stood outside of it, smoking cigarettes.

"Is Tyler in there?" I asked who I assumed were his glam squad.

The taller of the two shook his head. "Haven't seen him. We were waiting to freshen up his makeup, but he hasn't showed."

I felt a frown form, praying my star hadn't lost track of time in the tasting room. Just for good measure, I knocked on the trailer door, but it was answered by a slim girl in a hairdresser's apron, who informed me Tyler was not inside. She hadn't seen him since after the last demo.

After making rounds to the tasting room, the dining pavilion, and backtracking through the festival grounds again, I came up empty. I glanced at my phone, noting the time. Ten minutes until our demo was to start. I bit my lip. I wasn't sure guests would stick around if Tyler was an hour late with the final event like he'd been with the first.

I was about to give up and tell Gabby to go ahead solo, when a flash of movement in the vineyard to the left of the meadow caught my eye. The sun was falling lower now, and the landscape was growing dusky, casting shadows among the vines.

"Tyler?" I called out.

While no one answered, I thought I saw another flash of something, just beyond the first row of grapevines.

I followed it, jogging toward the vines, though as I peeked down the row, I saw nothing. I walked a few more paces, going one row over, hoping Tyler had snuck away to memorize lines or take a quiet moment apart from the crowds before his performance.

"Tyler?" I called again. "Tyler, we're about to start the demo."

Nothing but the breeze answered me. I could hear the dull roar of the crowd still, but it sounded far away. The stillness of the vineyard was almost eerie as the light quickly faded, darkness seeming to wrap around me from all angles.

I stepped one more row over.

And then I saw it.

White T-shirt, jeans, and a now-tussled mess of red hair that sat atop a face whose expression was frozen in shock, bright blue eyes staring unblinking up at the night sky.

Tyler Daniels.

And judging by the lifeless stare and pool of blood growing around his still body, he would not be doing any more cooking demonstrations.

Ever again.

CHAPTER TWO

I heard a long, gut-wrenching scream that in hindsight was most certainly mine. Then I felt my legs turn and flee, as if they had a mind of their own and it was telling them in no uncertain terms to run—run as far away from the gruesome scene as possible. I vaguely remembered stumbling back toward the festival grounds and falling into Ava's arms, incoherently babbling about dead bodies and blood.

So much blood.

She'd had the good sense to call 9-1-1 then pour me a glass of Zin and sit me in a chair in a quiet corner as she instructed Jean Luc to calmly start ushering guests out before the police arrived and the festival turned into a crime scene.

It felt like hours before the faint sound of sirens approached, but in reality it was probably more like minutes. As the last festival stragglers unsteadily awaited their Ubers, the sky was suddenly bathed in the red and blue lights of local law enforcement arriving en mass. Uniformed officers swarmed the scene. Ava directed several toward the south vineyard as one young officer in a rumpled uniform and glasses asked for my version of events, electronic tablet open to take notes.

I took deep breaths, trying to calm my thoughts into something at least mildly coherent. I slowly relayed my movements that evening, from looking for our wayward star to finding him very much unable to greet his public. As I replayed the scene, the hairs on my forearms stood at attention and my eyes shut as if they were trying to stop the disturbing image from gushing in.

"Emmy?" I opened them to find a plainclothes detective had joined the young officer.

He was tall, over six feet, and had broad shoulders, dark hair that lay several days past needing a cut along the nape of his neck, and deep brown eyes with small golden flecks that were now staring back at me with a note of concern.

Detective Christopher Grant, Violent Crimes Investigations Unit of the Sonoma County Sheriff's Office.

I'd first encountered Grant a few months ago when we'd had an unfortunate incident in our wine cellar. He'd struck me then as thorough, stoic, and harboring maybe just a little danger beneath the surface. Since then I'd seen some softness peek through that hard shell, and possibly even a little flirtatiousness. The last time I'd seen him was on what was to be our first date, at Ashton's restaurant downtown. Only, we'd just ordered the appetizers when a home invasion had occurred in Petaluma, and Grant had had to cut the evening short. We'd been promising to get together again ever since, neither of our busy schedules quite matching up enough to make it happen.

"I guess all it takes is a dead body to get a second date," I said, trying at humor to cover the fear still making my hands shake even as I held them together in my lap.

The corner of Grant's mouth lifted ever so slightly as he crouched down to meet me eye to eye. "You okay?" he asked, his voice low and deep and feeling more intimate than a detective usually got with his witnesses.

I sighed. "I will be."

He gave me a long look like he was only half convinced, but he nodded. "Good." He stood back up and pulled another chair over to sit beside me. "Can you tell me what happened?"

I took a deep breath, willing myself to relive the whole thing again. "There's not a lot to tell," I said honestly. "Tyler was missing. Then I found him." I paused, swallowing down the image. "Dead in the vineyard. There was a lot of blood." My voice must have betrayed the host of emotions still coursing through me, as Grant put a protective hand on my back. While it was a small gesture, the warmth felt like a beacon of safety.

"How well did you know Tyler?" Grant asked.

"I didn't. I mean, I just met him today. Jean Luc secured him for the event."

"So Jean Luc knew Tyler?"

I nodded. "I think he used to work for him. Years ago in one of his restaurants. Back when Tyler was first starting out on TV."

"Right. Tyler was some sort of celebrity?"

I let out a small laugh. "I take it you don't watch the Cooking Network?"

He shook his head. "Enlighten me."

"Well, Tyler's been the star of the network for a few years. He's had several shows—*Kitchen Battle, On the Chopping Block, Tasty Treats with Tyler.*"

"So this guy was a big deal," he surmised.

"In the foodie world, yeah. His most recent is *Eat Up*, a daily morning show he co-hosts with Gabby."

"That would be Gabriela Genova?" he asked, pulling his notebook out to consult it. Unlike the other officers, Grant still used old school paper. I could see his hastily scratched notes covering the page he flipped to.

"Yes. She and Tyler had a fun banter on the show. I think that's what people tuned in for even more than the recipes."

"And she was here with Tyler today?"

I nodded again. "They did a chicken demonstration together earlier. They were supposed to do a cake presentation tonight and a barbeque thing tomorrow." I bit my lip as it sunk in that those plans were as dead as my MC. No Tyler meant no demos, no presentations, no celebrity draw. Though, I was pretty sure the press would be swarming in droves. I closed my eyes again, thinking of the salacious headline I was sure Bradley Wu was typing up right now. He had a flair for the dramatic, and little was more dramatic than a victim in the vineyard.

"When was the last time you saw Tyler?" Grant asked.

I opened my eyes to find him scribbling down more notes. "I-I'm not really sure. Maybe seven. Eight? He was in the tasting room."

"And you went looking for him when?"

"About an hour later. He was supposed to do another demo soon, and Gabby was afraid he'd be late again, which is when I went looking for him and..." I trailed off, not wanting to go over the rest again.

"Did you see Jean Luc then?"

"What?" I snapped my thought away from Tyler Daniels' dead body and back to present.

"Jean Luc. Did you see him while you were looking for Daniels?"

"I-I don't think so. Why do you ask?" I scanned Grant's expression for any indication of his thoughts, but he had his stony Cop Face on now, all of the previous concern replaced by a blank look that gave away nothing.

"Did you look for Tyler in the tasting room?"

"Yes," I hedged.

"And Jean Luc was there?"

I pursed my lips, thinking back. "No, I didn't see him here. But he was probably in the cellar, grabbing more bottles for tomorrow."

"Did you see him in the cellar?" Grant pressed.

I shook my head slowly. "No, but, I didn't specifically go there either."

"When was the last time you saw Jean Luc at the bar?"

"Maybe eight thirty? It was getting dark, and we'd started pouring the Zinfandel to pair with Tyler's dessert."

"Eight thirty." Grant made a note in his book.

"Whose alibi are you looking for?" I asked point-blank. "Jean Luc's or mine?"

Grant's eyes flickered up to mine. "Did you kill Tyler?"

"No!" I scoffed.

The corner of Grant's mouth ticked up a notch. "I didn't think so."

"But you think Jean Luc did?" I asked, reading between the lines.

Grant drew in a deep breath through his nose, nostril flaring. "Jean Luc and Tyler had a history together."

"The foodie community is small—lots of us have histories together," I countered. "Jean Luc worked for Tyler. But that was a long time ago."

"It was his idea to have Tyler MC this event?"

I nodded slowly. "Yes. Tyler was a big draw. Local boy done good and all." I paused again. "Why?"

"Jean Luc was seen arguing with Tyler this evening."

That stopped me. "He was?"

Grant nodded. "Any idea what it was about?"

I shook my head. "This is the first I'm hearing of it." I wasn't sure if that looked better or worse for Jean Luc. "When was this argument?"

Grant looked at his notes again. "Around seven. Witnesses say Tyler was at the bar, and he and Jean Luc seemed to get into it pretty loudly. Jean Luc was even overheard threatening Tyler."

"No!" I said empathically. "No way. Jean Luc would never hurt a fly."

Grant quirked an eyebrow at me. "He was quoted as saying, 'I'll kill you if you do.'"

I bit my lip. Well that didn't sound good. I almost hated to ask... "If he did what?"

But Grant shrugged. "I don't know yet. That's all that was overheard. So far," he added.

"Look, whatever the argument was about, I'm sure it was just Jean Luc being dramatic. That's his thing. But I know he would never hurt anyone."

"Do you know if he owns a gun?" Grant asked, switching gears.

I sucked in a breath. "Is that what killed Tyler?"

He nodded. "Single GSW to the chest. He would have expired instantly."

Well at least he hadn't suffered, but I still felt myself shiver despite the warm night. "I didn't hear a gunshot," I told him.

"That far off from the festival, with all the noise going on? Even if someone did hear it, it could have easily been mistaken for the pop of a wine cork."

Of which there were plenty that night.

"Jean Luc didn't do this," I repeated.

Which must have come out as small and helpless as I felt in that moment, as Grant's Cop Face softened a bit and his hand went to my back again. "Don't worry. We'll sort it all out," he promised. "In the meantime, maybe you want to have Ava spend the night?"

I nodded. The idea of being alone at the winery that night was not one I relished.

Grant stood, but before he could walk away, I stopped him.

"Uh, about the Food and Wine Festival..."

Grant turned his attention back toward me.

"Are we shut down?" I felt callous even thinking of the event with a man dead. But I knew the vendors and other participants had counted on this publicity as much as I had—not to mention had invested in four days' worth of food and ingredients that would go to waste if we had to close. I hated to let them all down if we didn't need to. Granted, I wasn't even sure anyone would show up after they heard about the death, but I didn't want everyone's hard work to be for nothing.

Grant must have seen the warring emotions in my eyes as he took a beat before answering. "The crime scene is contained to the vineyard. We've sealed Tyler's trailer for now, and we may need access to the surrounding area if forensics deems it necessary, but I don't see a reason to secure the festival grounds."

"So, that's a yes on reopening tomorrow?"

He gave me a tentative nod. "I would ask that your wine steward make himself available for questioning, though."

I bit my lip as I watched Grant turn and join the small gathering of uniformed officers chatting at the bar. The way they kept gesturing at the spot where Jean Luc had spent most of the day was not reassuring. Neither was Grant's thinly veiled "don't leave town" request. I had a bad feeling that my sommelier had suddenly jumped from wine steward to murder suspect.

*　*　*

Ava slept in the guest room of my small cottage at the back of the winery property, and I tossed and turned in my bedroom across the hallway, images of Tyler's smirk, his larger-than-life persona with the crowd, and his lifeless body all swirling together to take over my subconscious. By the time the pale first light of morning came peeking through my curtains, I gave up and threw myself into a hot shower.

In lieu of a good night's sleep, I added extra eyeliner and mascara, completing the look with a pale mauve lipstick that gave my nude lip just a hint of color. I almost reached for a black sheaf dress, but considering the morbid circumstances of our festival, I rejected it, going instead for a sunny yellow sundress and a pair of cork wedges that felt sturdy enough to traverse the grounds while still adding a bit of style to the outfit. I was just securing the small pearl stud earrings that my grandmother and namesake, Grammy Emmeline, had handed down to me, when I heard Ava on the landing outside my door.

I peeked my head out. "Hey, you're up."

"Unfortunately." Ava's usual shampoo commercial perfect hair was matted to one side in a bedhead that was totally social media worthy. "You get much sleep?" she asked.

"Negative." I shoved the backing on my earring and led the way down the stairs to the small living room/kitchen combo. The cottage had been built in my grandfather's time, along with most of the small buildings that comprised our winery— including the tasting room, offices, converted barn that housed our wine production equipment, and The Cave, our wine cellar dug deep in the earth to keep our bottles cool and preserved. My parents had added small upgrades to the cottage over time, but it was still what real estate agents referred to as "cozy." But since the only inhabitants were me, myself, and I, it worked. Especially since the guest room doubled as my overflow closet.

"Coffee?" I asked Ava.

"I'd kill for a cup." She froze, immediately cringing. "Sorry. Poor choice of words."

I shook my head. "It's okay. I have a bad feeling that Tyler's death is all anyone will be talking about today." I crossed to my kitchen counter, where I had a small coffeemaker set up. Normally I took all my meals—including morning coffee—in the large kitchen down the little stone pathway. There was little reason to fuss around in my tiny house when I had a well-appointed (if slightly dilapidated) commercial kitchen just a few steps away. But today, I didn't want to get in the way, as I knew Conchita, our house manager, would be running the kitchen like a drill sergeant to get all of the appetizer trays ready for the guests.

Assuming we had any.

I shoved that thought aside and loaded a pod into the machine, thankful for the instant gratification of hot, aromatic liquid pouring out in response. I handed the first mug to Ava and did a repeat for myself.

"I saw you talking to Grant last night," Ava said as she sipped. "I don't suppose he gave any indication of what happened to Tyler?"

"Gunshot," I said, trying not to picture it.

"Who on earth would have a gun at the festival?" Ava asked, sipping her coffee. "Mmm. Heaven."

I made a cheers motion with my mug. "Ditto." I paused. "But I got the impression that the police think Jean Luc might have had something to do with it."

"No way! Even Grant?"

I nodded, replaying our conversation for her. "You didn't happen to see Jean Luc argue with Tyler, did you?"

She shook her head. "No. I thought they were friends. Didn't Jean Luc used to work for him?"

"In one of his restaurants. But I don't know the details." I sipped again. "Any chance you saw Jean Luc before Tyler was found? Between like eight and nine?"

"You mean, can I provide an alibi?" Ava sipped, her eyes going to the ceiling as she thought. "I was outside watching the sunset for a while with a couple of retirees. I'd just sold them some matching silver rings in a feather motif. Really cute."

I nodded. "I remember those."

"Anyway, after that I took a break to grab some food myself. I stopped at the booth with those stuffed mushrooms. Super yum. I guess that was around, maybe nine? Nine fifteen?"

"So you weren't near the tasting room at all?"

She shook her head. "Sorry. I'm not much help, am I?"

"It's okay," I assured her. "I'm sure someone saw Jean Luc." At least I hoped.

"Have you talked to Gabby yet?" Ava asked. "About the fate of the festival?"

I shook my head. "To be honest, I'm a little conflicted about the whole thing. It feels like we should shut it down in reverence to Tyler, but I hate to put all the vendors out like that."

"Not to mention the guests who have come in from out of town," Ava noted.

I sighed. "If they stay."

"Okay, how about this," Ava offered. "Let's see what kind of turnout we get today. If it's a flop, maybe we close up a couple of days early."

I nodded. "That way the vendors at least have a fighting chance to make back what they've put into their booths."

"And you wouldn't have to refund all of the guests' tickets. Just half."

I inwardly groaned. That was still enough to put us in the red on the entire thing. That coupled with the bad publicity was likely to have my accountant, Gene Schultz, crying in his spreadsheets.

I picked up my phone and dialed Gabby's number. Unfortunately, her cell went to voice mail, but I wasn't sure how to properly express both my condolences and our intent to carry on as planned in a thirty second soundbite. So I just asked her to please call me back when she could. I didn't blame her for screening her calls. As much as Tyler's death had jarred me, I could only imagine how his co-host was taking it.

"No answer?" Ava surmised from my end of the conversation.

I shook my head. "She's staying at the Sonoma Country Inn. Think we should visit in person?"

"Give me twenty minutes to shower, and I'm in."

* * *

Forty minutes later Ava and I were pulling up to the upscale hotel and spa near the Plaza. Ava parked her vintage mint green GTO convertible in the underground lot, and we rode the elevator up to the main lobby, which sported a large fountain in the middle, a lounge to the right, and a long, sleek reception desk done in white marble that gleamed under the crystal chandeliers.

While the clerk at the desk was pleasant and helpful, he told us he could not give out Gabby's room number, for obvious security reasons. Instead, he rang up to her room where, thankfully, she did not screen his call. After a little back and forth on his end, he told us she would come down and meet us in the lounge.

Being that it was barely nine in the morning, the bar was closed, but a coffee machine and various pastries had been set out on a side table for patrons to enjoy while chatting in the club chairs and small groupings of tables.

Ava and I each grabbed a second cup of coffee and chose a table near the windows, overlooking a small courtyard garden, featuring a sister fountain to the one in the lobby, large flowering hydrangeas, and several tall shade trees. The entire scene would have been very serene if we hadn't been there to discuss a murder.

We didn't have to wait long, as a few quick minutes later, Gabriela Genova floated into the room. As with the previous day, she was again in a body hugging dress that showed off curves I seriously doubted had ever ingested an ounce of the decadent pasta dishes she created. Today's ensemble was a deep navy blue, capped off with a pair of nude heels in a much more subdued design than the fire engine red ones of the day before, though they were no less tall and precariously spiky. Maybe it was the murder on my mind, but they looked like they'd make excellent weapons.

While it was relatively early, it was clear Gabby had already been up, as her hair was poofed into a large mane of dark waves and her makeup was impeccably camera ready. I noticed her eyes were clear and dry beneath her long, thick lashes. If she was in mourning, she was hiding it well.

"Gabby," I said, standing to greet her as she approached our table. "I'm so sorry for your loss."

"Thank you," she said, sitting. Her eyes went from me to Ava, though they held little emotion. "It's been a shock."

"How are you holding up?" Ava asked.

Gabby let out a long sigh. "I've already fielded several calls from the press. My publicist is in an absolute tizzy."

Apparently having your co-host die was quite the inconvenience to one's image.

"I tried to call you earlier," I started, struggling for the tactful words.

"Yes, I got your message," she told me. "I assume you're here about the festival."

I shifted awkwardly in my seat. "Actually, we are."

Gabby nodded. "I'll do it, but I want what Tyler was being paid."

I blinked at her, not sure I understood. "You'll do it...?"

"MC the festival. That's what you're here about, right?"

"Uh..." I looked to Ava. "Well, yes, we've tentatively decided to keep it going. At least for today," I amended.

"We feel we owe it to the vendors," Ava added. "And ticket holders."

"Sure," she said, brushing our reasoning off. "I'll take over the full duties, but I want the same rate you were paying Tyler *and* access to his glam squad."

I wasn't sure what I'd expected Gabby's reaction to us continuing the Food and Wine Festival to be, but negotiating for better pay had been last on my list. "Uh, okay," I agreed. I looked to Ava again, but she just shrugged. "I hope you don't find this insensitive of us," I said.

Gabby arched a perfectly shaped eyebrow my way. "Insensitive?"

"To go on with the show, so to speak," I explained, feeling my cheeks heat even as I said the words out loud.

Gabby let out a sharp bark of laugher. "God no. This is Tyler Daniels we're talking about. The man posed for the cameras in his sleep. Crass publicity was practically an art form to him."

While I had to agree with her sentiments—I hadn't found the late celebrity terribly endearing in life—her lack of emotion at his death was a little jarring. "I take it you two were not the best of friends off camera?"

Gabby snorted. "Tyler didn't have friends. He had an entourage and underlings."

"And you were considered an underling?" I asked, finding this new insight into their relationship interesting.

"It is *Tyler's* show," she pointed out. Then she paused, quickly correcting herself. "Or was."

"How long had you been doing *Eat Up* with Tyler?" Ava asked.

"Two years," Gabby answered. "Longest two years of my life. Every day that I had to endure him aged me ten. Look at these crow's feet. Just look!" She pointed to nonexistent wrinkles at her eyes.

"Tyler was difficult to work with, then?" Ava asked.

"You met him. What do you think?" Gabby countered.

I thought Tyler had been *almost* as much of a diva as Gabby was, but I figured the question was rhetorical.

"Look, Tyler played nice to the cameras," Gabby went on, "but I'm not going to pretend he was a humanitarian now just because he's dead."

"So why did you stay with the show so long?" Ava asked. I could see the frown on her face, betraying the fact she was at least a little disappointed that the onscreen relationship between the two was pure fiction.

"Well, he was my meal ticket, wasn't he?" Gabby reasoned. "Even if he was a hack."

"Hack?" I asked, jumping on the word. "What do you mean?"

"I mean, all he brought to the show was his name. I was the one who provided real content. You said it yourself—it was my family's stories that brought our recipes to life. But who got the bigger salary? Tyler Daniels. With his stupid catchphrases and career built on yelling at other chefs. Anybody can yell. Ask if he could actually cook."

"Could he?" I couldn't help complying.

She smirked. "You saw the demonstration yesterday. The most complicated thing the man cooked was chicken breasts. Good thing the crowd didn't actually have to eat them, too. Dry as the freakin' air in this little town."

"Surely he was just having an off day," I said.

But she just shrugged. "I'd put my homemade pasta up against his dry chicken any day."

Clearly there was no love lost between the stars, but I wondered how much of Gabby's accusations were born of jealousy and how much had a seed of truth. You didn't get to be Cooking Network royalty like Tyler Daniels without at least having some culinary chops.

"Where were you before the second demonstration was supposed to start?" I asked, wondering just how badly Gabby might have wanted out from Tyler's large shadow.

Gabby blinked at me as if not understanding the question. "I was on the stage. Waiting for Tyler. You saw me."

"I mean before that," I clarified. "Between eight and nine?"

She frowned. "I was getting a bite to eat. I never perform hungry. I was at the booth that served those little crostinis."

"With Alec?" Ava asked.

She frowned deeper. "No. I was alone. He said he needed to take some photos for his webcast." She paused. "Why?"

"The police think that's when Tyler was killed," I said, watching her reaction carefully.

"And you think I had something to do with that?" She barked out another laugh. Nothing like the warm tinkling thing she pulled out for the cameras every morning. "Please," she scoffed.

"It's clear you weren't a fan," Ava pointed out.

Gabby scoffed. "No, but he has plenty of those who tune in to *his* show. But he dies—so does the show. Why would I want to be out of a job?"

"You think the network will cancel the show now?" Ava asked, and I could tell it was at least partly as a concerned fan.

But Gabby just shrugged again. "I have no idea. My agent hasn't been able to get hold of anyone there yet."

Though I found it interesting she'd tried.

"So, do we have a deal or not?" Gabby asked, looking from me to Ava.

"Deal?"

She rolled her eyes. "The pay rate. *And* the glam squad," she added, stabbing a long red fingernail my way.

I licked my lips. "I can agree to the pay rate," I told her. Truth was, that was already in our budget. "But Tyler brought in the hair and makeup crew on his own." I paused. "Honestly, I'm not sure how they're getting paid now."

Gabby waved a hand in my direction. "I'm sure Mark will take care of all of that."

"Mark?"

Gabby nodded. "Mark Black. He's Tyler's business partner. He runs the corporation, oversees the flagship restaurant here in town, holds the purse strings." She barked out a laugh. "Holds them quite tightly, in fact."

"Oh?" Ava leaned forward in her seat. "Are you saying he and Tyler didn't get along?" I could see her inner Charlie's Angel perking up—never a good sign.

"Mixed about as well as oil and vinegar," Gabby answered. "Tyler liked to spend, and Mark liked to save. Why the two ever thought they could work together peacefully, I can't imagine."

"So they fought?" Ava asked, shooting me a meaningful glance.

"All the time," Gabby confirmed. "In fact, I overheard Mark threaten him just a couple of days ago."

I had to admit, now my inner seventies diva detective was perking up a bit too. "Really? What did he say?" I asked.

"It was right after we flew in for the festival, on Friday. Tyler wanted to film a segment at his flagship restaurant while we were all in wine country. Total puff piece. Blatant self-promotion, but you know…whatever Tyler wants." She frowned. "Or wanted," she corrected herself again.

"So what happened with his partner, Mark?" I prompted.

Her eyes went wide, and she shrugged again. "Search me! But the two seemed at each other's throats the entire time. Tyler was so preoccupied that we had to shoot the segment, like, fifteen times before he could get his lines right."

"And you said you overheard a threat?"

"Yeah, just as we were leaving. Alec and I were packing up to drive to the hotel, and I passed by the back office. Mark and Tyler were arguing about something, and Mark said that if Tyler didn't fix it, Mark was cutting him out."

"Fix what?" Ava asked.

But Gabby just did more blinking, her eyelashes fluttering like dark little butterflies. "Beats me. *I* don't stoop to eavesdropping. All I know is Mark was mad as I've ever seen him, and now Tyler's dead."

I had to admit, that was interesting timing.

CHAPTER THREE

———

"So what do we think of Gabby's story?" I asked Ava as we trekked back to her car.

"I think Gabby's colder than her gazpacho," Ava decided.

I tried to stifle a laugh. "She didn't seem to be too broken up about Tyler's death, did she?"

"She also didn't have an alibi," Ava pointed out.

"Or motive," I countered.

"True," Ava admitted as we got back into her GTO. "Unless…" she said.

"Unless?"

"Unless she plans to propose the same thing to the network that she did to you."

"That she could step into Tyler's shoes?" I thought about that for a second. "You may be right—especially if she really did have the cooking chops and Tyler just had the catchphrases."

"So, Gabby overhears Mark argue with Tyler," Ava said as she backed out of the parking space. "And she takes the opportunity to kill him at the crowded festival, then blame the business partner while she steps into the starring role and becomes the solo host of *Eat Up*."

"That's possible," I mused. "But I'd be curious to know what Tyler and his business partner argued about the day before he died. What do you think 'fix it' could have been referring to?"

Ava shook her head. "Just about anything, I guess."

I pulled my phone out of my purse, googling Tyler's Place in Sonoma. An address in downtown off E. Napa came up, along with a pretty decent Yelp rating. Nothing there that immediately screamed in need of fixing.

"Is there a phone number listed?" Ava asked, glancing over at me.

I nodded. "The police are saying Jean Luc argued with Tyler before he died. But if we could give them the name of someone else who *also* fought with Tyler, you think it might help Jean Luc?"

"I think it can't hurt," Ava responded.

I took a deep breath and dialed the number for Tyler's Place, getting a recording that said they didn't open for dinner until five and to leave a message.

"Hi! This is Emmy Oak from Oak Valley Vineyards," I said at the tone. "I, uh, spoke with Tyler yesterday about possibly stocking our wine in your restaurants."

Ava shot me a look from behind the wheel. I did an innocent palms-up thing. Okay, so it was a little white lie, but really, Tyler *had* seemed to like the wine. Who knows—maybe he would have ordered some?

"Uh, anyway," I continued, "I'd appreciate it if you could give me a call back when you're free." I quickly rattled off my number before hanging up.

"Possibly stocking your wine, huh?" Ava teased. "Maybe you should have gone for broke and said he already ordered it."

"Just drive," I mumbled, giving her a playful swat on the arm.

* * *

By the time we got back to Oak Valley Vineyards, guests were already starting to arrive for day two of our festival. I felt a bubble of hope lift in my chest at how many cars were parked in the lot—almost as many as the previous day. Though, as we got out of Ava's GTO and began walking up the stone pathway to the festival grounds, I realized that at least half the bodies in attendance were not ticket holding foodies but press. I spotted a woman in a blazer and microphone with our local NBC affiliate's logo on it giving a narrative to a cameraman in front of the tasting room entrance. Bradley Wu had Eddie cornered near the stage, peppering him with questions that had my winery manager visibly sweating. And several other people had cell phones out, taking pictures of everything from the culinary booths to the vineyard, fingers furiously typing up headlines that I feared would be all over both social media and legitimate news outlets in moments.

"This isn't good," Ava said beside me, stating the obvious.

"Aren't they trespassing or something?" I asked, glancing around for any sign of Hector, who might be able to shoo them off the property.

"Possibly. But do you want to go viral as being an unwelcoming winery as well as deadly?"

"It's a lose-lose, isn't it?" I said, feeling all bubbles of hope die with a resounding pop.

"Cheer up. Maybe the reporters will try the Pinot Noir and get hooked."

I shook my head. "You have a lot more optimism than I do."

"You're still in training." She gave my arm a comforting squeeze before heading off to man the Silver Girl booth.

I took a deep, fortifying breath and made my way to the stage to rescue Eddie from Bradley Wu's clutches. Bradley had forgone the tweed today in deference to the heat, but he'd compensated with a loud, paisley printed shirt that stretched over his rotund belly. Standing next to Eddie, who was dressed in a double breasted seersucker suit in lilac, the two made quite a fashion statement. I only hoped the clothes were the only statements being made.

"...so you don't deny that Jean Luc has a difficult streak," I heard Bradley ask Eddie as I approached.

"No!" Eddie blinked at the reporter. "Wait, yes! I do deny. I mean, he's *not* difficult."

"But you just admitted that he yelled at you for moving his corkscrew."

"Well, really, what's a *yell*? He was loud, and he wasn't happy, but—"

"And he called you incompetent."

"I-I may have provoked him a bit—"

"And threatened you with bodily harm?"

"N-now, I'm sure it was just a saying. You know, 'touch my barware again and I'll feed you to the goats.' Haven't we all heard that figure of speech?" Eddie pulled a checked handkerchief from the pocket of his suit and moved to mop the fine sheen of sweat that had collected on his brow. He must have seen me approach, as his shoulders sagged in relief. "Emmy! You're here."

"Eddie," I greeted him then turned my attention to the vulture beside him. "Bradley."

"Emmy Oak, just the woman I wanted to see." Bradley's eyes twinkled with glee, like I was the main course after his Eddie appetizer. "I just *must* ask you about this terribly tragic occurrence."

While every instinct I had wanted to tell Bradley to waddle himself right back down our oak lined drive, Ava's words echoed in my head, and I pasted a smile on my face, doing my best to play nice to the press. "What is it you wanted to know?"

Bradley pulled out his phone, presumably to record my words for all posterity in the cloud. "Can I get a quote from you on the tragic demise of one culinary legendary Tyler Daniels on the grounds of your winery?"

"It's tragic," I said.

Bradley's smile faltered for a second. "Yes, I just said that. What are *your* thoughts?"

"I think it's tragic?"

I thought I heard Eddie shift beside me. Or possibly he was trying to sidle away unnoticed, which would be quite a feat for a two-hundred-pound man in head-to-toe lilac seersucker.

Bradley cleared his throat. "Okay, well, what about the rumor that your wine steward—"

"Sommelier," I corrected automatically. I knew from experience that Jean Luc preferred that term. It probably stemmed from the fact that he preferred the French anything to American.

"Yes," Bradley agreed. "Your sommelier, Jean Luc, is being questioned in the death."

"That's quite a rumor," I told him.

"But is it true?" Bradley pressed.

"*I'm* not questioning him."

"But are the police?"

"You'd have to ask them."

"Come now, Emmy," Bradley said, sending me a smile that was practically predatory. "You know how many nice reviews I've given your Petite Sirah. Surely you can give me a little something in return…hmmm?"

I pulled in a long breath. As much as I hated it, he was right—he had given us some good press, even using the words *heavenly* and *divine* in the same article about a recent luncheon I'd catered. While I was dreading the column he was currently cooking up, I knew that Sonoma was a small community, and making an enemy of a syndicated food columnist was a mistake I could not afford to make.

"Fine," I relented.

Bradley moved his phone in closer. Eddie, I noticed, had all but disappeared. Smart man.

"Tell me," Bradley prompted. "Is Jean Luc guilty of murder?"

"No," I said empathically. "It's all a big misunderstanding. I'm saddened by the tragic loss of Tyler Daniels, but I can assure you that no one connected to Oak Valley Vineyards had anything to do with his death."

Bradley looked slightly disappointed for a moment. Then his eyes focused on something just beyond me, and that twinkling lit them again.

"I see," he drawled. "Then, I wonder—why are the police hauling off your *sommelier* now?"

My heart jumped in my chest as I spun around, just in time to catch the scene Bradley had witnessed through the windows of the tasting room. I spied at least three uniformed officers gently guiding Jean Luc away from the bar—along with one plainclothes detective I recognized only too well.

Grant.

"Uh, excuse me…" I mumbled to Bradley, barely giving him a backwards glance as I jogged toward the tasting room doors. I caught up with the group just as Grant ushered Jean Luc down the short hallway that connected the tasting room to the kitchen.

"What's going on?" I demanded.

Five pairs of eyes turned my way—four accusatory and one so full of fear that I had to stop myself from throwing my arms around Jean Luc.

Grant stepped forward first, looming over me, clad in worn jeans, black boots, and a button-down shirt that pulled tightly against his broad frame. His expression was unreadable. Even the golden flecks in his eyes were at a standstill, giving nothing away.

"We need to ask Jean Luc a few questions," he said simply.

"Emmy, please, tell zee police I do not know what zay are talking about," Jean Luc pleaded, his mustache twitching with every syllable.

I looked from Jean Luc to Grant, the tension between them almost palpable.

"Can we go somewhere private? My office, perhaps?" I suggested, hoping to avoid a scene.

Grant gave me a curt nod, gesturing for Jean Luc to walk the short distance down the hallway ahead of him before following. Grant mumbled something to the uniformed officers, and they opted to wait in the hallway, leaving the three of us alone in my office as Grant closed the door.

"Have a seat," he told Jean Luc. Clearly an order, not a suggestion.

My sommelier did, sinking into one of the chairs opposite my desk. He had the expression of a kid about to get a strong talking to in the principal's office. Facing Cop Mode Grant, I was feeling a little antsy myself.

"What sort of questions do you have?" I asked, sounding bolder than I felt as I took a defensive position standing behind Jean Luc's chair.

Grant leaned casually against my desk, crossing both arms over his chest. "ME was able to pull the bullet that killed Tyler. A 9mm."

"Any way to trace it?" I asked.

"We're working on a striation match. If there's a record of bullets with similar patterns in the database, we can match them to the same weapon." He paused. While he'd been addressing me this whole time, I could see his eyes on Jean Luc. If I had to guess, he was watching for any small hint of reaction.

"What does that have to do with Jean Luc?" I asked, feeling like there was something he was holding back.

"Zay think the gun is mine!" Jean Luc shouted out, his accent thick with distress.

"What?" I barked out. "That's crazy. You don't own a gun." I paused. "Do you?"

"A Ruger SR9c 9mm is registered to a Jean Luc Gasteon, purchased six years ago at a trade show in Pomona." Grant leveled my sommelier with a stare.

Jean Luc looked from me to Grant, his eyes misting. "I-I told zee policia man. Yes, I did own a gun. I bought this gun for protection when I lived in Los Angeles. It's dangerous there, *mon amie!*"

Apparently it was dangerous here in wine country too.

"Where is your gun now?" I asked him.

"I-I put it in a case before I move. I keep it under my bed. I have not taken it out since I arrive in Sonoma."

"You're sure?" I asked.

"*Oui, oui!*" He nodded vigorously. "I never take it out of its case. I swear!"

I turned to Grant, who had been silent during our exchange. "Then that bullet didn't come from Jean Luc's gun."

Grant breathed slowly, his eyes never leaving Jean Luc. "How long have you known Tyler Daniels?"

"A long time. Seven, eight years. Maybe more." Jean Luc seemed to calm down a bit at the change of subject.

"You worked for him previously, correct?"

Jean Luc nodded. "Yes. I tended bar at his restaurant in LA when it first opened."

"Tyler's Place," I supplied.

Jean Luc nodded. "*Oui.* Though, Tyler was just starting his TV career then, so he was not so famous yet, you know."

"How long did you work there?" Grant asked.

Jean Luc licked his lips, his mustache doing a little dance. "I do not know. Eh…maybe two years. Not so long."

"Why did you leave?" Grant asked, the question coming out more like a demand. The unspoken accusation in his tone had me taking a step closer to Jean Luc and putting a protective hand on his shoulder as he answered.

"I, well, I moved on."

"It had nothing to do with you being fired?"

"Fired!" Jean Luc shouted, his eyebrows hunkering down in a deep frown. "Who tells you zees?"

"Ashley Daniels," Grant supplied. "She and Tyler were married then, weren't they?"

"Yes," Jean Luc admitted. "But it's not true. I quit. Tyler, he was—how do you say?—difficult to work with. Demanding. He yells a lot."

"It's his trademark," I explained to Grant. "It's how he earned his reputation in the celebu-chef world on *Kitchen Showdown*."

But Grant's eyes only flickered to me with the briefest of interest before focusing in on Jean Luc again.

"So there was bad blood between you two?" Grant clarified.

"No!" Jean Luc shook his head so hard his dark hair flopped onto his forehead. "No, we parted ways. Zat is all."

"Parted ways a long time ago," I added for emphasis. "Jean Luc has worked here for at least five years, right?" I asked, turning to him for confirmation.

He did more nodding, displacing more shiny black hairs. "*Oui*. At least."

"And how much contact did you have with Tyler in that time?" Grant pressed.

"None! Why would I? I promise you, when I call him to come work Emmy's event, it eez the first I talk to Tyler in years. I hadn't even seen him before today."

Grant stared at Jean Luc, his eyes narrowed as if trying to decide if he believed him.

"Look, even if he was difficult to work with, that was years ago," I pointed out. "What reason would Jean Luc possibly have to want Tyler dead now?"

Grant's eyes flickered up to meet mine. "That's a good question." Then his gaze settled on his prey again. "What did you and Tyler argue about yesterday?"

Jean Luc paused, seeming to sink into the chair more, his slight frame shrinking before my eyes. "It was nothing," he said so softly it was almost a whisper.

"Witnesses overhead you threatening him."

Jean Luc sucked in a deep breath, but he remained silent.

I felt my heart squeeze. Clearly he was holding something back. While I knew he was innocent, I also knew this did not look good.

"I'm sure it was a figure of speech," I piped up on his behalf. "People say things when they're heated. It doesn't make them killers."

Grant grunted noncommittally, his gaze still on the man shrinking in his chair before my very eyes.

"Was there anything else?" I challenged Grant.

He sucked in a slow breath, and I could see a whole host of thoughts running through the golden flecks in his eyes, but the only one he apparently decided to voice was, "Not at the moment."

"Then, if you'll excuse us, we have a hundred thirsty guests and no sommelier on duty," I told him, hearing a lot more bravado in the statement than I felt. Honestly, in the confined space with Grant, I felt a little like I was poking a caged lion. But at this point it was either poke or let him devour Jean Luc.

Luckily, Grant let it go, giving me a curt, impersonal nod before opening the door to my office and stalking out into the corridor, the waiting uniformed officers a quick step behind him.

I let an audible sigh of relief as soon as he left, and I could feel the tension draining from Jean Luc as well. While I itched to dig into exactly what he'd said to Tyler the day before, I wasn't lying when I'd said someone needed to be at the bar pouring.

"I'm so sorry, Emmy," Jean Luc said, his voice sounding small and pitiful. I ached to scoop him up in a fierce hug, but I knew his sense of pride would only take more injury if I did.

Instead, I shook my head. "No need to apologize. You've done nothing wrong. Of that I am sure." I sent him the most reassuring smile I could muster, having just been on the business end of Bad Cop.

He smiled back, hinting at some of his usual flair. "*Merci.* But I will understand if you do not want me to stay on for the festival—"

"Nonsense," I said, quickly shutting that down. Both because I had absolute faith in Jean Luc and because I had zero faith in Eddie's abilities to fill his void. "Take a moment to freshen up, and then your public awaits, Monsieur."

He grinned again, this one looking a bit stronger as he stood. "I shall not disappoint," he promised as he left the office.

CHAPTER FOUR

———

The crowd was slow to pick up as the morning turned into afternoon, and it was clear that the majority of foodies who'd come to see Tyler Daniels put on a show had stayed away that day. Though, whether it was due to the absence of the star or the fact that our vineyard was now a crime scene, I wasn't sure.

I roamed the stalls, stopping near the main stage as Gabby put on a show of making Fettuccini Pomodoro from scratch in a way she deemed easy enough for any home cook to follow along. While Tyler had been the larger-than-life personality of the two, Gabby had a certain friendly charm about her as she cooked, deftly breaking eggs into a little well of flour as she regaled the crowd with stories of her Nonna making Sunday dinner back in the old country. Her tone was easy and conversational—nothing like the woman I'd come to know offstage. I had to admit that her dish looked very enticing and smelled even better, the heavenly aromas wafting over the small crowd as she tossed together garlic, fragrant basil, and San Marzano tomatoes.

My stomach growled, reminding me I'd yet to take time out to eat that day. I took a detour to the banh mi booth, where I picked up two sandwiches, and then headed toward the Silver Girl display to deliver one to Ava, whom I suspected hadn't taken time for herself that afternoon either.

Only, as I approached, I realized she was not alone.

Standing next to her table of handcrafted jewelry was a woman in a flowy, floral printed sundress and a man I knew all too well.

He looked up as I approached, and a wicked grin snaked across his dark features. "Well, there's my little wine and dine girl," David Allen said, taking a sandwich from my hands and digging in before I could stop him.

"I'm a woman, not a girl," I shot back automatically. "And I'm definitely not *your* girl. And *that* was *my* dinner." I handed the other sandwich to Ava. She gave me a grateful smile that said my guess at how busy she'd been was right.

"Well, well. I see we're in a feisty mood today," David teased, offering back the banh mi he'd taken a large bite from.

I shook my head and shot him a look.

David Allen and I had a complicated relationship. When I first met him, he was my prime suspect in the murder of his stepfather. While he'd turned out to be innocent of that particular crime, there were several gray areas of the criminal law code he traversed on a regular basis, including making a tidy living as a card shark. Not that he needed the cash. David came from a wealthy though highly dysfunctional family (see murdered stepfather reference above). He lived in the guest house of their vacation estate, had a healthy trust fund to keep him flush with video games and weed, and when he wasn't bilking unsuspecting poker players at the country club of their hardly earned cash, he showed his moody paintings at local galleries. Money was not something David Allen needed—he just liked the thrill of getting it.

While I didn't totally approve of David's extracurricular activities, he had displayed some chivalry recently when I'd been in a jam at the Sonoma Links golf club, coming to my aid at just the right moment. I was eternally grateful to him for it, but to say we were in the friend zone would be overstating the situation some. We coexisted peacefully.

Mostly.

"We were just talking about you," David told me, a gleam in his eyes that made me instantly nervous. "You seem to have created quite the excitement up here at your deadly little winery."

"Ha! Excitement is one way to put it," the woman in the sundress said. Up close I recognized her as Ashley Daniels, food critic and Tyler's ex-wife. Though, she looked as if she was as far as possible from mourning—decked out in a sunny red straw hat, high heels, and even more jangling bracelets than the previous day.

"Ms. Daniels," I greeted her. "I'm so sorry for your loss."

"Oh, honey, don't be. Do I look like I'm at a loss?" she asked with a wide smile, voicing my very thoughts.

"David stopped by just as I was telling Ashley here that we were on the fence about running the full four days of the festival," Ava jumped in.

"Well, I applaud you for going on with the show today," Ashley said, actually clapping her hands together, making the bracelets clack like castanets. "I'm sure Tyler caused you enough inconvenience in life—don't let his death spoil this for you."

David chuckled, leaning against Ava's table. "Wow, and I thought I was cold."

"Oh, honey, pure ice runs through these veins," Ashley responded, still grinning. "That's what a decade of living with Tyler Daniels' ego does to a body."

David nodded his understanding. Before devouring the rest of my dinner.

"Uh, well, I'm not sure we'll be continuing the festival tomorrow," I hedged.

"Oh, what a shame." Ashley frowned. "I bought a four-day ticket."

So had at least two hundred other people, the income from which I was counting on to keep us in the black next month. "I really don't know how many people will even be back." I glanced around at the sparse crowd.

"Look, if you close, you have to refund, correct?" Ashley asked.

"Well, I—" I looked to Ava, not wanting to admit anything until I checked my bank account balance. Could I even afford to refund everyone?

"But if you stay open and people decide not to come on their own…well, that's their choice, isn't it?" she reasoned.

"I-I guess that makes sense," I admitted. I still wasn't sure we were paying proper respect to the deceased star, but I was starting to think I was in the minority there.

"Really," Ashley went on as she picked up a silver necklace, turning it over in her hands, "it's not like anyone can blame *you*. You didn't kill Tyler." She paused. "Did you?"

"Wh-what? No!"

She winked at me. "Just teasing. Though, I would like to shake that man's hand." She paused again. "Or woman's," she amended.

"You were close to Tyler—who do *you* think did kill him?" Ava asked.

But Ashley just laughed. "Oh, honey, it's been years since I was even in the neighborhood of close with Tyler. He sends alimony checks. I keep my distance. That's it. I lived the Tyler show for almost ten long years. Plenty long enough to know the real man behind the catchphrases. And his personality was not as pretty as his pictures."

"Then you were married to Tyler when Jean Luc worked for him," I said, recalling my previous conversation with Grant. "At his Los Angeles restaurant?"

Ashley nodded. "Yes. Jean Luc tended bar, so I saw him occasionally."

"You told Detective Grant that Jean Luc was fired."

Ashley blinked at me. "H-how would you know that?"

"Emmy and Detective Grant are close," David said, infusing the statement with much more meaning than made me comfortable. "*Quite* close, in fact."

"We're…acquaintances," I said.

David raised one dark eyebrow into his long hair but thankfully didn't say anything.

"Oh, I see," Ashley said, eyes going to the silver necklace in her hands again. "Well, yes, the detective did ask me about Tyler and Jean Luc's relationship, and I did say he'd been fired."

"Was he?" I pressed, knowing that was not my sommelier's version of events.

"Well, yes. I mean, I assumed he was. Wasn't he?" She glanced up at me, blinking innocently. "He and Tyler were always at each other's throats. Tyler's explosive personality was one thing he didn't have to fake for the cameras. And Jean Luc—well, those French are just so expressive!"

I had a feeling that not every person from France could be or would appreciate being described that way, but I let it go. Mostly because, well, it did describe this particular person to a tee.

"But you didn't actually witness Tyler fire Jean Luc? Or hear Tyler mention it to you specifically?"

Ashley shrugged. "Like I said, I assumed. But it wasn't like Tyler and I engaged in late-night pillow talk or anything. Back then Tyler's head was usually on someone else's pillow."

David snorted, quickly covering it.

"Tyler cheated on you?" Ava cut in, her tone sympathetic.

But Ashley laughed again, as if she'd long ago spent all negative emotion surrounding that subject. "That man couldn't walk the line if he was on a tightrope. The bigger the bust the better. And, of course, as soon as his TV shows started airing, the man had hordes of foodie groupies. That was the last straw for me."

"How long ago was this?" I asked, hoping I didn't seem like I was prying as much as I actually was. But if Ashley Daniels had harbored animosity toward Tyler for cheating, it was a lovely motive to want him dead. And she was far from a grieving widow—or even ex-widow.

"That was ages ago!" she said, waving my question off with the same airy attitude she'd had throughout the conversation about her dead ex. "Look, we both got what we wanted—Tyler was free to make sweet, sweet cupcakes with whatever foodie floozy he wanted, and I got a lovely alimony check each month."

Which meant she had very little reason to want him gone. No Tyler, no more alimony checks.

My disappointment must have been plain on my face, as Ashley laughed again. "Sorry, darling, but really, Tyler had reason to want *me* dead, not the other way around. My divorce decree was ironclad. Even his fancy attorney couldn't get the payments lowered."

"His attorney tried to lower your alimony payments?" Ava asked, sympathy in her voice again.

Ashley shrugged. "Yes, but like I said, he was unsuccessful."

"Did Tyler say why?"

"I didn't speak to Tyler, my dear. That's like chatting with a brick wall." She laughed at her own joke. "But his attorney said it was because of the lawsuit."

"Lawsuit?" I asked. "Someone was suing Tyler?"

"Well, yes." She blinked at me as if it was common knowledge and she was surprised I had to ask. "Alec Post."

That was news. "Gabriela's boyfriend?"

"Well, I suppose he is now, but Gabby met Alec through Tyler. Alec used to work for him. He cooked in his Sonoma restaurant, actually."

"What was Alec suing him over?" Ava piped up.

But Ashley just shrugged. "Haven't the foggiest. You'd have to ask Alec."

* * *

I left Ashley haggling over the price of the silver necklace with Ava and noticed David Allen followed me away from the booth.

"Well?" he asked as I slowly wound through the festivalgoers.

"Well what?"

"Well, aren't you going to fill me in on the victim in your vineyard?" He grinned mischievously at me.

"Et tu, David?" I asked.

The grin grew. "Meaning?"

"Meaning, I'm afraid all anyone is here for today is sensationalism." I sighed, venting my general frustrations his way. "This is not how I wanted people to be talking about Oak Valley."

"Aw, poor Ems," David said, laying an arm around my shoulders in a move that was just a little too familiar to feel comfortable. His shirt smelled faintly of marijuana and some spicy aftershave, which was a much more pleasant combination than I would have guessed, and his lazy grin held the slightest hint of something predatory beneath it as he added, "Come have a glass of wine and tell me all about it."

"Hard pass," I decided. Chatting with David always made me feel like a small fish swimming precariously close to the big shark. If I was lucky, the shark would protect me from the big fish. If I was unlucky, I didn't want to know what those teeth could do.

Though, if David was offended, he didn't show it. "Well, at least tell me we're going to find out why Alec Post was suing his former employer."

"I doubt Alec Post will want to discuss the finer details of a lawsuit against a murder victim with me," I reasoned.

David shook his head. "You don't need him to. If the suit was filed in California, it will be public record. All civil court records are."

I paused, feeling my left eyebrow go up. "Since when do you know the California legal system so well?"

"Since I started playing poker with Judge Tomlinson."

"Poor Judge Tomlinson," I mused.

David laughed. "Well don't feel too sorry for him. The old goat's a total racist and plans to cut his gay son out of his will."

"So now you're card sharking for humanity?"

David shook his head at me. "Don't confuse sentiment with intention, Ems. You know I'd shark my grandmother, given the chance."

Interesting statement, since his grandmother was in jail. The Allen/Price family was *highly* dysfunctional.

"So you think we could access details of Alec's lawsuit online somewhere?" I asked David as I pulled out my phone.

"Possibly. How many details depends on how recently it was filed, but we could at least get an overview."

He looked over my shoulder as I opened a browser and typed in *Sonoma County Court.* A search engine directed me to the Superior Court's website, where, with a couple quick clicks, I found a page to search civil cases by date and keyword. I had to guess at a few parameters, like whether we were talking small claims court or high dollar, but after trying a few dates, I finally found a hit for *Daniels* in the unlimited civil cases section—claims over twenty-five thousand dollars.

Details were, unfortunately, sparse—just a case number, the names of the two parties, *Post v. Daniels,* and the claim of the action: Fraud.

"Fraud?" I frowned at the word. I wasn't sure what I was expecting, but this threw me. "What could Tyler have been fraudulent about that could have hurt Alec?"

"Hard to say," David answered.

"You think it had something to do with when Alec worked at his restaurant? Like, maybe Alec saw something or overheard something?"

"It really could be anything. Suit was just filed a couple of months ago," he noted. "No judgment yet."

"Which means?" I asked.

"Anybody can sue anybody else for just about anything. Frivolous lawsuits are brought all the time. Since it's still pending, it's hard to know if Alec was just tying up Tyler's time and money or if there was a legitimate claim."

I bit my lip, staring at the screen. The SCV court that was listed as scheduled to hear the case dealt in claims twenty-five thousand…and up. Meaning we could be talking several hundred thousand or even millions. If Tyler's lawyer had actually tried to get Ashley's alimony payments lowered, that made me think we could be talking about a significant amount. And it also seemed as if his lawyer thought there was at least some merit to the claims.

I glanced toward the stage where I'd last seen Alec, standing supportively on the sidelines when Gabby had demonstrated her chicken Milanese. No sign of either now, but a couple of Tyler's former glam squad members were milling around, glasses of wine in hand. With David on my heels, I quickly threaded my way through the crowd toward the raised stage and addressed the taller of the two bleached blonds.

"Excuse me?" I called up.

He paused, turning his attention my way.

"I'm looking for Alec Post. He was here with Gabby earlier?"

"Tall guy? Kind of young?" he asked.

I nodded. "Have you seen him?"

But the blond shook his head. "Sorry, I think they left. Gabby said she had a headache from all the pollen in the air."

I bit back a snide comment. The pollen count today was at moderate to none. "Any idea if they went back to the hotel?"

But the blond just shrugged. "Sorry."

I thanked him, trying not to feel too dejected as I turned away. I could try calling Gabby to talk to Alec, but this was honestly the type of conversation that I wanted to have face to face—where I could see the millennial's reactions.

"So, what now?" David asked, leaning casually against the stage.

I glanced at the time readout on my phone. Just after six. While Gabby might be done for the day, there was one place that was now open for business. Tyler's Place, in downtown Sonoma. Where Tyler's business partner, Mark Black—who still hadn't gotten back to me—worked.

And I still hadn't eaten.

"Feel like grabbing dinner in town?" I asked.

One of David's dark eyebrows rose into his hairline. "What happened to the hard pass?"

"Are you coming with me or not?" I sighed.

"Oh, I'm coming," he assured me, his eyes still twinkling with mocking humor. "You think I'd pass up a date?"

I scoffed. "This is *not* a date. You should be so lucky."

"Hmm." He narrowed his eyes at me, a grin spreading across his face.

"'Hmm' what?"

"I do get on a lucky streak now and then." The grin grew. "Just ask Judge Tomlinson."

"Just for that, you're buying."

CHAPTER FIVE

———

Half an hour later we pulled up to Tyler's Place on E. Napa. While the restaurant had started as a fine dining establishment, garnering some nice reviews early on that had gotten Tyler noticed on the foodie scene, it was now a kitschy monument to Tyler's onscreen persona, covered in neon writing and a large picture of Tyler's sparkling white smile ten feet high on the side of the building.

David parked the white Rolls Royce that was a hand-me-down from his mother, and we walked into the restaurant, where a life-size cardboard cutout of Tyler greeted us. At its base, some patrons had put flowers, making for an unconventional memorial in the lobby.

Which, by the way, was packed. If Tyler's death had turned people off to my Food and Wine Festival, it had only brought them in droves to Tyler's Place. The lobby was wall-to-wall patrons awaiting tables—sitting on benches along the windows, lining the walls, and spilling out into the walkways. David and I fought our way through them to approach a woman at a wooden hostess station, whose nametag read *Mandy*.

"Wow, busy tonight, huh?" I noted.

She laughed. "You're telling me. I haven't even had a chance for a potty break since I got on shift."

I couldn't help a smile at her candor. "We were hoping to get a table for two," I told her, fearing how long that wait would be.

"Oh wow. Do you have reservations?"

"Uh, no, not really," I admitted.

She pursed her lips together. "Well, the wait is about an hour for a table right now." She glanced at the packed waiting room.

"I'm guessing you're not always this busy," I said.

She shook her head. "God, no. But, well..." She bit her lip and lowered her voice. "One of the owners died." She gestured toward the makeshift memorial.

I nodded. "Yes, I heard about Tyler."

"It's been crazy here. The fire marshal almost fined us when he saw vigil candles outside, and security had to take a couple of nuns out who wouldn't stop praying at the silverware station." Then she paused, leaning in close. "You didn't hear it from me, but we've been so busy, management even raised the prices on the signature burger by a whole buck today." She pulled herself back upright. "So crazy, right?"

"Nuts," David agreed with a grin.

"Any chance of a spot at the bar?" I asked.

Mandy glanced behind her. "I could check. But honestly, the stools are super uncomfortable. You won't want to sit there for too long."

"Hashtag no filter," David mumbled to me.

I tried to cover my grin again. "Thanks, but I think it would be fine."

"'K. Lemme check," Mandy said, stepping away for a minute.

I watched a couple of ladies in all black wearing comical veils come in the front door, sniffle into actual handkerchiefs, and lay roses at cardboard Tyler's feet.

"Even in death he's got groupies," David mused.

"Seems people either loved him or hated him," I noted.

"Or killed him." David sent me a wink.

I was about to respond when Mandy hurried back, letting us know she had two stools near the bathrooms that had just opened up. Though, "we didn't hear it from her," the bathroom plumbing had been backed up by someone trying to flush a picture of Tyler down the toilet earlier, so it might not smell the best. I saw David having second thoughts, but I quickly assured her we'd take the chance and let her lead us to the only two empty barstools at the polished chrome bar top.

"Excuse me, Mandy," I asked her before she slipped back to her podium. "Do you know if Mark Black is in tonight?"

She nodded. "You're friends?"

"Possible business associates," I fibbed. "Emmy Oak. I own Oak Valley Vineyards."

"I'll let him know you're here," she promised before hurrying off to greet the three couples who'd come in the door after us.

"Business associates?" David Allen asked as we perused the bar menu.

I shrugged. "It's possible he may want to stock our wines here. Possible even Tyler mentioned doing so before he died."

"Possible or actual?"

"Semantics," I told him.

We both ordered Tyler's signature "Turn Up the Heat" Burger (even though it was a dollar overpriced), and I added a glass of the Zinfandel, which was good, though it wasn't as full-bodied as ours. Obviously I was a bit biased, but maybe Mark Black really should consider doing business with us.

I was halfway through my burger—which was juicy with a spicy aioli that was perfectly balanced between tangy and creamy—when a tall, thick man stepped up behind the bar where we were seated. "Emmy Oak?" he asked.

I awkwardly swallowed the massive bite I'd been chewing. "Yes?"

"I'm Mark Black. My hostess said you wanted to talk to me about some wine?" His voice was husky and deep, hinting at a bit of a New York accent. He was stocky, and his dark hair was liberally shot with gray at the temples. I put him in his mid-to-late-forties, around the same age as Tyler, though his face was much more weather worn than his camera-ready partner's had been. He was dressed in simple gray slacks and a navy button down shirt, rolled at the sleeves in an approachably casual way, and his nose was just slightly crooked, having spoken of being broke at some time in his youth.

I quickly dabbed at my lips with my napkin. "Uh, yes. I actually called you earlier today as well."

"My apologies. It's been a rather hectic day. I haven't had a chance to check my messages yet." His voice was appropriately solemn for someone who had just lost a partner and possibly friend. But the sentiment didn't quite reach his eyes, which shifted from me to David as if sizing us up.

"Please, no need to apologize," I told him. "And I'm so sorry for your loss." I felt like I'd been repeating that line a lot lately.

And as with the other times I'd uttered it, the person on the receiving end seemed less than broken up about it.

Mark simply nodded, as if I were telling him the burger had arrived cold.

"Tyler was actually at my winery for the Fall Food and Wine Festival when he..."

"When he expired so very tragically and prematurely," David jumped in.

Mark's gaze flickered to him, taking in the black T-shirt, overly long hair, and worn jeans.

"David Allen," my companion offered, sticking a hand out Mark's way. "Friend of the winery."

Friend might be overstating our relationship a little, but I let that go.

"Mark Black." He shook it warily before turning back to me. "And, yes, Tyler told me he was working a winery event. Sorry, I didn't put the name together until now."

I shook my head. "No, I'm sure you've had a lot to deal with today."

He sighed. "You can't imagine. Press have been calling since dawn, and the morbid mourners were lined up on the sidewalk even before we opened." He nodded toward the lobby, where I saw a busty woman placing a bouquet of pink roses at the feet of Cardboard Tyler.

"I imagine this has all been twice as difficult considering the strained terms you two were on," I said, watching his reaction closely.

I didn't have to watch too hard, as his gaze whipped to mine. "Excuse me?"

"I heard that you two fought the last time you saw him. Didn't you?"

His eyes narrowed, his jaw clenching. "You heard?"

"Uh, Gabby told me she overhead you two. Not that she was eavesdropping. She was just...concerned." I hoped I hadn't just thrown the Italian diva under the bus. The way Mark was glaring at me, I had a feeling he was mentally driving it into someone right now.

He sucked in a long, slow breath, gaze flickering to the couple drinking mojitos beside us, as if making sure no one was paying attention to us before continuing. "Yes. We had words. But it was just business."

"People kill over business all the time," David casually threw out there.

The look Mark Black shot him could have frozen a volcano.

"Just an observation," David covered smoothly. "I'm sure you didn't kill your business partner. I mean, why would you, with the way business is clearly booming here?" He punctuated the statement with a wide smile.

Mark's eyes narrowed in return.

"Gabby said there was something you needed Tyler to fix?" I asked gently.

"Gabby said that, huh?" Mark asked, crossing his arms over his chest.

I nodded.

"Gabby has a big mouth," he shot back.

Agreed. But by the way Mark was starting to turn red and his jaw clenched tight, I had a feeling she wasn't entirely a liar.

"Was Tyler in trouble, Mr. Black?" I asked. "Maybe some sort of trouble that got him killed?"

His gaze bounced from me to David as he tried to make diamonds out of his back teeth a little more. Then finally, he must have decided we were relatively harmless and let out a long sigh. "Yeah, you could say Tyler was in trouble. Or more accurately, he *was* the trouble."

"How so?" I prodded.

"He had booked a commercial shoot at the restaurant next month."

"That doesn't seem terrible," I said, shooting a questioning look at David. His eyebrows were drawn down in a frown of confusion too.

"No, it wouldn't be," Mark went on, "if we hadn't just shot a very expensive commercial last month. And one three months before that. Both of which lost money hand over fist, but Tyler said he needed to shoot a fresh spot to air during his show." He sighed again, as if trying to yoga breathe his frustration away.

"So, Tyler was playing loose with advertising funds?" I clarified.

"Tyler played loose with *all* funds. Look, the guy knew how to work a crowd, but he knew nothing about running a business. He breezed in every two months like clockwork, flashing his smile around and pretending to actually have a hand in this place. But I'm the one holding it all together here." He paused. "Or trying to."

"So the 'fix it' was…?" David asked.

"Cancel the commercial shoot! Tyler said he'd prepaid for the crew, but I told him to get a refund. No way did we need another losing commercial when we had two in the can already."

"I take it Tyler did not get a chance to fix it before he died," I assumed.

Black shook his head. "No. Once again, I'm left to clean up the mess."

Which was plenty of reason to be angry at Tyler, but I wasn't sure it was reason enough to want him dead.

"Alec Post used to work here, correct?" I asked him, changing gears.

"Alec Post?" Black blinked at me a couple of times, as if trying to place the name.

"He has a webcast now called The Digest, but I believe he used to work here under Tyler. As a chef?"

Black nodded, recognition dawning. "Right. Sous chef. That was back when Tyler actually spent time in the kitchen." He snorted.

"I suspect he did less of that when he landed the TV show?" David asked.

"Show*s*," Black corrected. "Plural. And he was not one to let us forget that."

"Did you know if there was any animosity between the two? Alec and Tyler? Any sort of falling out?"

He frowned, his bushy eyebrows taking on that menacing look again. "No. I mean, that was what—five years ago?"

"Alec recently filed a lawsuit against Tyler," David jumped in. "For fraud."

The bushy eyebrows moved north, but Black didn't respond.

"Any idea what that was about?" I asked.

He shook his head. "This is the first I'm hearing of it."

"So, Tyler didn't do anything that strikes you as fraudulent while they worked together?"

Black shrugged. "Look, Tyler was no prince. He was loud, arrogant, and often just downright mean. Did he make this Post guy angry enough to sue him? Probably. But you'd have to ask him."

Believe me, it was on my to-do list.

"Well, at least it appears Tyler's posthumously bringing in some revenue," David said, gesturing behind him to the packed restaurant.

Mark grunted. "This won't put a dent in what Tyler's done to our accounts." He paused. "But you're right. It doesn't hurt."

It was clear no one was mourning Tyler. Or, correction, no one who knew him was mourning. There were plenty of people—mostly women, I noted—in the lobby who looked like they'd been running their mascara over his demise. But I'd yet to encounter someone from his day-to-day life who wasn't speaking ill of this particular dead. While Black said he was left cleaning up Tyler's mess again, he did now have comfort in knowing it was the last time he'd be put in such a situation.

"Mandy said you wanted to talk about your wines?" Black said, pulling me out of my thoughts.

"Huh?" I blinked at him, trying not to see a potential murder suspect.

"Mandy," he said, gesturing toward the hostess who'd seated us. "She mentioned something about possibly serving your wines here? That Tyler suggested it?"

"Oh. Right." I cleared my throat. Knowing I was terrible liar, I tried to stick to the truth as much as possible. "Well, I know the tourist crowd always appreciates when they're served local wines. We've got a Pinot Noir, Chardonnay, Pinot Blanc, Zinfandel, and a few cases of small run Petite Sirah."

"Impressive. How large did you say your winery is?"

"Just under ten acres. But we use it wisely, and it's been in the family for generations."

He nodded. "I'm assuming you'll sell at wholesale prices?"

"Of course," I agreed, mentally trying to calculate our profit margins on those.

"Okay, tell you what? Bring some samples by, and I'll consider it."

"Sounds great," I told him, meaning it. While it had been a cover story, it was an opportunity that could be lucrative for us. Especially if people kept pouring into Tyler's Place in droves of hungry mourners.

* * *

"Well he was pleasant," David said, laying on the sarcasm thick as we left Tyler's Place and drove back toward the winery.

"He wasn't very cut up about Tyler, was he?"

David shook his head. "It doesn't appear anyone was."

"You think he killed Tyler to keep him from hemorrhaging cash from the business?"

"Well, it's possible. But I imagine the celebu-chef's draw is going to wane quickly now that he's gone."

"True, but the food was good."

David shot me look. "You're adorable."

I felt an instant blush. "What?"

"Ems, no one is coming to Tyler's Place for the food. They're coming to be close to the TV God."

"I'd hardly call him a god," I mumbled, trying to quell the heat in my cheeks—both at the quasi-compliment and the insinuation that I was naïve in the ways of celebrity marketing.

"Well, I highly doubt the restaurant will have the same draw as *Mark's* Place," David pointed out.

"I wonder just how bad things were," I mused as I looked out the window, watching darkness slowly envelope the valley.

"What do you mean?" David asked.

"Well, was Tyler eating up profits, or do you think he was actually borrowing money for his commercials and such? Taking the partners into debt." I paused, turning to face him. "There's a big difference between making a few bucks less and seeing your business facing bankruptcy." As I well knew. My accountant, Gene Shultz, had yet to say the *B* word to me, but I knew we were in a precarious position with Oak Valley. I could only imagine the desperation I'd feel if I had a partner who seemed oblivious to it or, worse, even contributing to it.

"It's an interesting question," David agreed. "But I still like Alec for the kill."

"Oh?" I asked.

"A lawsuit definitely says something was going on between the two." He paused. "Plus, he's too cute."

I laughed. "Call the detectives. We have our smoking gun."

"I'm not sure we need to call them," David said, his mood shifting as we pulled up the oak lined driveway to the winery. "Looks like they're already here."

While the parking lot was still emptying of the last few festivalgoers, one car stood out among the rest. A black SUV, parked near the entrance to the winery.

And standing in front of it was Detective Christopher Grant.

CHAPTER SIX

As David pulled to a stop, my mind raced, trying to come up with a good reason for Grant to be there. I could think of a lot of reasons—but none of them were good. I felt him watching me as I got out of the Rolls, making me antsy. David mumbled a quick excuse and beat a hasty retreat back down the oak lined drive in his luxury car, clearly feeling a little antsiness himself. Law enforcement had that effect on the card shark.

As my feet itched to follow David's lead and retreat, I sucked it up and made my way toward the winery entrance. Grant was leaning against his SUV, arms folded over his chest, legs crossed at the ankles, looking casual and perfectly at ease in comparison to my nerves at seeing him. Then again, he wore the gun, so there wasn't a whole lot for him to be nervous about.

"Emmy," he greeted me as I approached.

"Grant," I countered. I hesitated to ask, but… "What are you doing here?"

One eyebrow rose ever so slightly. "That's not exactly a welcoming greeting."

I straightened my spine, making the most of my 5'6" self. "Well, the last time you were here, you were interrogating one of my employees."

Some of the Bad Cop softened out of him, his arms uncrossing, shoulders relaxing. "I know. I'm sorry about that."

That was surprising. "You are?"

He nodded. "Look, I know you and I have a little history—"

Very little. Like, half a date's worth.

"—but I can't let personal feelings interfere with a murder investigation."

As far as apologies went, that one sucked. But my focus was immediately drawn to one phrase. "You have personal feelings?"

The corner of his mouth quirked up. "I might have one or two."

While it was hardly an admission of undying love, my body still heated in response to the mischievous little golden flecks dancing in his eyes as he looked down at me.

I willed my hormones to play it cool.

"Well, I wouldn't want any of those feelings to get in the way of your investigation, but I'm telling you now that Jean Luc is not your man."

At the mention of my sommelier, some of the flirt left his eyes. "Emmy, I know he's your employee—"

"And friend," I cut in. While Jean Luc had a distinctly prickly side at times, I'd always thought of him as sort of like the eccentric uncle I never had. He was part of the Oak Valley family.

"Okay," Grant said. "And friend. But I can't ignore evidence."

"You don't have any evidence that Jean Luc did this," I stated boldly. I knew because I was sure he did not do it.

Grant sighed. "The bullets."

"Which did not come from Jean Luc's gun!" I protested. "Jean Luc's gun is under his bed."

Grant sucked in another breath, not saying anything. But he gave me a hard stare.

"What?" I asked. There was something he was holding back.

"We searched Jean Luc's house this afternoon."

Crud. "And the gun? It was there, wasn't it?"

Grant slowly shook his head in the negative.

I closed my eyes and thought a dirty word. Only, when I opened them again, Grant was still there, all Cop Face now that didn't even hint at any "personal feelings."

"You searched his *entire* house?" I asked.

Grant nodded. "Our warrant included the garage, his dwelling, and anywhere on the property. No gun."

"So maybe someone stole it," I offered.

"Jean Luc didn't report it stolen. No sign of a break-in."

"Maybe it's just misplaced, then," I said. "Maybe it got lost in his move up here. He said he never even took it out of the case."

"What did Jean Luc argue with Tyler about?" Grant asked. If I had to guess, the change of subject was deliberate to catch me off balance.

Luckily, after years of walking in heels, I was excellent at maintaining mine. "I have no idea," I told him. "But I do know of someone else who argued with Tyler. The day before he died, even."

Grant raised an eyebrow my way. "I'm listening."

"Mark Black, his business partner."

"And what did *they* argue about?"

"Money," I told him. "Tyler was spending too much, and Mark wanted him to stop. Namely, cancel a commercial shoot that Mark said they didn't need."

Grant nodded. "Who told you this?"

"Mark Black," I said without thinking.

Grant's other eyebrow went up. "He just admitted to a stranger that he was having business issues?"

I shrugged. "Hey, you're not the only one who can interrogate suspects."

"I should be," he told me, his tone deeper and more commanding. "Emmy, you need to stay out of this."

I shook my head. "Nuh-uh. Not gonna happen. Especially when you're getting false information," I added with bravado I certainly didn't feel as his eyes went darker and darker.

"Excuse me?" he countered, his voice holding an edge to it now.

I licked my lips. "Ashley Daniels. She told you Jean Luc was fired by Tyler. But she was mistaken."

"And you know this how?"

"I talked to her."

His eyes narrowed. "You 'interrogated' Ashley Daniels too."

"*Talked to,*" I said, backpedaling on my own words. "And she said Tyler and Jean Luc fought a lot, and she *assumed* Jean Luc was fired. But she didn't actually know for sure."

"They fought a lot?"

I rolled my eyes. "You're focusing on the wrong part."

Grant's mouth did a quick upward twitch. "Am I?"

"Yes. Jean Luc quit. He didn't lie about that. And he isn't lying about anything else, either."

Grant let out a long sigh, lifting his chin as he stared me down. "I'm sure you want to believe that, Emmy."

"And you don't?" I challenged him, "You want my sommelier to be guilty?"

"Don't put words in my mouth," he warned, that edge returning to his voice. "I'm not working on emotion here. I'm simply following the evidence."

"Well, follow it somewhere else," I shot back, feeling my own anger start to rise. "And by the way," I added. "That was a lousy apology!"

I didn't wait for an answer before I turned and stalked into the winery with as much dignity as I could muster.

* * *

The rest of the evening wound down uneventfully, and as thankful as I was when the last guest had gone and I was free to spend some quality time with my beckoning pillow, sleep came in fits and starts. My mind refused to shut down as it mulled over my argument with Grant. I wasn't sure how the conversation had gone downhill so quickly, but what should have been a win on my side—I'd given him a new suspect and effectively killed the testimony of one of his witnesses!—actually felt like a loss on both. Any thoughts I might have harbored of getting that other half date faded away into fantasyland. Grant said it himself—he was no emotion, all business. And unfortunately, at the moment that business seemed to be pinning Jean Luc for a murder.

I refused to believe that Jean Luc really was involved, but I had to admit the missing gun was just one more thing pointing a big red arrow his way. Truth was, I'd been down this road with Grant before—him playing by the books and me trying to convince him that play was leading him in the wrong direction. I didn't doubt Grant's ability to do his job. But sometimes the facts didn't always add up the way forensics saw them. Sometimes there was something else at play—one little missing piece that made all the facts fit at totally different angles. And that red arrow of guilt would suddenly flip one-eighty and point somewhere else.

I just wished I knew where it would be pointing this time.

I was almost grateful when the first light of dawn peeked through my bedroom curtains, even though well-rested was a bit beyond my grasp. I peeled myself out of bed and cranked up the heat in my shower, letting the warm steam grow around me, clearing my head. I pulled on a pair of white Capri pants, a flowy asymmetrical blouse, and Grecian sandals with rhinestones along the straps. There was little I could do about the bags under my eyes, but I added an extra bit of mascara and peachy lip gloss to try to detract.

By the time I had my first heavenly cup of coffee in hand, vendors were starting to arrive to set up for day three of the festival. What was left of them. I noticed a couple abandoned stations where chefs had presumably decided our post-murder turnout wasn't worth their time. I said a silent prayer that some guests would arrive today as I walked among the stalls. The cool morning fog still hovered in the air, giving it a chill and a fresh scent as the sun struggled to reach us.

I was winding back toward the kitchen for a second cup of liquid energy when I spotted Tyler's glam squad doing their thing under a plastic canopy beside the still sealed RV. One of the platinum blonds was furiously throwing different shades of powder around Gabby's face while the hair stylist twirled and spritzed her hair. And Gabby was shouting at both of them that neither was doing their job right. I was just about to duck away from the scene before Gabby could spot me and toss a couple complaints my way, when I spotted Alec Post exiting the makeshift tent, pausing to chat with the other platinum blond.

"Alec," I hailed him.

He looked up, his dimple flashing in his cheek as he smiled back in greeting. "'Morning, Emmy."

"How's Gabby today?" I asked. "Allergies okay?"

Alec chuckled. "If they are, I'm sure it will be the heat or the bugs." He winked at me. "She's not really an outdoorsy type."

"Go figure." I grinned back. David Allen was right about one thing—Alec was too cute. And charming. I was having a really hard time putting him in the role of killer with his pearly white smile flashing my way. I cleared my throat. "Actually, I was looking for you yesterday after you left. I wanted to ask you about something."

"Shoot," he said, giving me his full attention.

"The lawsuit."

He sent me a blank look.

"The one you brought against Tyler."

His smile disappeared, his face instantly transforming from boyishly handsome to something much harder and decidedly not friendly. "Where did you hear about that?" he demanded.

I licked my lips. "It's public record."

He leveled me with an intense look. "Sure. And I supposed you just go searching for court records on the regular."

I ignored the goading, standing my ground. "The lawsuit alleges fraud."

"Is there a question in that?" His face gave nothing away.

"What was the fraud about?"

He narrowed his eyes, his jaw clenching. It was a whole new look on him—one that almost had a menacing edge. Suddenly he looked nothing like a cute boy and fully like a six-foot-three man made of solid muscle who was capable of just about anything.

"I don't think that's any of your business, is it?" he shot back.

"Was it over something at his restaurant? When you worked there?"

"Exactly what are you getting at? I was suing Tyler, so I must have killed him?"

Well, yes. But I hadn't planned to put it that bluntly.

Alec shook his head. "Look, it's true I didn't like Tyler, but *nobody* liked Tyler."

I had to agree with him there. "But was he also a fraud?" I pressed.

Alec let out a small chuckle that held zero humor. "Yeah. I guess he was."

"What did he do to you?" I pressed again.

"What he did to everyone. He used me. Then stomped all over me."

"When you worked at Tyler's Place?"

He nodded. "Tyler had the charisma to have any audience eating out of the palm of his hand. But he had the creativity of a cardboard box when it came to food. Fried chicken, burgers, diner food—that was all Tyler had up his sleeve."

"Unlike you," I said, following where he was going.

Alec shrugged. "I added some magic to a few of his recipes. Some Calabrian chilies here, some miso there, a little sriracha and a bit of unexpected flavor that elevated the diner fare into something people would pay premium prices for."

"So what went wrong?" I asked.

"What went wrong is Tyler started saying the recipes were his." There went that hard look in his blue eyes again.

"You did create them while working in Tyler's kitchen," I hesitated to point out. "Technically, that does make them his property."

"Technically, sure. Hey, they can serve my miso mac and cheese all day long in his restaurants and make bank off it if they want." He paused. "But when Tyler goes on TV and says *he* came up with the clever twist of adding jalapeño to the cheddar burger and *his* grandfather's farm inspired him to add bacon to the patty, that's where I drew the line."

I had to admit, I could see where he was coming from. If someone suddenly started using my personal stories as their own, I'd probably be a little miffed too. Or maybe more than a little... "How much were you suing Tyler for?"

"Just what I was due. You know how much he made on *Eat Up*?"

I shook my head.

"A hundred thousand. Per episode."

Wow. I was so in the wrong business.

"And I watched every single one. Every time he used one of the tricks that I brought into his kitchens and claimed it was his own, that was fraud. That hundred thousand should have been mine. Fifteen instances in the last two years."

"Which comes to a million and half in damages?" I said, doing quick mental math.

Alec nodded. "Only what I was due."

"Did Gabby know you were suing Tyler?"

Alec laughed. "Whose idea do you think it was in the first place?"

I lifted an eyebrow in his direction. "Gabby suggested you sue her costar?"

Alec shrugged. "I complained, and she said I should do something about it. She was right. My attorney thought I had a pretty solid case."

Tyler's must have too, considering he was trying to lower alimony in anticipation of having to pay restitution.

"Look, Gabby told me the network wasn't happy with Tyler, so I knew if I wanted to recoup anything I was due, I had to do it quickly."

"Wait—the network wasn't happy with Tyler?" This was the first I was hearing of it.

Alec shook his head. "Tyler's ratings were slipping. I mean, the catchphrases and angry chef shtick were getting stale."

"I can see that," I agreed. Mostly to keep him talking.

"Honestly, the network would have gotten rid of him last season if it weren't for his contract."

"With the network?"

"Yeah. Tyler was a jerk, but he wasn't stupid. He was contracted to stay on as host of *Eat Up* for two more years. Even if the network fired him, they still had to pay him, so, you know, he had them over a barrel."

"And Gabby told you all of this?" I wondered why she'd left it out of the narrative she'd given Ava and me.

"Sure. I mean, who do you think the network wanted to take over the show if they could ditch Tyler?"

"Gabby," I guessed. So she *had* been angling for Tyler's job.

"That's right." Alec puffed his chest out with something akin to pride. "Gabby's the real star anyway. I mean, look at her. The woman does not deserve to be a sidekick. Especially not to some hack like Tyler Daniels." That last part was said on a sneer that told me Alec still had plenty of emotion toward the dead man.

And while anger could be a mighty motivator to want someone dead, greed was an even better one. Gabby hadn't just been indulging in professional jealousy—she'd actually been in talks with the network to replace Tyler. And if the only thing standing in Gabby's way toward having her own show was Tyler's ironclad contract, there was one surefire way to terminate it—by terminating Tyler.

As if on cue, Gabby emerged from her hair and makeup tent, looking like she'd just stepped off a movie set. Her slinky dress was fire engine red today, hugging her body so tightly it was clear she didn't have an ounce of fat on her. Her dark hair was curled into a silky mane around her head, luminous waves cascading down her back. And her heels were tall stilettos that caused her to wobble a little as they sank into the wet grass.

"Good morning, Emmy," Gabby said, clearly in good spirits, having been properly glammed up.

"Good morning," I greeted her. "Alec and I were just talking about you."

Her smile faltered for a half second before resuming its place. "Oh?"

"About how you really do deserve your own show."

The smile came back full force, showing teeth and everything. "Well, thank you. It's always so nice to meet another fan." Then she turned to her boyfriend. "Alec?"

"Yeah, babe."

"I need coffee. Nonfat almond milk, one stevia, cooled to room temperature."

Alec shot her his charming dimple-studded smile, all signs of the harder Alec having diminished at Gabby's appearance. "Anything for you." He gave me a wink as he led her away toward the booth that our local coffee shop, the Half Calf, had set up. I saw a line forming already under their logo of a cow lounging on a crescent moon.

I took my own empty cup in hand, resuming my quest for more, as I watched the two walk off. They both seemed to have the Jekyll and Hyde sides to them—able to turn their charm on and off at the drop of a hat.

Or the mention of Tyler.

The only question was, which one had more at stake to do away with the star?

CHAPTER SEVEN

I made my way into the kitchen in search of French Roast. Only, as soon as I stepped foot inside the doors, I knew something was up.

Ava, Eddie, and my house manager Conchita all stood at the kitchen counter, eyes glued to something. Something that, as soon as Eddie looked up and saw me, he quickly shoved at Conchita to get rid of.

"What's going on?" I asked.

"Well, good morning to you, Miss Sunshine!" Eddie started. "The birds are singing, the flowers are blooming, and—"

"And the employees are hiding something," I finished for him.

His jovial smile faltered. "Uh, whatever do you mean?"

I glanced around him to where Ava had found a spot on the floor infinitely interesting and Conchita was fussing suspiciously with her apron.

"Conchita?" I asked, picking the weak link.

"*Sí?*" She blinked up at me, her brown eyes wide in her round face. Married to Hector, Conchita had been a fixture at the winery ever since I was a child and often clucked over me like a mother hen. Not that I minded, since her clucking usually came along with delicious baked goods. Today, her salt and pepper hair was pulled back in a floral clip, and the apron tied around her thick waist was liberally doused in flour. And had a large lump underneath it.

"What are you hiding in your apron?"

"Eh...nothing?" she said. Though it came out with a distinct question mark at the end of that statement.

I turned to Ava. "Come on. Whatever it is, it can't be that bad."

"Can't it?" Eddie asked. I could see a fine sheen of sweat had developed on his upper lip.

A small niggle of dread took hold in my belly. "Guys?"

Finally Ava cracked, letting out a long sigh. "You might as well show her. She's bound to see it sooner or later."

Conchita bit her lip, reluctantly pulling an electronic tablet from her apron and setting it on the counter. I knew she usually used it to pull up recipes or cooking videos while in the kitchen, but today the screen was filled with the *Sonoma Index-Tribune* and a headlining article by Bradley Wu entitled "The Deadliest Little Winery in Sonoma."

I heard a groan, and it took me a moment to register that it had come from me.

"See, I told you we should hide it from her," Eddie said, chiding the other two as he adjusted the lapels on his jacket. Pinstriped today, in a periwinkle blue, with a baby pink shirt beneath.

"No, I can take it," I said.

"Here," Ava offered, grabbing my empty coffee cup from my hand. "Let me get you some fortification."

I sent her a grateful smile as she turned to the coffee machine and I turned to the column that put yellow journalists everywhere to shame.

On Monday, Oak Valley Vineyards, the deadliest little winery in Sonoma, struck again, this time claiming celebrity chef Tyler Daniels as its victim.

"My winery didn't kill him!" I protested out loud.

"I know, honey," Eddie said, patting my back.

Conchita made a sympathetic clucking sound as I read on.

The Sonoma County Sheriff's Office has yet to make an official statement—

I thanked God for small favors.

—though sources close to the case have revealed that Daniels was shot to death in the winery's vineyard. As loyal readers will recall, this is the second body to be found at the

winery this year, after a murdered man was found in Oak Valley's cellar last spring.

I closed my eyes and thought a really dirty word.

Conchita gasped.

Oops. Maybe I kinda thought it out loud.

"Here. Coffee will help," Ava said, handing me a steaming mug.

"Does it have whiskey in it?" I said, only half joking.

She raised an eyebrow at me. "It could."

"You didn't even get to the good part yet—*ow!*" Eddie said, rubbing his shin where Ava may or may not have just kicked him.

"It gets better?" I moaned. I took a sip of coffee as I steeled myself for the worst, scalding my tongue in the process. But it was nothing compared to the sinking sensation in my stomach as I read on.

Police have been spotted questioning Oak Valley's wine steward, Jean Luc Gasteon—

I internally cringed, knowing the only thing worse than Jean Luc being named a suspect was being referred to as wine steward instead of sommelier.

—in connection with the death. When asked for her thoughts, winery owner Emmy Oak said, "I'm saddened by the tragic death...connected to Oak Valley Vineyards."

"That's not what I said!" I yelled at the tablet again.

"I knew it was all lies!" Conchita said then she spat on the floor.

"I mean I did say this," I said, mentally going back over the quote I'd given. "But the dot, dot, dot! There was a lot in the dot, dot, dot. This is completely out of context!"

"I'm sorry, Emmy," Ava said, sympathy lacing her voice.

I lay my head down on the cool counter, closing my eye and wishing for a do-over of this day. Week. Year?

"I wonder if this other source is misquoted too," Eddie said, scrolling down the article.

"Who is the other source?" I asked. Though with my face smooshed into the counter, it might have come out more like *who if de offer orse.*

Luckily, learning to speak Emmy mumble was one of the few skills Eddie had acquired. "I don't know. She's just called 'Unnamed source close to the business partners.'"

"Partners?" I lifted my head to glance at the evil tablet again. "You mean Tyler and Mark Black?"

Eddie nodded and pointed to the section.

I looked over his shoulder and read the line out loud. "*A source close to the business partners alleges that Black and Daniels argued quite frequently over money matters at the restaurant.*" I paused. "Well, that much we knew." Though I wondered who the source was as I read on. "*The close source said, 'You didn't hear it from me, but Tyler Daniels accused his partner of...embezzlement.*"

"Embezzlement!" Ava said. "Whoa. Talk about your motive for murder."

I shook my head. "Remember, this is Bradley Wu we're talking about. See that dot, dot, dot?" I stabbed my finger at the spot in the article. "That could say anything. Like 'accused his partner of *nothing like* embezzlement.'"

Ava shrugged. "Good point. Hard to say what the source actually heard."

"Or who she might be," Eddie added.

I read back over the line again. While I was 90% sure Bradley was tweaking the words for his own sensationalism, I also recognized one phrase as likely authentic. *You didn't hear it from me.* Mostly because I *had* heard it from her the night before: Mandy, the hostess at Tyler's Place.

"Actually, that one I might know," I said, filling them in on the conversations I'd had at the restaurant, both with Mandy and Mark Black.

When I was done, Ava's eyes were shining with a look that instantly made me nervous. "We definitely need to talk to this Mandy again," she decided.

"And say what?" I said hesitantly.

"Look, if this source is Mandy, and if Mark was embezzling and if Tyler found out about it and Mandy overheard him confront Mark, that's a huge reason to want Tyler out of the picture."

"It's also a lot of ifs."

"So, let's go talk to Mandy and eliminate a couple of them."

I paused, looking from Eddie to Conchita. "Think you two can manage the festival for an hour or so?"

Conchita nodded "*Sí, sí*. We have everything covered. Go."

Eddie nodded in agreement, glancing down at the article again. "Jean Luc needs you," he decided. Very kind of him, considering the fact that Jean Luc did, on a regular basis, yell at Eddie and call him incompetent. In Jean Luc's defense, Eddie *was* incompetent, but as he was demonstrating now, he also had a heart of gold, which was worth just as much to me at the moment.

I turned to Ava. "Okay, you win. Where do we start?"

*   *   *

Turns out a first name and place of employment were not a lot to go on when it came to tracking down a person. Our first try was the Tyler's Place website, but the only name listed was—no surprise—Tyler Daniels. Then Ava tried typing in *Mandy employed at Tyler's Place* into a search engine. Luck must have been with us, as we got a hit on the LinkedIn website. Unfortunately, as we clicked through to LinkedIn, luck took another long hike, and we realize we had not one hit but thirty-five.

I groaned. "How could there be this many Mandys who work at Tyler's restaurants?"

Ava shrugged. "He does have four locations."

"Yeah, that's still like nine Mandys at each one!"

"Not all of these look like they're active," Ava said, clicking on the first one—an Amanda Cline who lived in Illinois. She was listed as working as a server at Tyler's Place in Chicago two years ago. Last active date on the LinkedIn site was one year and nine months ago.

"Okay, so our Mandy is not Amanda Cline," I cleverly deduced as Ava switched back to the list. "Who's next?"

"Armando 'Mandy' Rodriguez. Dishwasher at the Los Angeles restaurant." Ava paused. "This might not be so hard to weed through after all."

She was right. After clicking through each name on the list of thirty-five, we finally narrowed our search down to two Mandys—Amanda Brooks and Mandy McIntire, both listed as hostesses at Tyler's Place and both living in Sonoma. After some quality time with our friend Google, we found a social media page for Mandy McIntire, where all of her recent posts had to do with her being eight months pregnant with twins. Amanda Brooks was our Mandy.

And, after a couple of quick white pages searches, we had an address just south of Sonoma Valley High School.

Since it was turning out to be a beautiful day, at least as far as the weather was concerned, we decided to take Ava's GTO convertible. With sunglasses on and ponytails flapping behind us, I'm sure we looked to all the world like two blondes without a care. Good thing they couldn't read my mind and hear that every thought running through it had to do with murder.

The address our search gave us was an older townhouse complex. Ava parked semi-legally in front of the garage for number 17B, and I rang the bell of the small corner unit. At first I feared Mandy wasn't at home, as I heard the chime echoing inside but no movement to accompany it. I waited a good thirty seconds before ringing again as Ava chewed on a fingernail beside me. I was about to give up when I finally heard shuffling footsteps on the other side and the sound of a lock being unlatched.

The door opened, and a sleepy-looking Mandy stared out at us. "Yeah?" she said, stifling a yawn. She was in a pair of pink pajama pants bearing a Victoria's Secret logo and a white tank top, and her hair was sticking out a wild angle on one side.

"Sorry to wake you," I said automatically.

"'S okay." She blinked at me. "What do you want?"

"I'm Emmy Oak. I own Oak Valley Vineyards."

She gave me a blank stare. "Do I know you?"

"Uh, not really. I was in the restaurant last night."

"Yeah, a *lot* of people were," she said.

"Right. Well, I was wondering if I could ask you some questions..."

"Wait, you're not a reporter, are you?" She narrowed her eyes at us and crossed her arms over her chest. "Because that last one totally misquoted me."

I opened my mouth to reassure her that we were not reporters, but before I could get a word out, Ava beat me to it.

"Yes! We are reporters."

I shut my mouth with a click and shot her a look. "We are?"

"Yes." Ava nodded enthusiastically. "We're with the, uh, *Sonoma Truth Tellers*."

Mandy cocked her head to the side. "I've never heard of that paper."

"We're mainly digital," Ava said, waving that minor detail off. "But, what we do is get to the real truth behind the sensation. We like to set the record straight. And when we read Bradley Wu's piece this morning, we just knew it wasn't the whole, unedited truth."

Well, at least that much was true.

And it seemed to have the desired effect, as Mandy's defensive posture relaxed.

"Seriously! That guy can totally twist someone's words," she said. Then she seemed to stop herself, realizing she might be giving away her anonymity. "I mean, so I heard."

"Any chance we could come in and ask you a few questions?" I jumped in.

Mandy thought about it for a second. "Okay, but as long as you promise you won't print anything that isn't 100% the way I say it."

"Cross my heart," I told her. Which was an easy promise to make, considering we weren't planning to print anything at all.

Mandy stepped back, allowing us both entry into the townhouse. The living room/dining room combo was small but homey, furnished with a loveseat and armchair situated to face a TV above a gas fireplace. Beyond that, I could see an eat-in kitchen and a stairway that led up to what I assumed were bedrooms. Mandy plopped herself down on the armchair, crossing her bare feet up under her, and Ava and I sat on the sofa.

"So, what did you want to know?" Mandy asked.

"Well," I said, "for starters, I'd love to know what you actually said to Bradley Wu that was misquoted."

Mandy's face colored. "Why do you think it was me who talked to Wu?"

"Just a hunch." I gave her a reassuring smile. "But it was you, wasn't it?"

She let out a long breath. "Okay, fine. Yeah, I talked to the guy. He came in last night—after you," she said, gesturing to me. "At first I didn't even know he was a reporter. He just wanted to know all about Tyler. I thought maybe he was a super fan or something. But then what do I see this morning? My words all misquoted in print. Ugh!"

I knew the feeling.

"The article mentioned you overheard an argument?" I asked.

Mandy nodded. "Dude, Mark and Tyler argued every time Tyler was in town. Most of them went pretty much the same. Mark yelling that Tyler was spending too much, and Tyler asking Mark whose name was on the sign."

"So Tyler didn't accuse Mark of embezzlement?" I asked.

Mandy shook her head, her bed head flopping around her ears. "No. Tyler accused Mark of being a—" She paused. "Can you quote swear words?"

Ava shook her head. "We're a family paper."

"Okay, well then, he accused Mark of being a big 'poo-poo' head." She did air quotes, indicating the part that might not have originally been family friendly.

"So there was never any talk of embezzlement?" I asked, feeling my hopes sink.

"Oh, sure there was."

"Oh?" Hope perked back up.

"Yeah, but it was just talk. I mean, I heard Tyler say that thing about Mark then Mark said something back about Tyler being an egotistical—" She paused, stopping herself just in time. "Egotistical 'other word for a donkey.' Then Tyler said something about missing money, and Mark said embezzlement was ridiculous."

"Then what?" I asked, feeling on the metaphorical edge of my seat.

But Mandy shrugged. "Then one of the dishwashers walked by, and I didn't want him to see me hanging around Mark's office."

"So what was this missing money?" Ava asked.

"Search me. I don't even know if any money was missing. I mean, like I said, Mark said it was ridiculous."

Which didn't mean it wasn't true.

"Hey, you aren't going to use my name on this, are you?" Mandy asked. "I mean, I'm not sure my boss will like me talking to the press, even if it is to set the record straight."

I shook my head. "I promise your name won't end up in print anywhere."

* * *

"So it is actually possible that Tyler accused Mark of embezzling," Ava noted as we got back into her car.

"Tyler just said 'missing money,'" I reminded her. "It's also possible that Tyler found ten bucks missing from the bar register. 'Missing money' is a pretty broad term."

"But Mark did say the word embezzling," Ava countered.

"Yeah, as in it was ridiculous."

"Which is exactly what an embezzler would say!" Ava said, eyes shining as she pulled out of the townhouse complex.

"You are almost as bad as Bradley Wu," I told her.

"Ouch." She shot me a look of mock hurt. "Low blow, girl."

I laughed. "Okay, fine. For the sake of argument, let's say there was money missing."

"You said Mark admitted that they were in bad financial shape, but what if it wasn't really because Tyler was overspending but because Mark was skimming funds?"

"Tyler finds out and confronts Mark," I said, picking up her narrative.

"And Mark kills Tyler to keep it quiet. And," Ava added, "conveniently points the finger at Tyler as the reason their funds are running low. Tyler's not around to dispute it, and it would be easy enough for Mark to juggle the books to make it look like Tyler had wasted the money away."

"What isn't as easy is proving any of this is true," I pointed out. "All we have is 'you didn't hear it from me' Mandy and a lot of guesswork."

"If only we could get a look at Tyler's Place's books," Ava said, drumming her fingers on the steering wheel, her eyes getting a faraway look in them.

"Oh no," I said.

She blinked innocently at me. "What?"

"I know that look. It's your *Charlie's Angels* look."

"What's wrong with *Charlie's Angels*?"

"Nothing, but whenever you get that look, you're imagining us being badass crime fighters."

She grinned. "Admit it—you're kind of imagining it too."

"I'm imagining us getting arrested."

She scoffed. "What for?"

"For whatever scheme you're cooking up."

Ava waved me off with a laugh. "Look, I'm just saying, if we could get a look at the books, we could tell if Mark was cooking them to cover his embezzlement. That's all."

"And we would get a look at his private financial papers, how…?" I asked, waiting for the punch line.

She shrugged. "We could break into the restaurant when it's closed."

"That's it." I stabbed a finger her way. "That's what's wrong with the *Charlie's Angels* look."

Ava shook her head at me. "You're no fun."

"It's called being a law-abiding citizen. Wait—did you just roll your eyes at me?"

"Nervous twitch," Ava covered.

CHAPTER EIGHT

———

By the time we got back to the winery, the festival was in full swing. Or, as full a swing as I feared we could expect. If it was possible, even fewer guests were milling around today, and if I had to guess, press outnumbered them two to one. Ava quickly went to open her Silver Girl booth, and I went in search of Hector. All the empty booths from vendors who had not returned were starting to get depressing. If he could pull them down before we reopened again tomorrow, maybe our last day wouldn't look like I was serving appetizers in a ghost town.

I finally found him in our wine cellar—or The Cave as my grandma Emmeline had dubbed it years ago. As a kid I'd loved to play there, the cool, underground cavern a welcomed place to escape from the summer heat. As an adult, I knew it held our greatest assets—our stock in trade aged to perfection. In fact, I'd recently sold a couple of the older bottles at auction to raise funds needed for our harvest this year. Something I'd hoped we wouldn't need to do.

"Hey, kid," Hector greeted me. He sent me a smile through the weather worn wrinkles that comprised his face. Hector had been a fixture at Oak Valley ever since my father's time, having come on as a teen and practically growing up in the vineyard. He'd taught me everything I knew about the vines, and I'd even been the flower girl at his wedding to Conchita, which had taken place years ago right here at the winery. My parents had looked at them as family, and Hector had been the first one to alert me that something hadn't seemed right with my mom. I hadn't wanted to believe it then, but, as always, he'd been right. He also often made the weekly trips with me to visit her in the home in Napa where she spent her days trapped in memories that had become her jumbled reality.

I shook that thought off, focusing on the more immediate problems of the day.

"Hi, Hector," I returned his greeting.

"Just grabbing a few more bottles for Jean Luc. The guests are thirsty today."

I raised an eyebrow. "Guests or reporters?"

Hector gave me sympathetic smile. "I saw the article too. Chin up, kid. This will pass."

"Thanks," I told him, meaning it. "Let's just hope it doesn't bulldoze us down as it does."

He laughed, the chuckle deep and rumbling. "We've been through tougher things than this."

"Not a *lot* tougher," I countered.

But his smile didn't falter. "We'll be fine. Just think of all the reporters who are getting hooked on Oak Valley wines." He gave me a wink.

"There's always a silver lining, huh?" Despite the fact I only half believed that, I couldn't help an answering smile tugging at my mouth. "I wanted to talk to you about the empty booths up in the festival grounds."

"I noticed. There are quite a few, aren't there?"

"Unfortunately. Any chance you could pull some down before we open tomorrow? I'm afraid they're not sending the right message."

He nodded. "I'll get Charlie and José to help me when we close."

I sent him a grateful smile. "Thanks. At least we can try to finish with a bang."

Hector wagged a finger at me as he hauled a case of Zinfandel onto his shoulder. "A bang is what started all this trouble in the first place."

Wasn't that the truth.

I thanked him and closed the cellar doors behind us as he took his case toward the tasting room. I was just about to follow him, when something caught my eye a few paces down the stone pathway.

Gabriela Genova and Alec Post, just off the pathway, partially hidden by a grove of oak trees. Not that the pair were an odd sight, but I noticed Gabby was waving her arms wildly, her words coming out rapid-fire. I was too far away to hear what they were saying, but the body language was clear—the couple was arguing.

I did an angel-shoulder-devil-shoulder thing as I watched Alec fire some response back, his usually handsome features contorted with anger. He was Mr. Hyde Alec at the moment.

I really shouldn't eavesdrop. Whatever they were arguing about was clearly none of my business. However, if it had anything to do with Tyler's death and could help Jean Luc's case…

Devil shoulder won, as I tip-toed off the stone pathway, going the long way around the grove of trees to come up on the other side of the couple. A stone wall sat just beside the grove, making for excellent cover as I caught the tail end of Gabby's response.

"…totally overreacting!"

"*I'm* overreacting?" Alec shot back. "You're the one getting all hot and defensive."

Defensive? That was an interesting word. Innocent people didn't usually need to defend themselves.

Gabby's response was loud, immediate, and half in Italian. I tried to think back to my high school Spanish classes for some help, but I could only pick up a few words.

"…lies!…with someone so *stupido*…believe me…*muerto*…"

I froze. Muerto I knew. It meant dead. Was she talking about Tyler?

I inched forward, trying to peek around the wall to see her face, but my foot must have landed on a stick, as a loud crack sounded through the air.

Okay, maybe loud was relative, but to someone crouching in the dirt trying to eavesdrop unseen, it felt like a herd of elephants.

And Gabby must have noticed it too, as her Italian tirade stopped. "What was that?" she asked.

"Don't change the subject," came Alec's curt reply.

"Why do you have to be so mean?" Gabby spat back.

"You know what? I don't. I don't have to take any of this!" I heard leaves rustling then footsteps on the pathway.

"Alec, wait!" Gabby called, her voice moving farther away from me and quickly accompanied by the distinct sound of heels click-clacking on the uneven stones.

I waited a full minute before moving, just to be sure they were both far away enough that I wouldn't be seen. Then I slowly stood, stomping some life back into my cramped legs as I made my way back to the path as well.

I had no idea what I'd just heard. Possibly a simple lover's spat. Possibly something much more sinister. Had they been discussing Tyler's death? Alec had sounded like he was accusing Gabby of something—possibly killing her costar? I tried to think of any way to delicately approach either party to pry into their argument as I followed the pathway toward the kitchen.

I never quite got there, as a loud commotion at the RV still parked behind the building caught my attention.

The crime scene tape had yet to be removed from the door, but the seal had been broken, and two guys with official looking CSI jackets were coming in and out of the trailer, Ziploc baggies in hand. At the base of the steps stood Grant, hands on his hips as he stared down at the instigator of the commotion—Bradley Wu.

The portly reporter was dressed in a dapper plaid vest today, looking much like the white rabbit from *Alice in Wonderland* as a gold pocket watch dangled from a chain on one side of it. His white shirt was buttoned all the way to the top beneath it, and as I approached the pair, I heard him lobbing quick questions at Grant.

"I hear the wine steward is the prime suspect in your investigation," Bradley said, goading Grant.

I involuntarily held my breath as I listened for the answer.

"The Sheriff's Office has no comment at this time."

I said a silent thank you.

"But you have been questioning him?"

"No comment."

"And searching his home?"

"No. Comment," Grant ground out, enunciating clearly.

"Maybe I could just take a teeny tiny peek at what your team is gathering from the trailer..."

Bradley made a motion to sidestep Grant, but the detective's hand shot to the gun at his hip.

"This is an active crime scene," he told Bradley hotly. "If you take a single step more, I'll arrest you for tampering with evidence."

Bradley's eyes went wide, and I stifled a laugh. While I would have loved to see the reporter hauled off in handcuffs, I wasn't sure what it would do to the mood of the few remaining festivalgoers.

"Everything okay here, boys?" I asked, stepping into the mix.

Two pairs of eyes swiveled my way, both holding a hint of relief in them.

"Emmy, my dahling, just the person I wanted to see," Bradley said, his features shifting from terror to glee in seconds flat.

"Bradley," I said, nodding his way. I glanced up at Grant. "Any problems here?"

"No problem," he said. "As long as everyone steps back and lets me do my job."

I wasn't sure if he was talking just to Bradley or a little to me as well, but I complied, backing up a few steps with my hands up in a surrender motion.

Bradley followed me, leaning in with a mock whisper. "He's tightly wound, huh?"

"If you only knew."

Bradley sent a questioning eyebrow my way, but I didn't take the bait. "Interesting article you published this morning," I told him.

"Thank you." He beamed.

"That was not a compliment."

The smile faltered a bit. "Now, Emmy, you know how the saying goes—all publicity is good publicity!"

"'Deadliest little winery'?" I quoted. I shook my head at him. "And here I thought we were friends, Bradley."

"Hey, a reporter's gotta do what a reporter's gotta do to keep readers. You know how few people still read newspapers these days? I have a better chance of catching the plague than a new subscriber."

"Aww." I gave him a sarcastic pout and pretended to play a violin in sympathy.

"Oh." Bradley scoffed and waved me off. "You make fun, but you know you need me just as much as I need you."

I hated how right he was. "Okay, fine," I said. "What about this? You leave Jean Luc alone in your column—"

He moved to protest, but I rode right over it.

"—letting the police decide if he's a suspect. And when the festival is over, I'll give you an exclusive interview detailing how I found the body." Which was the last thing I ever wanted to think about, let alone retell. But if it kept Wu off my back for 24 hours, it just might be worth it.

He paused, mulling that offer over. "You promise this is exclusive? No leaking similar stories to Sonoma Magazine?"

I held up three fingers. "Scout's honor."

He cocked his head to the side. "Why do I get the feeling you were never a Girl Scout?"

"Do we have a deal or not?" I pressed, sticking my hand out his way to shake.

Finally he must have realized it was the best deal he was going to get—and a lot better than Grant's offer to haul him off to jail—as he put his pudgy palm in mine.

"Deal. But as soon as the Food and Wine Festival is over, I'll be knocking on your door, Emmy."

"Looking forward to it," I lied through gritted teeth.

* * *

I left Bradley Wu waddling toward the stuffed mushrooms booth and went to check in on Jean Luc. With the police and press hovering in equally terrifying numbers, I could only imagine how my sommelier's mood was. But as I entered the tasting room, I noted that if he was feeling any foreboding, he was excellent at hiding it. He stood behind the bar, pouring with his usual flourish for the few scattered customers partaking of our samples. Though I noted most of them were not our ticket holders but press. I prayed that Hector's rosy outlook on the onslaught was true—reporters bought wine too, right?

As I approached Jean Luc, I noticed he was refilling a glass for one of the few members of the press I was happy to see still here—Ashley Daniels, the food critic for the *LA Times*. She was dressed today in a smart pencil skirt, two-inch pumps, a loose blouse that billowed flatteringly around her middle, and gold and silver bracelets at her wrist that tinkled together like wind chimes as she raised her glass to her lips.

"Ms. Daniels, I'm so glad to see you've stayed on for the rest of the festival," I told her, meaning it. A good review might not be enough to counter all the bad publicity the Bradley Wus of the world were dishing out, but it certainly couldn't hurt.

"Of course," she said, raising her glass my way. "I'm dying to see how this little drama all plays out." She shot me a wink.

I cleared my throat awkwardly. "Yes, well, that's why I'm here."

"Eez zere a problem?" Jean Luc asked, his mustache twitching, betraying that nerves were, indeed, hiding just below his calm surface.

I shook my head. "No, no, nothing like that. I just wanted to see how today's tasting turnout was."

His shoulders relaxed. "Ah. Good. Yes, we're busy enough," he responded, gesturing to the few patrons at the bar.

"How are *you*?" I asked, wishing there were some comforting words I could give him.

He straightened his already stiff spine. "Perfectly fine, I assure you."

I couldn't help smiling at his bravado. "Good. But let me know if you need a break."

He nodded curtly. "I am fine," he repeated.

"I was just telling Jean Luc here how sorry I was," Ashley cut in, gesturing to him with her wineglass. "You know, about the misunderstanding about him being fired by Tyler."

Jean Luc's mustache twitched indignantly at the word *fired*, but he nodded stiffly, acknowledging the apology. "It eez nothing, Meez Daniels. All eez forgiven."

"Really, I had no idea I'd cause any trouble for you with the police," she went on. "I mean, I honestly thought it was the case. But I should have known better than to run my mouth around the police anyway. It was just that detective. He was so…unnerving, you know?"

I nodded. "Oh, I know."

"Anyway, thank you," Ashley said, sending the comment Jean Lu's way. "For being so understanding."

He nodded at her again, his shellacked hair not moving an inch. Someone from the other side of the bar hailed him, and he politely excused himself, looking grateful for the excuse to abandon the uncomfortable conversation.

"I noticed a few more of your vendors didn't show today," Ashley said.

"Uh, yes." I bit my lip, hoping this didn't fare badly for her article. "But Gabby is still slated to do a wonderful baking demonstration later, and we still have a variety of food being served for lunch."

"And the Zinfandel is delightful," Ashley said, shooting me a smile as she sipped again.

I felt a small wave of relief.

"Join me for a glass?" she asked.

I hesitated a moment—I didn't usually drink while on duty, so to speak.

"Please," Ashley said with a smile. "No one likes to drink alone."

Well, she *was* from the *LA Times*…

I stepped behind the bar and poured myself a glass from the open bottle. "Please let me know if you'd like to try any of our other varietals," I told her. "We have some lovely whites too."

"Thank you. I may take you up on that. I have to say, this place is a little hidden gem here."

"Do you get up to wine country often?" I asked, taking my glass to the empty barstool beside her.

She shrugged, sipping. "Not really. Now and again for business. You do have a reputation up here for fine dining."

I nodded, feeling a small opening. "Speaking of dining, I was at Tyler's Place last night."

She laughed, the cackle ringing in my ears. "That is not the definition of fine, is it?"

I grinned, shaking my head. "No, not really." I paused, watching her. "I did chat with Mark Black though."

"Oh?" she said, sipping her glass.

"Do you know him well?" I asked, hoping I sounded like I was just making casual conversation.

She shrugged. "Of course. We're old friends…you know, from when Tyler and I were married." She paused, a small frown forming between her eyebrows. "Why?"

I shook my head. "Just curious. Do you know how long Mark and Tyler have known each other?"

She pursed her lips, eyes going to a spot on the wall as if trying to picture the meeting in her mind's eyes. "Gosh, ages. Fifteen years, maybe? They met when Tyler was trying to open his first restaurant here in Sonoma."

"The first Tyler's Place?"

She nodded. "But it was called something else back then. Wine Country Inn or some other generic term." She laughed. "Tyler never was one for much creativity."

"So I've heard," I mumbled.

She raised an eyebrow my way. "Oh, have you?"

I hesitated to talk about Alec's lawsuit, but with Tyler dead, it didn't seem like there was much point in keeping quiet. "Well, the lawsuit you said Alec filed against him…"

"Yes?" Ashley asked. "What about it?"

"It alleged that Tyler was using Alec's recipes as his own."

Ashley threw her head back, a torrent of hearty laughter erupting from her throat. "Oh, that is rich."

"You mean you don't think it's true?"

"Oh no." She shook her head. "No, I'm sure it's true. I just mean, it was pretty brazen even for Tyler. But what do you expect from a man with an ego three times the size of his brain?"

She shook her head as the laughter subsided, sipping from her glass again.

"Were you and Tyler together when Alec worked with him?" I asked.

Ashley shook her head as she swallowed her sip. "Only briefly. To be honest, Alec was really just a kid then, and I didn't pay much attention to what was going on in the restaurant. I already had one foot out the door, so to speak."

"So you don't know how the two got along?"

"I imagine not well, if Alec was suing him." She paused, that small frown going between her eyebrow again. "Why? You think Alec killed Tyler over this lawsuit?"

"Do you think he's capable of it?" I asked, trying to be as delicate as possible.

But she didn't seem phased by the question, quickly shaking her head. "I don't see why he would. I mean, if Alec thought he was going to win the lawsuit, it kind of defeats the purpose to kill Tyler before he can pay restitution, right?"

She had a good point. However, that assumed Alec thought he would win the lawsuit. Even if the fraud was true, it didn't mean Alec would win. Or, if he did win, he'd be awarded what he was asking for.

"What about Gabby?" I asked, switching gears as I thought of the argument I'd overheard.

"Gabby?" Ashley laughed again. "Kill Tyler? No way. Not a chance."

"You seem pretty certain."

Ashley leaned forward. "Why would she kill the man she was sleeping with?"

I blinked at her, the implications of that question sinking in. "Wait—Gabby and Tyler?"

Ashley nodded, still grinning at me. "You didn't know?"

I shook my head. "But what about Alec?"

Ashley laughed again. "Honey, Gabby would not be the first woman to cheat on a man."

"Who told you this?" I asked, still trying to process this new information.

"No one had to tell me. Look, I know the signs when Tyler is sleeping with a woman, okay? I spent years trying to deny them. All you had to do was watch them on the show, and it was obvious."

"You sure they weren't acting?" I asked, thinking of the way Gabby had displayed nothing but disdain for Tyler whenever we'd spoken.

Ashley nodded. "Positive. Sure, some of the cutesy banter was put on for the audience, but the way he looked at her, the way he'd touch her leg, the wolfish gleam in his eyes when her neckline was especially low? I know those all too well." Ashley jiggled her empty glass at me, signaling the need for a refill.

I took it and moved around the bar automatically, refilling as I digested this new bit of information. If Gabby had been sleeping with Tyler, that opened up a whole new dynamic—not just between her and Tyler but between Tyler and Alec too. Maybe Alec hadn't killed Tyler over the theft of his recipes—but over the theft of his girlfriend. Had that been what the couple was arguing about in the woods? I thought back to the words I'd overheard. Alec had definitely been accusing Gabby of something, but it felt like she was hotly denying it.

Though, whether that meant it was a valid accusation or not remained to be seen.

* * *

I left the tasting room with a whole new round of questions swirling through my head and a slight buzz from Zinfandel before lunch. After a quick stop to the Aldo's Restaurant booth, where I grabbed a couple of bowls of Caprese Panzanella Salad, I stopped by Ava's Silver Girl booth to feed her and fill her in on the argument I'd witnessed and Ashley's affair hypothesis.

"So you think Alec found out that Gabby was sleeping with Tyler, and he killed him over it?" Ava asked around a bite.

I shrugged. "I guess it does sound kind of soap operaish when you put it that way."

But Ava shook her head. "No, I think it could be possible. I mean, maybe it was a heat of the moment type thing, you know? Alec confronts Tyler, Tyler goes into his smug jerk act, and Alec just loses it."

"With a gun that he just happens to have on him? That just happens to be the same type as Jean Luc's?"

"You're right. Nix the crime of passion thing." She paused, stabbing a tomato and chewing thoughtfully. "But it doesn't mean it still couldn't be Alec. I mean, yes, it would require a little planning, but maybe he did. Plan it out, I mean."

"Over Gabby?"

"Well, let's say he was no big fan of Tyler already. Tyler stole his recipes," Ava added.

"But he was suing Tyler and by all accounts seemed to have a pretty good case. Even Tyler's own attorney was nervous about it."

"He was nervous about having to *pay*," Ava reminded me. "Remember Mark Black said their business was going into the red. Maybe Tyler's attorney knew he just didn't have the money to pay Alec if he lost the lawsuit."

"Maybe Alec found out how bad Tyler's finances were and realized that he likely wouldn't get a dime even if he did win the lawsuit," I said, following her breadcrumb trail.

"I'm sure Alec has had to pay out of pocket for his own attorney to file the lawsuit. What if he realized he wouldn't be likely to get any of that back even if he won? That he was essentially going to end up spending thousands of dollars just to get Tyler to stop presenting his recipes as his own."

"And he decided that killing Tyler was a much more economical way to stop him," I finished.

Ava nodded. "Could be finding out Tyler was also sleeping with his girlfriend was just the final straw."

I popped a stray piece of mozzarella into my mouth and munched it down. "It's a great theory, but it all hinges on one thing," I said.

"What's that?"

"How bad *were* Tyler's finances? Alec said he was making a hundred grand an episode. The restaurants would have to be losing a lot to eat that up too."

Ava nodded. "Unless, of course, Mark Black really was stealing from the business." She pinned me with a look, her eyes taking on that mischievous twinkle. "Gee, if only we could get a look at Tyler's Place's finances."

I paused, a bite of salad midway to my mouth. "Oh no..."

"You know they aren't open until five for dinner."

"Please don't tell me you're thinking..."

"It would be the easiest thing in the world to just slip in and get a little peek."

"Really? Breaking and entering—easiest thing in the world?"

"Come on, Emmy. You know this could be the key to knowing if we're on the right track or just going in circles."

While every fiber of my being screamed at me to deny it, I knew she was right. Whether it was the embezzling partner or the ticked-off former protégé who killed Tyler, both motives hinged on one thing—the state of Tyler's finances. I dropped the fork back onto my plate in surrender. "Fine," I said.

Her eyes lit up like a child at Christmas, and I kid you not, she actually clapped.

"But you're driving," I told her. "I've still got a Zin buzz."

Ava raised an eyebrow at me. "Drinking red before noon?"

"It's been that kind of week."

CHAPTER NINE

———

Ava circled the block twice, checking that the lot to Tyler's Place was empty before pulling up to the curb two doors down in front of a used bookstore.

"I don't know about this," I said for probably the tenth time since we'd left the winery. "You sure it wouldn't be better to come back later? Like, after dark?"

Ava shook her head beside me, her blonde hair floating along her shoulders. "We're hiding in plain sight like this. Look, the place is closed, and even the prep staff won't be in for a couple hours, right?"

"Right," I agreed. I knew that for a fact because I'd called "You Didn't Hear It From Me" Mandy earlier and gotten the staff schedules. The first person on it was the sous chef, who didn't start for another two hours.

"So, what's less suspicious—two fans coming to pay their respects to the late, great Tyler Daniels in broad daylight or a couple of dark figures lurking around in the middle of the night?"

"Fine," I relented. Mostly because while I wasn't a fan of sneaking in anywhere, I was definitely not up for lurking. "Let's get this over with."

"After you, Farrah," Ava said, getting out of the car.

"Farrah?" I asked.

"Farrah Fawcett. She's my favorite Charlie's Angel, but you can be Jaclyn Smith if you want?"

What I wanted to be was home in my cozy sweats, eating a pint of mint chip and watching a nineties rom com, preferably starring Drew Barrymore. But one did not always get what one wanted.

Ava grabbed the bouquet of roses we'd stopped for on the way as a prop. Her plan was to pretend we were a couple of the mourners who'd been flocking to the restaurant to pay their last respects to the cardboard Tyler cutout. It wasn't an altogether terrible way to get past the security cameras I could see mounted on the building.

"What time did Mandy say she'd be here?" Ava asked, shielding her eyes from the sun with one hand as she glanced at the two-story-high picture of Tyler's face on the sign.

"She told me twenty minutes."

Phase two of our plan had been to ask Mandy to let us in the building before shifts started. Ostensibly it was to take a few photos of the place to go along with our super truthful article. How we were going to segue from that to pawing through the financial records, I hadn't quite worked out yet. But I was hoping something came to me.

And quickly, I decided, as a red Kia pulled into the lot, parking just a couple spaces away from the door.

Ava locked her car, and we made our way toward the Kia, approaching just as Mandy got out of the driver's side door.

"Hey!" she called, waving to us.

Ava waved the roses back.

"Thanks for meeting us," I told her.

"Yeah, the photos will really give our piece the authenticity it needs," Ava jumped in, giving Mandy a smile that was all teeth. If I didn't know better, she was digging this Angels stuff.

Mandy shrugged. "Sure." She looked to Ava. "What's with the roses?"

"Prop," Ava told her. "Makes us look like mourners and not reporters."

"For the security cameras," I said, nodding my head in what I hoped was a surreptitious gesture to the two mounted near the front entrance.

"Ooooooh," Mandy said slowly. "Right. Don't want anyone to know I let reporters in, huh?"

I nodded again.

"Maybe I should go around back. Then unlock the door from the inside."

"Great plan," Ava agreed.

I nodded a third time, like a silent bobble doll who was feeling very exposed standing in the empty parking lot in front of a pair of cameras. As Mandy jogged around the building, I couldn't help looking over both shoulders as if at any moment someone was going to catch us in the act.

"Stop that," Ava muttered to me.

"What?"

"Looking around like that. It looks like we're up to no good."

"We *are* up to no good."

"No, we're up to *lots* of good," she corrected. "We're catching a killer."

Just as long as we didn't catch a breaking and entering rap, I'd be happy.

I reluctantly followed Ava to the glass front of the restaurant. The interior was largely dark, only the natural sunlight filtering in the windows, creating shadows in the empty booths. A sign that hung on the glass front doors read *Closed*, and Ava grabbed the handle, giving it a jiggle. It didn't budge.

"Just checking," she said.

"I hope Mandy hurries." I shifted from foot to foot as I stared into the empty lobby.

"Stand still," Ava hissed. "You're making me antsy."

"*Everything* about this is making me antsy," I hissed back.

Ava shook her head at me.

"What?"

"You are tightly wound lately."

I gave her a deadpanned look. "Gee, wonder why?"

"You need to get laid."

I choked out a laugh. "What?"

"Seriously, when was the last time you went out on a date?"

"I had half a date last month," I said, hearing how pathetic it sounded to my own ears.

Ava did more head shaking. "Half a date. With a guy who is now trying to put your employee in jail."

"He's just doing his job," I countered. Though, why I was suddenly defending Grant, I didn't know.

"If he was doing it *well*, he'd be looking at the Tyler's Place financial records and not Jean Luc."

"God, please do not let him think of *that* in the next twenty minutes," I muttered, more to myself than Ava. "And what is taking Mandy so long—"

I didn't get to finish that thought, as the sound of a lock being opened came from the door and I spotted Mandy on the other side.

"Hey," she said as she pulled the doors open for us. "Sorry. Back door is kinda sticky sometimes."

I let out an internal sigh of relief and quickly stepped inside and away from the cameras.

"So, what did you want to photograph first?" Mandy asked.

"Did Tyler have an office here?" Ava asked. I could see her eyes immediately going to the Tyler cutout with a pile of slowly decaying bouquets still at his feet.

"Sorry." Mandy shook her head. "Mark—the other owner—he keeps an office in the back. But Tyler wasn't here that often."

"How often was he here?" I asked, jumping on the opportunity.

"Hmmm. I dunno. Maybe like every couple of months? Mostly he just came in to do some publicity spots. Sign his cookbook, do a meet and greet—you know."

"And argue with Mark Black?" I asked.

She shrugged. "Yeah, and that." She paused. "Want to start in the kitchen?"

"Sounds great!" Ava said, a big smile on her face.

Mandy moved to lead the way then paused, her eyes going from me to Ava. "Where's your camera?"

I quickly grabbed my phone and held it out in front of me. "We're on a budget."

"The truth is awesome, but it doesn't pay much," Ava jumped in. She put her flowers down at Tyler's feet and pulled her own phone out of her jeans.

If Mandy found it odd, she didn't say anything, just shrugging as she led the way to the kitchen.

Ava leaned her head close to mine as we walked. "The financials must be in Mark's office."

I nodded. "How are we going to get at them?" I whispered back.

"Leave it to me."

I was about to protest that plan, but it died on my lips as we entered the kitchen and Mandy spun around to face us.

"So, this is where the magic happens!" She spread her arms out wide to encompass the room.

Ava gave her a bright smile. "Awesome!" She held her phone up, taking random photos.

I followed suit, and I had to admit that the kitchen actually was kind of awesome. A drool-worthy range, huge walk-in refrigerator, and more appliances than I could dream of ever stocking in our kitchen. And I had an envious feeling none of them were on the fritz.

"Hey, where's your restroom?" Ava asked, clicking away at the oven hood.

"Down the hall," Mandy said, sounding bored with the whole thing.

"Thanks. I really have to go." Ava paused. "Don't you have to go, Emmy?"

I pulled my attention away from the range and glanced up. "What?"

"To the restroom," Ava said. "Didn't you say you had to go too?"

This was her brilliant plan?

But luckily Mandy had pulled out her own phone and was so engrossed in whatever was on her screen that she didn't seem to notice.

"Uh, yeah. I do," I responded.

"Cool. I'll wait here," Mandy said, not looking up.

I quickly followed Ava as she ducked down the hallway.

"What are we, twelve? We have to go pee together?" I whispered.

"It worked, didn't it?" Ava grinned at me.

I had to admit, it had. "Okay, Farrah, where's Mark's office?"

"Mandy said in the back."

We passed a restroom and a supply closet before the hallway dead ended in a door on the left marked *Exit* and one on the right marked *Private*. We pushed open the private one and were treated to a view of a desk, office chair, and filing cabinets, all in utilitarian gray. Florescent lights buzzed above, and the linoleum floor was cracked and peeling. I wasn't sure what the inside of Tyler's trailer looked like, but I had the distinct feeling that Mark Black had the short end of this partnership stick.

"Well this is depressing," Ava said.

"Ditto. But let's hurry. Mandy's phone can't hold her attention forever."

Ava nodded, going immediately to the computer and switching it on.

On the off chance Black was analog, I opened the file cabinets. No luck. A six pack of domestic beer and three *Sports Illustrated* magazines with Chrissy Teigen on the cover. If Black got any actual work done back here, it was all in the cloud.

Ava sat behind the desk, the office chair creaking loudly in response.

We both froze. I half expected to hear Mandy's sneakers padding down the hallway, but after a couple seconds of total silence, I figured our noise had gone unnoticed. I let out a sigh of relief and turned back to the computer monitor, where Ava had the system booting up.

"Password?" she asked.

I gave her a blank look. "How would I know?"

She scrunched up her nose. "Well, maybe we can guess. You met Black. What kind of words would he use?"

I shook my head. "I met him once. For a few minutes. I have no clue. Birthday, pet's name, make of his car?"

"Know any of those?"

I shot her a look.

"Right, okay. Well, maybe he wrote it down somewhere…" Ava trailed off, going through the desk drawers.

I felt that antsiness come on full force again, wondering how much time would pass before Mandy decided we were taking the longest tandem pee on record. I glanced around the room for any hints. Unfortunately, it was, as Ava had said, a depressing room, holding little to no decor. There was a digital frame on the desk, but half the photos were showing error messages and the other half were pixilated to distortion. The furnishings were monochromatic and designed for cheap utilitarian purposes over style or esthetics. Walls were plain white, and the only thing hanging on them was a calendar with a photo of a model in a teeny-tiny bikini, lying on a beach in a way that was sure to get sand in some really uncomfortable places. I squinted at the woman's face and recognized the model.

"Try *Chrissy*," I said.

Ava glanced up at me then followed my line of sight to the calendar. She nodded, and her fingers hit the keyboard typing it in. "C-H-R-I-S-S-Y…and *enter*."

We held our collective breath as the screen switched to a loading logo then Black's desktop appeared.

"Genius!" Ava said.

"Men," I decided. "But yeah, it worked." I glanced up at the thankfully still closed door to the office. "Let's find the files quickly, huh?"

"On it, Jaclyn." Ava clicked an icon clearly and conveniently labeled *Accounting* on the desktop.

A bookkeeping program opened, and digital ledger pages appeared. Ava scrolled through a few of them, eyes narrowing as they scanned the screen.

"Any of this make sense to you?" she asked, turning to me.

I scanned the numbers. While it was easy enough to tell the accounts receivable and accounts payable, it would take a lot longer to sift through it all and see if one matched up with the other. And I wasn't really confident I'd be able to notice if something felt off, like someone had tampered with it. Our winery books were a lot more simple, and to be honest, this was the sort of thing I usually left up to my accountant, Schultz.

"Not really," I admitted. "But I'm not totally sure what I'm looking at." I glanced at the door again, expecting Mandy to pop through it any minute. "I wish we had more time."

Ava switched to a new screen, pulling up an internet browser window.

"What are you doing?" I whispered.

"Emailing the files to you."

"Won't Black notice?"

"I don't see how," Ava said, logging into her account at the email provider's home screen. "I mean, it's not like I'm using his account to do it. I'm using my own."

I bit my lip. "Just hurry, okay?"

"Hurrying," she promised, attaching the entire *Accounting* file to an email addressed to me.

I waited the longest thirty seconds of my life, watching the little loading bar slowly grow to 100% before she finally hit *Send* and whisked the ledgers off into cyberspace.

I let out a sigh of relief.

"Now to cover our tracks," she mumbled, logging out of the email account and going to the browsing history window, where she deleted any trace of our visit. I had to admit, I was kind of impressed. She was just closing all of the windows and shutting down Black's system when a sound came from just on the other side of the door.

My heart leapt up into my throat. "What was that?" I whispered.

"What?" Ava asked.

"Listen."

She did, the both of us silent and still. I felt my entire body suddenly buzzing with adrenalin as I heard it again.

And realized it was a key turning in a lock.

Instinctively, I ducked down behind the desk and felt Ava do the same beside me. My fingers gripped the edge of the battleship gray behemoth as if it were the one barrier between me and a criminal record as I listened. The key turned, the lock unbolted, and a door opened.

I said a silent prayer of thanks that it was not the one keeping us hidden but presumably the other door at the end of the hallway—the one that had been marked *Exit*—as I heard it shut again and footsteps echo down the hallway. As soon as they began to fade away, I turned to Ava.

"We have to get out of here," I hissed.

She nodded, the look in her eyes mirroring the fear coursing through me.

I stood, rapidly skittering the few steps to the door before opening it a crack and peeking out.

While I saw nothing, I could hear voices. One male and low and the other female—higher pitched and almost sounding a bit guilty.

"What are you doing here so early?" the male voice said. I recognized it as belonging to Mark Black and felt my legs go numb.

"I-I thought I'd help out Javier," I heard Mandy reply, the lie coming out on a stutter.

Mark said something back that I didn't quite make out, but his voice sounded low, deep, and menacing. Or maybe that was my fear reading into it.

"...help him prep. I mean, I know we'll be slammed again tonight, right?"

"Fine...appreciate your...going to my office."

I stifled a yip of fear and dove for the exit door across the hall. I felt Ava at my back, pushing me as I fumbled for the handle, my hands suddenly feeling like rubber. She shoved, I grabbed, and somehow we both stumbled into the alleyway behind the restaurant, the sunshine hitting my eyes like an assault. We both ran as fast as our heels would take us to the street, where we forced ourselves to slow down and walk the rest of the way to her GTO, lest we look suspicious running for our lives away from Tyler's Place.

It wasn't until we were both safely inside Ava's car that I took a full breath.

"I think I might have just had a heart attack," Ava said, leaning back against the headrest as she blew air out through her pursed lips.

"Ditto," I admitted. "I'm officially retiring as an angel."

CHAPTER TEN

My hands had finally stopped shaking by the time we got back to the winery. Ava left me at the front entrance, heading back to the festival grounds to reopen her Silver Girl booth in hopes of a growing cocktail hour crowd. A hope I feared was in vain as I took in the sparse group watching Gabby's gnocchi demonstration on stage. Even though the chef deftly pushed the potato through a ricer and mixed it lightly with flour as she spoke of the way her Nonna had made this recipe for her as a little girl, we were hardly drawing a crowd. More like a smattering. On the upside, I saw fewer press than I had that morning. Whether that meant we were entertaining real paying guests or just that everyone had already sent in their articles for the day, I wasn't sure.

I tucked that thought away as I quickly checked on Jean Luc in the tasting room (which I was happy to see was at least semi-full of sipping guests) and Conchita in the kitchen (prepping some delicious looking crab puff appetizers to circulate through the crowd), and the CSI team (still buzzing around Tyler's trailer like a bunch of busy ants at a summer picnic).

Two out of three seemed to be going smoothly, so I took those odds and slipped into my office to check out the email Ava had sent from Tyler's Place.

I closed the door behind me, feeling sneaky even in my own office as I sat behind the desk and jiggled my mouse to life. A couple of quick clicks later I had the Tyler's Place accounts open again. Luckily they used the same popular accounting program I did, which made it easier to view and navigate the files. Unluckily, as I'd noted at the restaurant, their books were a lot more complicated than mine. The sheer number of vendors they dealt with on a daily basis was ten times more than our operation—most of our goods being produced in house or bought in bulk, like the pallets of recycled wine bottles we used to hold our wares. Tyler's Place had a variety of different types of active accounts—including net 50, cash, and credit—for everything from napkins to fresh seafood to larger ticket items like signage and the commercials Mark Black was so against. As I noted the amount on the pages for the last commercial endeavor, I could see why. It had ranged in the tens of thousands of dollars just for a twenty-second spot. And that was only the bill from the production crew. I could only imagine what Tyler's glam squad, locations, and graphics might have cost them. No doubt about it—Tyler was spending a lot. And, if the files indicating the nightly gross receipts at the restaurants were any indication, it was also a lot more than the mogul was taking in. Even combining the receipts from all four Tyler's Places, it looked as if he was in the red on a consistent basis.

What I couldn't tell was if anyone was actually stealing money to line his own pockets and cooking the books…or if Tyler was just a really terrible businessman.

I stretched my arms above my head and blinked the strain out of my eyes. What I needed was someone who was an expert in these types of accounts. I paused a moment, wondering just how much I wanted to get my circle of trust involved in this, but as Jean Luc's nervous mustache twitched in my mind's eye, I made a split-second decision and picked up my phone.

"Gene Schultz," the voice on the other end answered after the first ring had barely finished.

"Hey, Gene. It's Emmy Oak."

"Emmy, my favorite winery owner. How are you? How's the festival?"

"Great," I lied.

"Don't kid a kidder, kid," he shot back. "I've seen the news, you know."

"Vicious lies."

He made a noncommittal *hmmm* sound in his throat but let the comment go.

"Listen, I was wondering if you could do me a favor?"

"Honey, I've been doing you favors all day. Your investors are not happy about the body in your vineyard, and I've been on damage control since dawn."

While the winery was still family owned, in order to cover harvest cost and up our inventory, we'd had to take on a panel of investors who earned a small royalty on each bottle we sold. It cut into our profits, but for the moment, it was what was keeping our doors open. Which meant we sorely needed their backing.

"How bad is it?" I hesitated to ask.

He sighed. "Remains to be seen. I'd say we're at yellow, but it could easily veer into red again depending on what the morning news has to say."

I felt a wave of nerves at that thought but shoved it aside. One crisis at a time.

"So what's this favor?" Gene asked.

"I need you to look at the books of this restaurant." I paused, wondering how much to divulge. "Tyler's Place."

"The dead guy's restaurant?"

I nodded at the empty room. "I spoke to his partner yesterday. We're, uh, looking at doing some business with them."

"What sort of business?" Schultz asked. I could hear the skepticism in his voice.

"They're thinking about serving our wines in their restaurant."

"Exclusively yours?"

"Uh, well, I don't know—"

"In all four restaurants?"

"Uh, sure…maybe?"

"Well, that might be something," he agreed. "You said you had some financials for me to look at?"

"Yes. I have copies of their receivables and payables."

"They gave you these?"

"Yesssss," I said, drawing out the lie in a much more tentative fashion than I'd intended.

"That's very forthcoming of them."

"Isn't it?" I put my hand up to my face to make sure my nose wasn't actually growing. "Anyway, I, uh, just wanted to make sure it all adds up."

"Adds up?" Gene repeated. "You mean you suspect something isn't on the up-and-up with them?"

I bit my lip. "Kind of. I…well, I just wanted to make sure their funds are being well-handled. You know, before we get into bed with them. Think you could look over it all for me?"

"I think I better," Gene decided. "Email it over, and I'll see what I can tell you."

I let out a sigh of relief. "Thanks. I'll send them over now."

We said our goodbyes—with me promising to turn our reputation around for the investors and Gene promising that if I didn't, he'd be visiting shortly. I tried not to take that as a threat.

I was just hitting send on the email with Tyler's accounts attached when a knock sounded at my door.

"Come in," I replied automatically, eyes still on the screen as the little icon whisked my stolen goods away.

"Hey, Emmy."

My eyes shot up at the sound of the familiar voice to find Grant's broad frame filling my doorway. His dark hair looked like he'd run his hands through it one too many times that day, appearing tousled and more enticing than it should. His chin was dusted in a five o'clock shadow, even though the hour hadn't yet approached, and while his stance held the same intimidating authority it always did, I noticed his shoulders looked a little more rounded now, as if he'd gotten little sleep last night and it was catching up to him.

I immediately shut my laptop, hoping the guilt I felt wasn't written on my face. What was the minimum penalty for cyber stealing and sending to your accountant?

"Uh, hey yourself," I responded, quickly standing and walking around the desk to put some distance between myself and the guilty laptop.

"I didn't mean to interrupt…" Grant trailed off, gesturing to my desk.

"Nope!" I responded a little more emphatically than I meant to. "Not interrupting a thing. Not one single thing." I shot him a big smile with teeth and everything.

"Okaaaay," Grant said, drawing out the word. "Well, I just wanted to let you know that the CSIs are done with Tyler's trailer. We're releasing it." Grant took a step forward, and suddenly the space between us shrank, his presence taking up all the air in the room.

I instinctively took a step back, coming up against the edge of my desk. I tried to lean against it casually, as if his presence had no effect on me, even while my heart was pumping hard enough I swore I felt it banging against my ribs. I told myself it was guilt and not Grant's woodsy aftershave. (Hey, I was on a roll with the lies today. What was one more?)

"They locked everything up," Grant said, handing me a couple of keys on a metal ring. "I trust you can get these to the appropriate party?"

I nodded. "Don't suppose you found anything interesting in the trailer?"

Grant smiled but shook his head. "No comment."

I shrugged. "Can't blame a girl for trying. So the crime scene tape is gone, then?"

"CSI took it down when they left," he said.

"Good. I think it was scaring away customers."

The corner of his mouth quirked upward. "You think *that's* what's scaring off customers. It's not the fact that you're the 'deadliest little winery' in Sonoma?"

I felt very mature about the fact that I resisted the urge to stick my tongue out at him.

"All publicity is good publicity," I countered, repeating the hollow line Bradley Wu had fed me earlier that day.

Grant cocked his head to the side, studying me as if trying to figure out if I really believed that. "I hope so," he finally said.

"You do?"

He nodded slowly. "You know I don't want anything to happen to this place."

I swallowed, the sudden switch from Cop to Actually Caring Human taking me off guard. "Well, thank you," I responded.

"Look," Grant said, breaking eye contact to run a hand through his hair as I suspected he'd been doing. "I'm not any happier about all of this than you are. But I've got to go by the book on this."

"Seriously? Who are you, Sergeant Friday?"

This time he actually let out a small laugh. "Point taken. Man, you don't let anything slide, do you, Oak?"

The way his warm chuckle floated over me, almost leaving a physical chill behind, I was ready to let just about anything he said slide.

But I was too much of a strong woman to let him know that.

"No. Not much," I told him, crossing my arms over my chest.

He took a step forward, his eyes going back to mine and his voice going lower. "Good. I like that about you."

I swallowed, my throat suddenly dry at the way the gold flecks in his eyes were smiling mischievously down at me. Had the big bad cop just said he liked me?

"You do?" I asked again.

Grant nodded slowly, his eyes never leaving mine as he took another step forward. So close I could reach out and touch him.

I licked my lips. "Like, you like-like me or just like me? Or is this more of a general like, like you kind of like the way—"

Grant cut me off with a crooked grin and a deep low whisper of, "Shut up, Emmy."

Then I watched in slow motion as he leaned in, that slow, sexy grin moving toward me. My eyes tracked the movement of his lips as they moved toward mine. I almost went cross-eyed as they came closer and closer, finally skimming my bottom lip ever so softly.

Someone sighed out loud, and I had a bad feeling it was me, as he kissed me—softly, slowly, and so warmly I felt my body tingling in all sorts of places that hadn't tingled in months. Possibly even years, but who was counting?

My entire being melted into a puddle of pure hormones for a wonderful two seconds.

Then, just as surprisingly as it started, it was over— much too fast. My lips suddenly felt cold and abandoned where his mouth had just been as he pulled away. I must have closed my eyes against the onslaught of sensations at some point, as I found myself slowly blinking them open now as if coming out of a dream.

A really nice one.

When I found my focus, Grant had stepped back, an arm's length away again, those delightful lips curling into a half smile as he watched my face.

"Have a nice night, Emmy," he said, his voice husky and deep as he opened my office door and stepped out.

And then he was gone.

* * *

In lieu of a cold shower, I closed up my office and went outside, not really sure where I was going but knowing I needed some air to clear my head. And my hormones. While Grant and I had flirted with dating, a kiss was the last thing I'd expected from him that day. Maybe ever, to be honest. Grant was tough, unreadable, and didn't do emotion as far as I could tell. Truth was, up until today I wasn't sure I'd even want to be kissed by him, the complication feeling like a little too much in my already overcomplicated life. But now? *All* I could think about was wanting to be kissed by him.

I tried to shake that unhealthy thought off and inhaled deeply the mingling scents of the dinner fare being cooked and served in the remaining few booths on the grounds. While the curry competed with the Thai spices and unmistakable woodsy tang of barbeque grilling to a caramel sweetness, the entire effect was a pleasant one, conjuring up images of county fairs and family picnics and good friends coming together over good food. It served to ground me back in reality as I walked among enticing aromas.

I spotted Gabby sipping from a glass of Chardonnay at the edge of the festival grounds, seated on a low stone wall that bordered the pathway to the tasting room. I was about to approach to ask how her demo had gone earlier, when she tipped her head back to take a sip, and I saw that her cheeks were wet. Gabby was crying.

I paused, unsure whether I should intrude, but it appeared she'd already seen me. She swallowed, swiping at her cheeks with the back of her hand.

"Gabby?" I asked softly, approaching her.

She sniffed loudly, turning her head away from me as she wiped under her eyes for traces of running mascara. "What?" she said, her voice brusque and annoyed. As per usual.

"I, uh, wanted to see how the demo went. The gnocchi? Everything go okay?"

She sniffed again, finally turning her head so I could see her face full on. Her eyeliner was smudged, creating faint dark circles under her eyes that made her look tired and probably close to what her actual age was. Her foundation had streaked with her tears, leaving the tone of her skin looking uneven and betraying the fine lines that her expert makeup job had covered.

"It was fine," she said quickly.

"Are *you* okay?" I asked, feeling the first wave of sympathy for the woman I'd experienced yet.

"Do I look okay?" she shot back, heavy on the sarcasm.

Some of my sympathy waned at her argumentative tone, but I bit my tongue. "You look like you've been crying," I pointed out. I paused, remembering the scene I'd witnessed earlier that day. "Does this have anything to do with Alec?"

She let out a deflated breath on a sob but quickly swallowed it back up, shutting her mouth tightly. "How did you know?"

I shrugged. "Just a guess. Things felt…tense between you two today."

"Tense is one way to put it," she muttered. "Childish jerk is another."

"Alec?"

She shook her head so hard that her hair fell out of its clip on one side. "Tyler freaking Daniels. Would you believe he's still screwing me over even in death? That—" She continued in Italian, and while I didn't speak the language, I got the gist as she finished with a snarl and spit in the dirt at her feet.

"What did he do?" I asked.

"Whatever he could to make my life miserable. Well, look at me now. Do I look miserable enough for you?" she asked, looking up to the sky. "Huh, do I? You two-faced son of a—" And off she went with more cursing in the most romantic language on earth.

Through her tirade I thought back to the allegation Ashley had made, reading into the body language Tyler'd had with Gabby on their show. While this woman didn't look like she was mourning the loss of a lover, I had to ask...

"Gabby, what was your relationship with Tyler?"

"Tyler was a snake," she spat out, tears starting to send more makeup running south. "What more do you want me to say?"

"Were you sleeping with the snake?"

She scoffed and shot me an incredulous look. "Wh-where on earth did you hear that nasty rumor?"

I shook my head. "Doesn't matter. Is it true?"

She pursed her lips together, and I had the feeling she was about to deny it. But instead the tears won over and she broke down, shoulders sagging with defeat. "God, why even try to deny it any longer?"

Score one for Ashley the ex-wife. "So you *were* having an affair with Tyler."

Another scoff escaped her. "Affair sounds so dramatic. Yes, we were sleeping together, okay? Look, he was charming." She paused. "Or could be when he wanted to."

"And he wanted to with you."

She nodded. "At first. The chemistry between us was real on the show—that's part of what made it so good. The audience can feel when you're faking it, you know?"

I wasn't sure about that, as I'd seen her faking warmth on stage several times this week, and the audience had seemed to enjoy it. But I didn't interrupt, instead nodding my understanding as she continued.

"What can I say—Tyler was hot. All that energy and confidence. I fell for it."

"Did Tyler feel the same way?" I asked.

She barked out a self-deprecating laugh. "I thought he did, but it turns out he was a better actor than I gave him credit for."

"How so?"

"Look, he played me, alright? He was only sleeping with me to boost his precious ratings." She paused. "They were slipping, you know."

"Oh?" I said, feigning ignorance even though I'd heard that particular rumor as well.

She nodded. "Every shtick gets stale eventually. And Tyler knew the network wasn't happy."

"But he had an ironclad contract, right?"

She shot me a look. "How did you know about that?"

"I, uh, read the trades," I mumbled. "But it's true the network couldn't fire Tyler, right?"

"No," she admitted. "But they could move him. Give someone else more lucrative his timeslot and bury him in the midafternoons."

"So he decided he needed publicity," I mused. I paused, still not quite getting it. "But if your affair was secret...?"

"Yeah, that's the rub. *I* thought it was our little secret. But then Tyler told me he planned to leak the affair to the press. What could be more enticing than the two co-hosts entangled in a romantic relationship, right? The *bastardo* said he even had photos of us. Photos! He'd been taking pictures of me the entire time we were together."

"And he planned to give them to the press."

She nodded. "I begged him not to. I mean, I could only imagine what that would do to Alec."

"He didn't know about the affair?"

She moved to shake her head but paused. "At least he didn't then." She let out a shaky sigh, and I could see real emotion behind her eyes. "I-I don't know anymore. Maybe he's guessed by now."

I watched her reaction carefully as I asked, "Gabby, is there any chance Alec found out about the two of you *before* Tyler died?"

Her eyes shot up to meet mine. "What are you implying?"

I did an innocent, palms-up thing. "Nothing! I just wondered if Alec might have confronted Tyler."

"And killed him, you mean?" She shook her head. "No, Alec is not like that. He's kind. Gentle."

At least one side of him was. I'd see him turn the charm on and off just as easily as she did. I knew Gabby had seen it too, from the scene I'd witnessed in the oak grove. I wondered if she was in denial or covering for him.

"Gabby, you said you were getting something to eat when Tyler was killed. Do you know where Alec was?"

She bit her lip, red flecks of her lipstick coming off on her teeth. "No," she said quietly.

Which meant Alec Post had no alibi.

CHAPTER ELEVEN

———

"So you think maybe Alec killed Tyler not over the lawsuit but because he was sleeping with Gabby?" Ava asked, her eyes shining almost as brightly as the large crystal pendant she was wearing around her neck on a silver chain.

After my conversation with the emotional Gabriela Genova, I'd gone straight to the Silver Girl booth and filled Ava in on all the gory details, including Tyler's plan to leak the affair to the press for his own gain. Ava had gasped and *ohmigod*ed at all the appropriate parts, and when I'd finished, she'd hit on the same conclusion I had.

"I think it's possible," I decided.

"But, you know, it's not like they were married or anything," Ava mused, scrunching up her nose as she stared out at the hilltops.

"What do you mean?"

"Well, Alec and Gabby were just dating. I mean, there weren't any kids or house or shared finances at stake. No real vow of monogamy. And, not to be a pessimist, but it wouldn't be the first time a girl cheated on her boyfriend."

"So, you're thinking Gabby cheating on Alec with Tyler wasn't enough to push Alec to homicide."

Ava shrugged. "I dunno. I guess it all depends on how short Alec's fuse is."

I thought back to the way he'd transformed in seconds flat when I'd confronted him about the lawsuit. "If I had to guess, it's not all that long," I told her.

"Well, I suppose it's possible he was angry enough." Ava shrugged, rearranging a couple of amethyst earrings set in sterling silver on the black tray at the front of her table. "But, you know, if Gabby can't provide Alec with an alibi, that means Alec can't provide *her* with one either."

"So your money's on Gabby as the killer?"

"Depends on how badly she wanted to keep those photos of her and Tyler private."

I picked up a pendant shaped like a tree, turning it over in my hands as I thought about that. "She seemed pretty upset about it all when I talked to her."

"But she is something of an actress," Ava countered.

I nodded. "I guess if she can fake warmth on stage, she could fake tears for me."

"So, what if she was telling you the truth—that Alec really didn't find out about the affair until after Tyler died. What if the clue that tipped him off about it was something in Gabby's mannerism after Tyler's death? Like, somehow he guessed she killed Tyler and why?"

I thought back to the argument I'd witnessed between the two. "Alec did seem to be accusing Gabby of something."

"Right!" Ava said, stabbing her finger in the air at me. "What if it had nothing to do with the affair and everything to do with her killing Tyler?"

I was turning that theory over in my head when my phone buzzed with a text. I quickly glanced at the readout, seeing Gene Schultz's name pop up. I swiped my phone screen on to read his message.

Got info on the accounts you sent. Call me.

My pulse immediately picked up as I read the words.

It must have shown on my face, as Ava leaned over my shoulder. "What? Who is it from?"

"It's Schultz. I think he may have found something in Tyler's Place's books," I explained as I hit the call button and put him on speaker. It only rang once before his voice picked up.

"Gene Schultz," he answered.

"It's Emmy. I got your text."

"Hey, kid. Listen, I know you're gung-ho about this partnership with the restaurant, but after looking at the paperwork you sent over, I'd have to advise against it."

"Oh?" I asked.

One of Ava's eyebrows went into her bangs, and her lips broke into a grin.

"Yeah. Listen, something shady is going on with these guys, and I'd steer clear."

Bingo. "What kind of something shady?" I asked. "Like…say, embezzlement?"

Gene paused on the other end. "How did you know that?"

Uh-oh. I shot Ava a *help me* look. But she just shrugged and did a palms-up thing.

"Uh, I kinda just got a vibe from them," I said, hoping I sounded vague enough that he didn't press it.

"Well, I'd say trust your vibes in the future, kid. Yeah, it looks like one of the partners was skimming funds. It took some doing to find it, but there are a lot of lines that are just ghosts."

"Ghosts?" I asked.

"Fakes. Entries in the books that don't actually correlate to any payments being made to real companies. For example"—I heard some papers rustling on his desk—"Personal Services Corporation."

"That sounds generic. What is it?"

"No clue. As far as I can tell, it doesn't exist. But the AP shows the business having paid them over fifty thousand dollars last year."

I felt an eyebrow rise, mirroring Ava's expression. "And there's no record of this actual payment?"

"Well, there are withdrawals for that amount but no record of the funds going to that company—no canceled checks, no account transfers, nada. And no record of the company anywhere except in the account ledger. No contracts or mentions of services rendered. Nothing I can see."

"Fifty thousand is a good chunk of money," I mused, though I wasn't sure it was quite enough for a man to kill his partner over.

"Sure, but it's not the only ghost I've found."

Now he had my attention. "How many others?"

"Maybe half a dozen. And that's just what I've found sitting with these books for an afternoon. I have a feeling if I dug deeper, I might scare up even more."

"So we could be talking hundreds of thousands?"

"Or even millions, over time. Hard to say how long this has been going on."

Ava did a low whistle beside me. Millions. Now that was definitely a motivating number.

"Would you say you have definite proof of embezzling?" I asked, thinking of how to slip this info to Grant.

But Gene answered in the negative. "Sorry, but I'm no forensic accountant. This is just my impression based on what I'm seeing here. These ghost entries show up every two months, but it would take a lot more to prove the cash was going someplace other than where it was supposed to."

Which was a bit of a downer, but something else he said suddenly clicked.

"Wait, did you say every two months?"

Ava shot me a questioning look, but I ignored it, focusing on Schultz's answer.

"Yeah." I heard more rustling on the other end. "Almost exactly. Why?"

"Nothing," I lied.

"Well, like I said, kid, I'd steer clear of this deal if I were you. Too much risk involved that you can't afford to take right now, you know?"

"Thanks," I told him before I said good-bye and hung up.

My mind buzzed, puzzle pieces rearranging themselves as the tidbit of new info sunk in.

"What?" Ava asked, still giving that same questioning look as I put my phone back into my pocket. "What am I missing?"

"When David and I were at Tyler's Place, Mark Black said Tyler visited the restaurant every two months like clockwork."

I could see the mental gears working behind Ava's eyes as she digested that info too. "Wait, so you think that *Tyler* was the one making these entries?"

I nodded. "If Mark had been cooking the books, he had all the time in the world to do it. But if the entries only showed up when Tyler was in town…"

"That means the partner embezzling funds from Tyler's Place was not Mark Black. It was Tyler."

I nodded. "That puts a whole new spin on things."

"Spin? It puts a Tilt-A-Whirl on it," Ava said, chewing her bottom lip.

"*If* it's true," I said. "Like Schultz said, while the ghost entries are a red flag, we're taking a leap saying Tyler made up the companies and took the money for himself. I mean, where would he put it?"

Ava shrugged. "Offshore accounts? Switzerland? Bonds?" She paused. "Sorry, I'm not rich enough to have these kinds of problems. My savings are in a coffee can."

I was suddenly jealous. I didn't even have a coffee can.

But I could think of one person who did know about the problems of the wealthy and devious.

David Allen.

"Feel like hitting up a friend for a drink?" I asked Ava.

She sent me questioning look again but shrugged. "Sure. We've been chatting nearly half an hour, and not a single customer has hit the booth."

I tried to shove down the wave of desperation on my bank account's behalf at that comment and pulled my phone out again, swiping through my contacts until I found his name.

It rang five times and was about to go to voice mail when David finally picked up. "Ems, my love, to what do I owe the pleasure?"

I swallowed annoyance at the *my love* part. I was not *his,* and whatever tolerance we had for each other was a far cry from *love.* But, since I was calling to ask him a favor, I let it go.

"Ava and I wanted to pick your brain about something. You busy?"

"Just grabbing a couple of games at the club," David said. The club was the Links golf club just outside of town, and the games I knew meant card sharking the members as they indulged in their whiskey after rounds.

"Mind if we swing by for a few minutes?" I asked.

He was quiet for a beat, then: "You know I'm always thirsty for your company, Ems."

I was never sure if David Allen was specifically trying to get a rise out of me or if it was just his default mode to make people in general uncomfortable. But I decided to take advantage of the offer this time.

"We'll be there in twenty," I promised him as I hung up.

*   *   *

The Links club was an exclusive golf club at the base of the rolling hills that spanned several acres of pristine green courses, had a well-appointed clubhouse used for all manner of high society functions, and boasted several bars, both indoor and outdoor, where the handshakes and secret endorsements that made the upper crust run were made. Ava and I had visited the club on a few occasions in the past, though neither of us quite fit the criteria for membership—namely a fat bank account.

We valeted my Jeep and passed through the glass front doors that whispered opened automatically at our approach. The lobby was cool and serene, with quiet flute music being piped in through hidden speakers aimed at instantly melting members' stress away as they entered their home away from home. A long walnut reception counter sat against one wall, where we gave our names to the clerk on duty as guests of David Allen and were directed to the lounge where the clerk said David was expecting us.

Our heels clicked loudly on the polished marble floor as we made our way down a short hall before entering a large, comfortable room overlooking the green that was brimming with happy hour activity. Several older men in slacks and polo shirts with paunches that extended well beyond their belt lines guffawed at bawdy jokes over whiskey glasses, while slim, Botoxed women in short, sporty athletic skirts and slimming sundresses sipped Chardonnay and champagne from elegant glasses while tittering quietly amongst themselves. The one incongruent figure in the mix was the tall, slim guy in dark jeans, a black button down shirt rolled at the sleeves, and too long hair pulled up today into a small man-bun at the nape of his neck. He waved a small glass of amber liquid in our direction when he spotted us, hailing us to join him at a table near the windows.

"Lovelies," he said, standing in a gentlemanly manner as we approached.

"David," Ava responded.

"Thanks for meeting us," I told him.

"Can I get you anything?" he asked, signaling a server to our table as Ava and I sat in the empty chairs.

"I'd love a rosé," Ava decided.

I shrugged. Well, if he was buying... "Make that two."

David put in our order before turning back to us. "So, what is it you wanted to pick my disgustingly large brain about?" he asked with a smile, draping an arm casually over the back of my chair.

I cleared my throat, trying to ignore the overly intimate gesture. "Well, we have a question about where to put money."

"Dear Aunt Sally suddenly leave someone an inheritance?" he asked, raising one questioning eyebrow.

I shook my head. "Not our money."

"Tyler Daniels'," Ava supplied.

David's other eyebrow rose, and he turned to me. "You're still looking into his death?"

I bit my lip, not really sure I wanted to commit to that statement. "Jean Luc is still a suspect, and I'd like it if the police had somewhere else to look."

"Hmm." David sipped at his drink, eyes never leaving mine over the rim of the glass. "I'm not sure I like you two girls running around unchaperoned."

"Give me a break," I told him. "We're not going to a high school dance."

David's mouth quirked up, showing off a dimple in his right cheek that I'd never noticed before. "Just trying to keep my Emmy out of trouble. Not sure my poor heart can handle another incident like last time."

My stomach clenched at his words. I knew he was referring to a recent incident where he'd come to my rescue just in the nick of time. While I'd appreciated the heck out of his timing in that moment, it wasn't a scenario I wanted to repeat.

"We *women* can keep *ourselves* out of trouble, thank you very much," Ava supplied for me.

David waved her off, still grinning. "No need to go all Ginsberg on me, honey."

Ava narrowed her eyes and pursed her lips. If David hadn't just bought us both drinks, I had a feeling he would have gotten an earful.

"We're making a few discreet inquiries," I assured him. "That's all."

David turned his gaze toward mine again, his eyes assessing. "And you're inquiring of me where Tyler Daniels put money?"

I nodded. "We have a suspicion that he may have been embezzling cash from Tyler's Place," I said, filling him on everything I'd learned from Schultz as our drinks arrived.

When I finished, David was frowning. "So Tyler wasn't just overspending like his business partner told us."

Ava shook her head. "While it looks too coincidental that these ghost entries show up every time Tyler is in town, what we don't have is proof."

"So, you're thinking follow the money?" he asked.

"That's right," I jumped in. "Where did he put the money that he pulled from the business accounts." I paused. "So, if you were going to hide a bunch of stolen money—"

David turned to me, eyebrows going toward his hairline in mock innocence, as if I were accusing him of something.

"I said *if*."

He grinned.

"—where would you put it?"

He cocked his head to the side and looked out at the green, eyes focusing on a guy in plaid pants trying to dislodge his ball from a sand trap. "Well, offshore accounts are always an old-school go-to. Cayman Islands, Switzerland, Belize."

"I thought of those," Ava said, looking pretty happy with herself.

"But, like I said, that's kind of old-school. I mean, the IRS has been on to that trick for decades."

"You mean they're not secure anymore?" I asked.

"I didn't say that," David hedged. "There are still places where your account info is protected, and it would be pretty difficult for the Feds—or anyone else for that matter—to find it unless they had some inkling where to look."

"But..." I said, feeling it coming on.

"But Tyler Daniels was a celebrity. And if he really was cooking his own books to hide stolen cash, well, I'd say he might fear being under scrutiny."

"So, the offshore accounts are a no-go?" Ava looked disappointed.

I patted her arm. Hey, at least she was still one coffee can ahead of me in the financial know-how department.

David shrugged in answer to her question, swirling the contents of his glass. "It's still possible but not where I'd sink my ill-gotten gains." He paused, giving me a mischievous grin again. "*If* I had any."

"So spill—where would you hide them?"

"I'd probably buy cryptocurrency."

I frowned. "Like Bitcoin?"

"Bitcoin is probably the best known one, yes. But there are others. It's all online, no real paper trail of money in and out of accounts, no physical cash to try to hide. Accessible from anywhere and very liquid." He paused again. "Or so I've heard."

I sat back in my chair, sipping my rosé as I thought that over.

"So, if Tyler Daniels converted the funds into cryptocurrency somewhere, how would we find it?" Ava asked.

"That's the beauty," David said, sitting forward. "Unless Tyler kept some sort of records of the transaction, you wouldn't. It's all handled on the currency's site under anonymous account numbers."

"Which means we're back at square one," Ava said, taking a rather generous sip from her drink.

David shrugged, leaning back against his chair again. "Sorry, ladies, that's the extent of my devious brain."

CHAPTER TWELVE

————

"So now what?" Ava asked as we waited on the valet to bring my Jeep around. I noticed a Tesla and a Porsche Cayenne had already line-jumped me. Apparently my Wrangler didn't rate. Or maybe the valet had an inkling how small his tip would be by my lack of a designer purse.

"Now," I answered, checking the time on my phone, "we need to get back to the festival before we lose the happy hour crowd."

Ava raised an eyebrow my way. "*Crowd*? I see you're working on that optimism thing again."

I couldn't help a laugh. "Leave me my delusions."

"Okay, how about this—I think we're both deluded if we decide Tyler Daniels stealing money from his own business didn't have anything to do with his death."

"*If* he was stealing money," I said. "So far all we have are coincidence and theory."

"So let's find out," Ava pressed. "Let's ask someone who knew for sure."

I shot her a look. "Mark Black, you mean?"

Ava nodded. "He must have known. If he really was the brain behind the business, the ghost entries couldn't have been fooling him for long."

I thought about that as the valet finally appeared in my red Wrangler. I handed him a tip that barely registered on his radar, and Ava and I both climbed inside, buckling our seat belts before I pulled away from the curb.

"You have a point," I told Ava finally.

"I do?"

"Mark Black definitely knows more than he was saying. At the very least, the argument he had with Tyler about 'missing money' means he had some idea what was going on."

Ava nodded. "Maybe that 'ridiculous embezzlement' line went something like, 'your embezzlement is ridiculous,'" Ava guessed.

I had to admit, it didn't feel like a terrible guess. "You know, yesterday I did promise to bring some sample bottles of our wines to Mark," I said, thinking out loud.

"That's our in!" Ava said, stabbing a finger clad in a polished silver ring at me.

I bit my lip. While I agreed with her, the enthusiasm in her eyes had me rethinking David's offer of a chaperon.

"Don't suppose you have a few bottles stashed in your trunk?" she asked.

I shook my head. "No. And I want to get a good sampling of our different offerings." I paused. "You know, on the off chance he's not a killer and does want to do business with us."

"Right. Okay, you grab a case of wine, I'll check in on the festival and make sure all is hunky-dory, and then we meet back in the parking lot in an hour. For Operation Interrogation."

I cringed. "How about Operation Subtle Discussion?"

"Po-tay-toe, Po-taw-toe—wait, did you just roll your eyes at me?"

"Nervous twitch," I told her.

*   *   *

By the time we got back to Oak Valley Vineyards, happy hour was in full force and the delicious scents of cumin and chilis wafted toward me from the kitchen as Conchita made her spice-crusted tilapia to serve to the upcoming dinner crowd. I stopped in for only a minute to sample the flaky fish before making my way to the tasting room to see how Jean Luc was faring.

Only, as I approached the bar, my French sommelier was nowhere to be seen. In his place was Eddie, pinstriped jacket abandoned, sleeves of his pink dress shirt pushed up his forearms as he wrestled with the cork of a bottle of Pinot Noir.

"Eddie," I said, a question in my voice as I approached. "Everything okay?"

"Oh, sure. Just a bit of a sticky cork," he said, his cheeks turning red as he twisted.

"You need to pull up as you twist. Rotate to the right," I tried to instruct him.

"I got it," he said under his breath, a bead of sweat forming on his upper lip.

I glanced down the bar, seeing a couple of customers waiting on their glasses.

"Where's Jean Luc?" I asked.

"Had…to…go…" Eddie grunted out one syllable at a time.

I felt a frown pull between my eyebrows. "Go where?"

"Storeroom…to get…more clean…glasses… There!" Eddie's cork popped out, nearly smacking him in the eye with the force as the bottle finally let it free, spilling just a little Pinot on the floor in the process. He turned to me, a wide grin going from one pudgy cheek to the next. "See? I knew I could get it."

He turned to the waiting couple. "Now, which one of you said you wanted the Zinfandel?"

I closed my eyes, silently praying for patience. "Eddie, that's Pinot Noir."

Eddie blinked at me then squinted at the label. "It is? But it's red."

"Pinot Noir *is* red," I informed him.

"Oh." He did more squinting. "I thought it was white. You know, *blanco* meaning white and all in Spanish?"

"That's Pinot Blanc. Different wine."

Eddie blinked at me. "There are *two* Pinots?"

I closed my eyes again and counted to ten. Unfortunately, when I opened them, Eddie was still there, blinking innocently at me.

"Well, whatever it is, I'm sure it tastes good," he said with a smile. Then he turned to the two waiting customers, who were looking at us like maybe they didn't need that glass after all. "Pinot Noir okay?" He shot them his ear-to-ear jovial grin.

Luckily it was infectious, and they both shrugged and passed their empty glasses toward him anyway. What my winery manager lacked in actual knowledge about wine, he sometimes made up for in personality.

Sometimes.

I quickly pointed out the Pinot *Blanc*, the Pinot *Noir*, and the Zinfandel to Eddie before leaving the bar just as Jean Luc arrived with a box of wineglasses and a frown at the spots of wine Eddie had spilled. I left them to hash it out as I made my way to The Cave.

I grabbed a carrier with our winery logo on it and filled it with a bottle of each of our varietals. Once I was happy with the offering, I made my way to the parking lot where, true to her word, Ava was waiting, her GTO idling near the entrance as she fiddled with the radio. She waved and popped the trunk for me as I approached, and we made the short drive into town, arriving at Tyler's Place to find a packed parking lot. Ava did a full tour of it twice before spotting a pickup truck that was just pulling out and snagging the slot near the back.

The lobby was, as on my previous visit with David, filled to capacity. There seemed to be even more morbid looky-loos filling the space than before, and the pile of flowers at Cardboard Tyler's feet had grown, filling the room with the faint sickly sweet smell of rotting foliage. I spotted Mandy at the hostess podium, her hair falling out of a messy bun, looking like she'd been on a heck of a shift so far. The line to chat with her was three deep, and we waited patiently, pushing one step forward at a time through the crowd until we were at the podium.

"Welcome to Tyler's Place—oh, it's you," she said, recognition dawning as she blinked at us. She did a quick over-the-shoulder look then leaned toward us, whispering. "Ohmigosh, Mark almost caught me letting you in earlier today. I had to, like, pretend I was here to help prep dinner. I've been here ever since."

No wonder she looked tired. I suddenly felt a little bad about asking her to put her job on the line for us. If Jean Luc hadn't had more at stake, I would have retreated right then with my tail between my legs. "Sorry about that. We slipped out the back when we heard him come in."

She nodded. "Yeah, I figured you'd made yourselves scarce." She paused. "So why you back? Didn't you get enough pictures earlier?"

Ava nodded. "We're actually here on official winery business today." She gestured to the carrier of wine in my hands.

Mandy blinked. "Oh. Huh. You know, I thought that whole *wanting to sell wine* thing was just a ruse to get in."

Maybe Mandy wasn't as dumb as she looked.

"You know, for the story," she finished.

"Uh, no. I mean, yeah. I'm a reporter, but I do own a winery too." Which sounded lame even to my own ears, but Mandy just shrugged.

"Sure. Whatev. Just keep it on the down-low that I let you in, right?"

"Mum's the word," Ava promised, doing a *zip the lips shut and throw away the key* thing. "We never give up our sources."

Mandy looked a little more comfortable at that and straightened back up to resume her usual stance. "So, did you ladies want a table, or…"

"We actually wanted to chat with Mark Black," I told her.

"Oh good. Cause we're, like, totally booked. It's an hour and half for a seat at the bar tonight."

Wow. Suddenly I kinda hoped Mark *wasn't* a killer and *would* stock my wines.

"Is Mr. Black in?" Ava asked again.

"Yeah, he's in the back. Gimme a minute and I'll let him know you're here."

Ava and I waited as Mandy left her post to go down the back hallway. A moment later she reappeared and directed us to his office. I didn't have the heart to tell her we already knew where it was.

We retraced our steps from that morning and found the office door open. Mark Black was sitting behind his desk, staring intently at his computer screen, and I knocked on the doorframe to get his attention.

"Uh, hi. Mr. Black?"

He looked up, eyes going from Ava to me. "Yes. Uh, Emma, right?"

"Emmy," I supplied, stepping into the room and shaking his hand. "And this is my friend Ava Barnett."

He nodded Ava's way then his eyes went to the wine carrier in my hands. "I see you brought some of your samples by?"

"Yes," I said, setting the carrier down on his desk. "This should give you a good idea of what we have to offer."

He picked up a bottle, turning it over in his hands. "Nice labeling."

"Thank you," I said, feeling a note of pride creep in. Hector had designed it himself last year, and I thought the simple gold oak leaf on the dark background invoked just the right balance of nature and elegance we strove for.

"Quite a crowd you've got out there," Ava noted.

Mark lifted his eyes from the bottle to meet hers, his bushy brows drawn downward. "Nothing attracts a crowd like a tragedy."

"I'm sorry for your loss," Ava told him.

But he just grunted.

"Uh, I was a fan of Tyler's," Ava went on. "I watched *Eat Up* every morning."

But Mark's attention was back on the bottle again, a slight nod in her direction the only indication that he'd even heard her.

She gave me a shrug, clearly not winning at engaging Mark in conversation. She nodded my way, tossing me the proverbial ball.

I cleared my throat. "Uh, I was wondering..." I said, eyes cutting to Ava as I tried to crack the tough nut. "You do plan on keeping the restaurant open now that Tyler's gone, correct?"

His head snapped up. "Yes. Of course. Why? What have you heard?"

"Nothing!" I assured him. "I just, well, I guess I just wondered about the future of the place. I mean, before we go into business together," I added, thinking of Schultz's warnings. "You, uh, did mention that the finances weren't in great shape."

He frowned. "Don't worry about that. I'll work them out. We're *not* closing." He said it with such emphasis that I wasn't sure if he was trying to convince me or himself.

"You mentioned there has been some overspending," I hedged. "On Tyler's part."

His frown deepened. "Yes. But, like I said, I'll take care of it. We'll be solvent soon enough."

I bit my lip. "Now that Tyler's gone, you mean."

"Yes." He paused as if realizing how that sounded. "What I mean to say is, it will be easier to balance the books without the extra expenses Tyler incurred."

"Right. Expenses." I shot Ava a look, wondering just how far I could push this. "Do you know exactly what Tyler was spending money on?"

Mark blinked at me as if not understanding the question.

"I mean...did you actually see receipts for the funds that Tyler withdrew, or did he just take out cash, or..." I trailed off, hoping he'd pick up the train of thought.

But instead he set the wine bottle down on his desk with a loud thud, eyes homing in on me. "Exactly what are you getting at?"

Oh boy. I took a deep breath, going for broke. "Was Tyler stealing from the business?"

The frown was a downright scowl now. "Who told you that?" he demanded hotly.

"Is it true?" I pressed.

I could see his chest rising and falling with the effort of keeping his temper in check, and I half expected him to throw us out. To my surprise, instead he finally just nodded.

"So Tyler was embezzling from the company," I clarified.

Mark let out a long sigh and crossed the room to shut the door from prying ears before answering. "Yes, he was. Though in Tyler's words, it was his name on the door, so it was all his money." Mark shook his head, as if trying to shake the memory away.

"So you confronted him?" I asked.

"I did. Look, when our last commercial lost so much money, I started looking at our finances more closely—looking for places we could tighten the belt so to speak."

"And that's when you found the discrepancies?" I guessed.

He nodded again. "I've known for a while that Tyler was playing loose with the money, but it wasn't until I started really vetting the purchases he made that I realized a lot of them weren't purchases at all. He was making up companies that he paid for fake things then pocketing the funds."

"Pocketing them where?" I asked, wondering if David Allen's theory had been correct.

But Mark shook his head. "No idea. I confronted him with it, and he just laughed. Said it was his cash to begin with. Cleary he didn't understand the meaning of the word *partnership.*"

"So what did you do?" Ava asked.

He shrugged. "What could I do? I told him it had to stop. That he was bleeding us dry."

"Did he?" I asked.

"I don't know." Mark sighed, sinking back down into his chair looking defeated. "Look, I told him to cut it out, and he just laughed. He had no idea what trouble we'd be in if what he'd been doing came to light. Faking expenses? Pulling tax-free funds from the corporation? The IRS would have this place shut down so fast it would make his pretty little head spin. And we'd be looking at real jail time. But did he care? No. He was Tyler Daniels. He always landed on his feet."

Except, this time he didn't.

"How much did he take?" Ava asked.

"All told?" Mark looked up, some of the apathy being replaced again with anger. "Almost two million dollars over the last year."

I sucked in a breath. That was a pretty penny. And while Mark might well have been worried about what the IRS would do if they found out about it, the truth was that a million of that was Mark's money, if the partners split profits 50/50. If someone had stolen a million dollars from me, I'd be tempted to do more than just tell them to "cut it out."

"When was the last time you saw Tyler?" I asked, watching his reaction.

His head shot up, eyes meeting mine. "Why? You think I killed him?"

The thought had crossed my mind...

"I'm just wondering what his state of mind was," I lied.

"Friday," he shot back. "When he was here at the restaurant filming his ridiculous show segment. I told him to cancel the upcoming commercial shoot, he refused, we argued."

"And then?"

"And then he left here. Alive." Mark stood, some of the fight returning to him as he towered over us.

Instinctively, I took a step back, running into Ava at the door.

"Now, is there anything else, Ms. Oak?" Black asked, a hint of sarcasm lacing his words.

I shook my head silently and felt behind me for the doorknob. Only, Ava already had it open, ushering me quickly outside the room, where we all but scampered back down the hall for the second time that day.

"I don't think he likes us very much," Ava noted, her heels click-clacking on the linoleum as we threaded through the crowd toward the front door.

"Ditto." I paused. "In his defense, we are pretty nosey."

"What do you think the chances are that he'll want to stock your wines now?" Ava asked as we hit the parking lot, dusk just starting to creep up over the hills.

I shook my head. "Slim to waif model."

"Sorry. Five bottles of wine wasted."

"Well, I guess you couldn't say *totally* wasted. We know now that Tyler definitely was stealing from his partner."

"And Mark definitely knew about it."

"And had a million reasons to want Tyler dead," I pointed out.

"That's a lot of reasons," Ava mused, unlocking her car and letting us both in. "You think he was telling the truth about not knowing where Tyler kept the cash he stole?"

I shrugged. "You're thinking he killed Tyler and stole back the two million?" I thought about it. "I guess it's possible he found out where Tyler had it hidden. Maybe Tyler let it slip when they argued. Or Mark threatened it out of him."

"Hmm." Ava pursed her lips together as she clicked her seat belt into place and turned the car on.

"*Hmmm* what?" I asked.

"Well, I was just wondering…do you think Alec knew?"

I swiveled in my seat to face her. "Knew what? About the embezzling?"

She nodded.

"How would he?"

"Well, I was just thinking. I mean, Alec knew how much Tyler was making per episode, but he also had a front row seat to Tyler's spending. The RV, the glam squad, the sports car he drove."

"Ferrari," I said, liking where she was going. "Go on."

"Alec had to have some inkling what the restaurants were doing. He used to work there. And, well, even Tyler's own attorney seemed concerned about where he'd get the money to pay off a lawsuit. So, when Alec sued Tyler, where did he think Tyler would get the money?"

I pointed a fingernail at her. "Good point." I sat back in my seat, thinking that one through. "Maybe Alec saw something, back when he worked for Tyler, that tipped him off. Or maybe he's known all along that Tyler was embezzling and was just waiting for an opportunity to capitalize on it."

"So where does that leave us?" Ava asked.

"With lots of motive," I told her, my mind still running over possibilities. "No proof and—" I added, looking at her dash clock, "—a dessert demonstration to get to." I sighed.

"Well, I can help you with one of those," Ava promised, pulling out of the lot and pointing her car back toward Oak Valley.

CHAPTER THIRTEEN

———

Twenty minutes later we were back at the Fall Food and Wine Festival, where the last demonstration of the night seemed to be going off without a hitch. Or at least with only a couple of minor hitches. When I'd arrived, Gabby had been yelling at the hair stylist about her hair being too frizzy, yelling at the bleached blonds about her eyelashes being crooked, and yelling at anyone within range of her voice that someone needed to find Alec. Fortunately, the hairstylist had frizz serum, the blonds reapplied Gabby's left eyelash, and Alec made an appearance just before Gabby was to go on stage—cradling a glass of Zin in hand and a scowl on his face. I wasn't sure what the current relationship status between the two was, but I'd say it was in the murky to muddy range.

But one thing I could say for Gabby was that she was a total professional when it came to her audience. Whatever foul mood she'd been in all day, she checked it at the stage and showed up for the crowd with a smile and a gregarious welcome to everyone assembled as she demonstrated her Summer Fruit Flambé. While the applause was sparse—as was the "crowd"— Gabby put on a show that had everyone enthralled as they watched her light her peaches ablaze with a flourish against the backdrop of the darkening sky.

That crisis averted, I made my way back toward the main building. Jean Luc was pouring in the tasting room for the last of the customers of the evening. While he said he was "perfectly fine, *mon amie*," I could tell the long days and the suspicion in the air were wearing on him—if nothing else, the droop of his mustache betrayed that much. Eddie promised to help Jean Luc clean up after the guests went home, and I left them to finish up a little paperwork before calling it a night myself.

Only, as I made my way down the hall and to my office door, I realized someone had beaten me to it.

I froze. Someone was in my office.

He had his back to me and was bent over my desk, as if searching it for something. It took me a moment to recognize the blond hair and slim build, but as I did, anger started to bubble up inside me.

"Excuse me," I said loudly.

Alec Post stood and spun around so quickly he almost knocked my stapler off my desk.

"Looking for something?" I asked, arching one eyebrow in his direction and doing my best to channel the stern, no-nonsense sound of my second grade teacher's voice.

Alec blinked at me, taking a moment to respond. If I had to guess, he was searching for a credible lie.

"Gabby sent me to find you."

"Gabby?" I asked, my tone probably giving away that I only halfway believed him. "You mean the Gabby who's on stage right now?"

His adorable features pulled down into a scowl. "*Before* she went on stage."

"What does she need?"

"She wants the keys to Tyler's trailer to get it back to LA. The police said they handed them over to you."

I crossed my arms over my chest as I watched his eyes ping around the room, not quite meeting mine. "They did. And you thought you'd just search through my desk until you found them...?" I left the question hanging.

His scowl deepened, but he had the good grace to at least temper it with a little guilt. "Look, I just thought if they were sitting in plain sight, I could save you the trouble."

"Sure." I narrowed my eyes at him. "In plain sight under the piles of papers you were riffling through, you mean?"

Alec lifted his chin. "I don't know what you mean."

"I find that hard to believe. You're a smart cookie, Alec."

He clenched his jaw. "Are you going to give me the keys or not?"

I paused, feeling an opportunity I might not later have. "How much did you know about Tyler's finances, Alec?"

"Wh-what?" I could tell the question surprised him.

"You mentioned earlier that you knew exactly what he made per episode. Did you also know how much he was spending on his celebrity lifestyle?"

He snorted. "I could guess. The guy was the biggest show-off alive. Even back when I worked at his restaurant, he was always pulling up in some new sports car, flying off to Europe, flashing Rolexes."

"Where do you think he got all that money?"

Alec cocked his head to the side. "What do you mean?"

"I mean, one could run through his TV salary pretty quickly if one spent the way Tyler did."

Alec shrugged. "Maybe he had money coming in from the restaurant chain."

I watched him, trying to decide if he really believed that. "Maybe. But one would have to wonder if it was enough to cover the amount in your lawsuit."

Alec shook his head. "Look, all I knew was he owed me. Where he got the money to pay up was his problem."

"Emphasis on *was*," I noted. "Past tense."

Alec took a step forward, his jaw clenching again. "What exactly are you implying, Ms. Oak?"

I shrugged, feeling some of the bravado at having caught him red-handed in my desk fading. Alec had me by a good six inches and sixty pounds—all of it gym-honed muscle from what I could tell. "Nothing," I hedged. "Just that it seemed like a gamble suing Tyler for money he might not have."

The corner of Alec's mouth quirked up ever so slightly in a snide smirk. "Oh, he had it."

"Did he?" I asked, suddenly thinking maybe Ava's theory was right. Maybe Alec *had* known about Tyler's embezzling. "How can you be so sure?"

But instead of answering, Alec took another step forward. The smirk was still on his lips, but his eyes were dark, menacing, and definitely not smiling. "What is this about, Ms. Oak? Hmm? Are you trying to say I killed Tyler over some worry he might not be able to pay the restitution in my lawsuit? That's a pretty thin motive to murder someone."

I tried to take a step back, coming up awkwardly against the doorjamb. "N-no. I didn't say that." I paused. "But Tyler has stopped stealing your recipes, hasn't he?"

Alec snorted out a derisive laugh again. "That he has."

"And," I said, watching his expression, "stopped stealing your girlfriend as well."

All trace of smirks, smiles, or laughter vanished as Alec took another step toward me. "I don't know what you're talking about," he ground out between clenched teeth. I tried to step back again, but I was pinned against the wall. Alec leaned in, his face just inches from mine, so close that I could smell our Zinfandel on his breath. "But if you know what's good for you, you'll keep your big mouth shut."

I felt my breath hitch in my chest, my body involuntarily bracing for the physical blow that his menacing posture threatened.

Instead he stepped back, quickly walking through the doorway and down the hall toward the tasting room.

I let out a long breath, leaning against the doorjamb and closing my eyes as I counted to ten to get my heart back to normal.

"Emmy?"

"Eep!" I screeched and felt my insides jump as my eyes flew open.

To find my best friend standing in front of me, her flowing boho dress floating around her ankles as she frowned at me.

"Whoa. You okay?" Ava asked.

I blew out a long breath. "Yeah. Just…jumpy," I finished, crossing the room and sinking into my desk chair.

"Why?" Ava pressed, plopping into a chair across from me. "What happened?"

I quickly filled her in on my run-in with Alec.

"Why do you think he wanted the keys so badly?" she asked when I'd finished.

I shook my head. "Search me. As far as I could tell, it was just Tyler's hair and makeup trailer."

"Unless he kept some personal items in there," Ava said, perking up. "Like, maybe some record of his embezzled funds?"

I shook my head. "Police have been all through there. If he had financial papers among his curlers and hairspray, I'm sure they're gone now."

She gave a resigned shrug. "You're right. Even if the records were digital, I'm guessing they took his phone and computer?"

I shrugged. "Probably."

Ava paused. "You didn't give Alec the keys, did you?"

I shook my head. "No. I should give them to Gabby though. I mean, if she really is going to haul that thing back to LA."

"Well, you'll have to wait until tomorrow. I just saw her leave," Ava informed me.

"How did the demo go?" I asked.

"Great! The flambéed peaches were really impressive. I think the crowd liked it."

"All five of them?" I joked.

Ava grinned. "Cheer up. At least tomorrow is the last day." As if just thinking about one more day made her tired, Ava yawned, stretching her arms above her head.

"Thanks for hanging in there with me," I told her. I knew she must not be making much with her Silver Girl booth, especially with having to pay an employee to run the store while she worked the festival.

She shot me a bright smile. "Hey, no worries. What are friends for?"

"Well, tonight," I said, "I think they're for thanking profusely with a girls' night. How about a pint of mint chip and a date with Bridget Jones?"

"Throw in a bottle of rosé, and I'm there," Ava said enthusiastically.

"Done!"

* * *

An hour later, we had Ava's booth closed down, the kitchen cleaned, and the tasting room and winery entrance locked up tight for the night. We both changed into our pajamas—Ava into the spare pair she kept in my guestroom for nights when she might have enjoyed the rosé just a *little* too much and me into a comfy cozy pink flannel set covered in tiny blue elephants. Ava had the movie cued up and the wine uncorked, and I ducked out quickly to raid the freezer of the big kitchen for the promised mint chip.

After digging waaaay in the back (I'd had a few mint chip moments lately), I finally found a pint that was only minimally freezer burned and almost full. I locked the kitchen back up and was halfway down the stone pathway back to my cottage when I passed The Cave and noticed that the cellar door was slightly ajar. With everything going on, Jean Luc must have been distracted and forgotten to lock it up that evening. Ice cream in hand, I made a small detour toward The Cave, pausing at the open doorway.

"Hello? Jean Luc?" I called out. The light at the far end of the cellar was on. Damp air surrounded me, along with the scents of oak barrels, tannins, and the cool musty aroma of the aging wood.

"Eddie?" I asked of the still air, wondering if my jovially inept winery manager had been down for a bottle and left the door unlocked.

But silence was the only response that came back to me. Even the sounds of the crickets under the moonlight were muted down here. I shivered as the cool air prickled over my bare arms, making the frozen dessert in my hands feel like an icicle. Satisfied I wasn't locking a wayward employee in, I shut off the light, plunging The Cave into darkness, and turned to go.

Only, I didn't get the chance to leave.

As soon as I spun around, something heavy slammed into the side of my head, making my vision go fuzzy and spinning me back into the cellar. The mint chip flew from my hand, and the ground rushed up to meet my face. My cheek hit the cool stone floor with a jarring force, causing a second explosion of light to go off behind my eyes.

Then all I saw was black.

CHAPTER FOURTEEN

———

The fragrant scent of grape leaves drying in the sun wafted toward me on a warm breeze, signaling the harvest would be upon us soon. The sun hit my shoulders beneath my flowered tank top, and a large oak tree provided shade for the man sitting beside me as he wiped his brow and looked out at the vast fields.

"All this will be yours one day, Emmy," my father told me, his deep voice washing over me in a familiar rumble that instantly made me feel safe and at ease.

"All of it?" I tried to wrap my young brain around the idea.

"Yes. Everything to the hills. The same acres your grandfather worked."

"I don't remember that," I told him honestly, my voice sounding very small beside his booming presence.

"That was before you were born, little bean."

"Oh." I followed his gaze, taking in the rows of grapevines planted in neat lines one after another on the rise and fall of the landscape. Sun glistened off the horizon, bathing the fields in its golden rays.

"Someday, you'll work the land just like I have," Dad continued. "Love the grapes. Be grateful for the harvest. Rise and fall with the sun."

"I can't work it all myself," I said matter-of-factly. "It's too big."

Dad chuckled. "You'll have help."

"Will you help me, Daddy?" I asked.

He smiled down at me but shook his head. "No. It will be your turn then, Emmy."

"But where will you be?"

Dad chuckled again, the sound filled with warmth from deep inside him. "I'll be old, Emmy. I'll be sitting on that front porch over there," he told me, pointing off toward our small cottage. "Enjoying a rocking chair and watching my grandkids play while your mom bakes us pies." He ended with a wink in my direction, knowing how much I loved my mother's apple pie.

And suddenly it hit me—Dad didn't know. He didn't know about the heart attack that would take him before my seventeenth birthday. That what he'd leave my mom and me with was a small winery still operating the old way it had for decades, even when the industry around us was rushing into the digital age. That no matter how hard Mom tried to make it all work, she would not only be battling the tide of change but also the changes in her mind that brought good days and bad ones. That eventually her whole world would be a jumbled mess of memories, all at an age that was way too young and too full of physical life.

The pain and unfairness of it all hit me so hard that it was almost a physical thing, making my head ache and pressure build behind my chest as I tried to be brave for him and keep tears inside.

I must not have done a very good job of it, as he turned to me, his eyebrows drawn down. "What's wrong, my little Emmy?"

I opened my mouth to tell him. To warn him. But no sound came out. I struggled for the right words to express the loss that I felt as if it were pounding in my head, ripping me apart from inside. There would be no rocking chairs. No pies. No enjoying the fruits of his years of labor. Just a sudden finality that would leave nothing but emptiness in its wake.

"Emmy?" he asked again.

My chest hurt. My head pounded. Tears behind my eyes wouldn't stay put, making the entire scene blur like a watercolor painting left out in the rain.

"Emmy? Talk to me, Emmy."

His voice was far away now, the sound as watery as my vision. I tried to bring him back into focus, but he faded farther and farther from me.

"No," I said, hearing my own voice come out small and weak.

"Emmy!" he shouted. Louder this time. Closer. Younger.

"There you are. Emmy, open your eyes."

I blinked, tears making my lashes wet as I struggled to comply.

But the face I found hovering above me was not the image of my father haloed in the sunshine, but Detective Christopher Grant, his concerned features shadowed by the dim light just outside my field of vision.

"G-Grant?" I asked, my brain slow to catch up to my eyes.

I heard him let out a long breath. "God, you scared me."

Something cold was beneath my head, and I realized I was lying on the floor. I blinked, taking in the dark ceiling of The Cave above me, the aging barrels to the right and the stone floor that smelled like dirt below me. I tried to lift my head, but pain exploded behind my eyes, forcing them shut again. "Uhn." My head fell back on the hard stones again.

"Don't try to move. You've got a big lump on your head."

"You don't say," I croaked out.

I thought I heard a soft chuckle in response, but it was forced and shaky. "I'm calling an ambulance."

"No!" I cried out on instinct. Then regretted it, as even talking hurt. "I-I don't have insurance."

"I'll pay for it," he told me.

I forced my eyes open to find him already dialing. "I'm fine," I said. Which would have been way more convincing if I wasn't lying on my back, struggling to form words.

Grant shot me a look that said as much. "You are so far from fine."

"Wait. Just, give me a minute, huh?" I pleaded. While he was right—I was not even fine adjacent—the thought of him having a bill of several hundred dollars for an ambulance I didn't need was too much. Almost as bad as envisioning myself trying to pay that bill.

I must have sounded slightly more convincing this time, as Grant did lower his phone from his ear. "You need to see a doctor."

I nodded. Slowly, as the pain seemed to rocket back and forth with each movement. "I will. But I don't need an ambulance." I forced myself up on my elbows again, fighting a wave of nausea as the world swayed with the effort.

"Here." Grant reached out, supporting me into a sitting position. His gaze roamed my face, as if assessing me. "Your pupils aren't dilated. Eyes are tracking."

"Is that good?"

He nodded, attempting a smile. "Yeah. That's good." He paused. "You've got a bruise forming on your cheek and a nasty bump on your head though." He reached out and gently touched the side of my face.

Even his featherlight touch made me wince and jerk involuntarily away from his fingers.

His eyebrow drew down in concern again, erasing the smile. "What happened?" he asked.

I took a shaky breath in, trying to recall through the pounding in my head. "The cellar door was open. The light was on," I remembered.

Grant nodded. "Go on."

"I-I came in and called out Jean Luc's name."

"Jean Luc. Why?" I could hear the immediate pounce in his voice at his prime suspect's name.

"I thought maybe he was here, stocking for tomorrow. But it turned out someone just left the light on and forgot to lock up."

"What happened then?"

"I shut the light off. But then something hit me."

"Something or someone?" Grant clarified.

I licked my lips. "I guess it was someone," I said, that realization sending a chill through me that had nothing to do with the cool air around me.

"Did you get a look at them?" Grant pressed, going into Cop Mode.

I started to shake my head then thought better of it as the pounding vibrated between my temples again. "No. I-it was dark," I stammered, trying to remember anything that might be useful.

"Did you hear anything? Smell anything?"

I bit my lip. "No. Sorry."

He took in a deep breath through his nose. "Not your fault."

While I knew that, I still could have kicked myself. "He was right here," I said, "and I didn't even get a look at his face."

"His?" Grant said, jumping on the word. "It was a man?"

I scrunched up my nose, thinking back. "Sorry. I can't be sure." I paused. "But whoever it was, I'm sure it had to do with Tyler's death."

Grant froze. "What makes you say that?"

I licked my lips. "I may have been asking a few questions about Tyler. To his friends. Or enemies, as the case may be."

Grant sucked in a deep breath. I could feel a whole host of swear words running through his narrowed eyes, but he was too much of a gentleman to let any of them out. "Okay," he finally said. "Who have you been talking to?"

"Well, Mark Black for one."

"Tyler's business partner?"

"He told me Tyler was embezzling funds from the company. Two million dollars, half of it Mark's money."

Grant's eyes narrowed. "He just told you this."

"Sure," I said, glossing over the details. "And then there's Alec Post." The mental image of his menacing face inches from mine earlier that day jumping to the forefront of my mind. "He threatened me."

"Threatened?" I had Grant's full attention now. "When?"

"This evening. I…I caught him in my office."

"Doing what?"

"Honestly, I'm not totally sure," I admitted. "I thought he was after the keys to Tyler's trailer."

"Did he say why?"

"He said Gabby wanted them to get the trailer back to the studio in LA."

Grant nodded. "Makes sense."

I had to admit, saying it out loud, it kind of did.

"So why did he threaten you?" Grant asked.

I licked my lips again, my mouth feeling dry. "I may have kind of insinuated that Tyler was sleeping with Alec's girlfriend."

Grant raised an eyebrow at me. "Gabby?"

I nodded. "He told me to keep my mouth shut if I knew what was good for me."

Grant let out a sigh. "Emmy, if you were saying things like that about my girlfriend, I'd probably tell you to shut up too."

"*Your* girlfriend?"

"*If* I had one."

"Oh." I felt myself blush and tried to get the conversation back on the rails to cover it. "Look, clearly I made someone nervous. Someone was sending a message to me. A warning."

His jaw clenched. "Or the cellar was left unlocked and you interrupted a burglar."

I rolled my eyes and quickly realized even that movement hurt. "Doesn't that seem coincidental to you?"

"You've had hundreds of people here for the festival, correct?"

Dozens was sadly probably more accurate, but I nodded slowly in agreement.

"And it's no secret your stock is kept in the cellar."

I bit my lip, hesitant to agree again. Mostly because he was making sense. While my gut still said this was related to Tyler's death, there was no evidence to suggest it wasn't a random burglary. And, the truth was, with everything else happening, maybe my staff and I hadn't paid the most attention to keeping The Cave secure.

"I still think it's not a coincidence," I said, though I could hear some of the conviction fading from my voice.

Grant let out a long breath, his features softening. "I think we need to get you home. Are you able to stand?"

I nodded, the thudding pain subsiding to a dull roar as Grant slowly helped me up. Once on my feet, the world went a little woozy for a moment, but with Grant's hands to steady me, I managed to avoid falling on my face. Which I took as a good sign.

I took a tentative step forward.

And my knees buckled under me.

"Whoa," Grant said, his arms suddenly going around my middle, pulling me up against him to keep me from slithering to the ground.

It was not an altogether unpleasant position to be in. I could feel his heart beating quickly through his shirt, warmth from his chest suddenly chasing away any lingering chill. His arms were strong and steady, encircling me in their safety. And as I looked up into his face, his eyes were dark, the golden flecks in them dancing down at me like twinkling stars. His lips parted, and I braced myself for their soft touch as his hand moved up to cup my head.

"Your hair is sticky," he said.

I blinked at him. "Wh-what?" I reached a hand to my hair and came away with melted mint chip on my palm.

"Ice cream," I moaned. "I was coming back from the kitchen when I was hit."

"That it?" he asked, eyes cutting to the floor.

I followed his gaze and saw the last of my dessert splayed across the stone floor. So much for my girls' night. Though, I was in no shape to clean it up at the moment. I decided to leave it for tomorrow as Grant helped me shut off the lights in The Cave again and lock the door behind us. Then I let him support me the short walk down the pathway to my cottage door.

I noticed my hands were shaking a bit as I fumbled with the knob, and as soon as I pushed the door open, Ava jumped up from the sofa.

"Finally. I was beginning to think you got distracted in the kitchen and—"

She froze as she spotted me—knot at my temple, doused in melted mint chip, Grant practically holding me up. "Ohmigodwhathappened?" she asked all in a rush, suddenly at my side, helping Grant ease me down onto the sofa.

Those worn cushions had never felt so good.

"I fell," I told her.

"She was attacked," Grant amended, his voice monotone as if making an effort to eradicate any emotion from it.

"What?" Ava gasped. She sat beside me, eyes roaming my body like Grant's had, as if mentally assessing me for damages.

"I'm okay," I assured her. "Mostly."

"She needs to see a doctor," Grant interjected, contradicting me again.

"We should call an ambulance," Ava agreed.

"That's what *I* told her." Grant gave me a pointed look.

"I'm fine," I protested again. "Just a little bruised."

"And battered," Ava added, frowning at the lump I could feel forming on my head.

"It's fine. I'm feeling better already," I lied, shooting the two of them a big smile with teeth and everything.

Which did nothing to erase the concern on either face staring back at me.

"Come on, guys. You know how much an ambulance will cost?"

"Em, you could have a concussion," Ava protested.

"Look, I'll go see a doctor in the morning," I promised. A cheap one at the walk-in clinic. Where I had a coupon.

Grant turned to Ava. "You're staying the night here?"

She nodded. "We were going to have a girls' night in." Her gaze went to the opened bottle of rosé that I would definitely not be partaking of now.

"Good. Wake her at least a couple times during the night. Watch for confusion or nausea. She can have Tylenol but not aspirin. And call me if anything changes."

Ava nodded. "No aspirin. Wake her up. Call you."

"I'm not concussed," I protested.

Grant turned his gaze on me, his eyes dark and filled with an emotion I couldn't read. "Emmy, you were unconscious when I found you."

Ava sucked in air beside me, her pale eyebrows pulling together again. "Thank God you were there," she told him.

"Yeah, what *were* you doing here?" I asked, the thought suddenly occurring to me.

Grant's eyes went to me, and he hesitated, as if he didn't want to say. "I came to see you," he finally let out.

I licked my lips. "Me?"

He nodded. Though the way his jaw clenched and his eyes avoided mine, I had the impression this had not been a social call.

"Why?" I asked.

He bit the inside of his cheek and crossed his arms over his chest, the stance instinctively protective.

Or combative.

"Grant, what did you come see me about?" I asked again, becoming less and less sure I wanted to know the answer.

His eyes went to a spot on the wall above me, his nostril flaring as he breathed slowly in and out, as if wishing he were anywhere but here at the moment.

"You can't leave me hanging here," I prompted again.

Finally he barked out two short words. "Jean Luc."

I felt that nausea roll through my stomach again. "What about Jean Luc?" I pressed.

"Nothing," he shot back quickly. Too quickly. "It can wait until morning."

"Oh, no way," I said, getting up from the sofa. Only, as I stood, the room wobbled again, and my body flopped back down all on its own. "You're not getting away that easily," I finished weakly.

He let out a long breath, shaking his head. "Look, I came to give you the heads-up. So you didn't have to learn the hard way tomorrow."

"Learn what?" I asked, dread strong enough that it was a physical sensation in my gut.

His eyes went from Ava to me, mentally stalling.

"What is it?" Ava asked. She reached over and took my hand in hers as protection against whatever it was Grant clearly was not happy about telling us.

He let out another long breath, this time accompanied by a hand running through his hair. "Fine. You're going to find out tomorrow anyway. The DA is getting a judge to issue a warrant for Jean Luc's arrest."

All the air was suddenly sucked from my lungs. "What?" I whispered.

Grant shook his head. "I'm sorry, Emmy." His voice was soft and sympathetic. "I know you're close to him."

"Close?" I shot back. "He's like family!" Some days he and the rest of the staff were pretty much the only family I had left. And I'd be damned if I was going to let Grant take them away from me. "No, you can't arrest Jean Luc."

"I'm sorry," he repeated. "But the evidence is strong enough that the DA wants to move forward with charges."

"What evidence?" Ava demanded, squeezing my hand in solidarity.

Grant shifted his gaze to her, some of his official cop mode covering the softness he'd let escape. "The murder weapon is the same make and model as Jean Luc's gun."

"Which is missing!" I pointed out. "You have no proof it's the same weapon."

Grant ignored me, continuing to address Ava as he listed out his case. "Jean Luc and the victim had a history."

"Ancient history," I argued.

"He was seen arguing with the victim just moments before his death."

"Allegedly," I shot back.

"And we have his fingerprints in Tyler's condo in downtown Sonoma."

That one took the wind out of my sails. "Wait—what?"

Grant ran a hand through his hair again in way that left it so sexily tousled that I almost lost my train of thought.

Almost.

"What do you mean you have his fingerprint in Tyler's condo?" I demanded.

"Just that," Grant told me. "CSI found a wineglass in the sink at Tyler's place. Recently used. Prints on the glass came back as Jean Luc's." He sighed deeply. "Which means Jean Luc lied to the police about not having seen Tyler prior to the festival."

"B-but that can't be," I protested. "Jean Luc would never lie about that. There must be a mistake."

But Grant shook his head, something akin to pity in his eyes as he stood over me. "I'm sorry, Emmy. There's no mistake."

I felt hot, angry tears back up behind my eyes, but I would not give him the satisfaction of seeing me cry. "Yes there is, because Jean Luc did not kill Tyler."

"Emmy—" Grant started.

But I didn't want to hear any more. "Get out." I blurted the words out without thinking.

I heard Ava shift uncomfortably on the sofa beside me, but I didn't take my eyes off Grant.

His jaw clenched again, and emotion flared behind his eyes. But it was gone too fast to read as his face shut down into Cop Mode again—giving nothing away.

I felt my heart beating rapidly in my chest, anger bubbling close to the surface as those tears threatened. "You heard me," I repeated. "If you're really going to arrest one of my family, you're not welcome here."

"Em," Ava said softly beside me.

But I ignored her. "Go," I told Grant.

He gave me one last long, hard stare before turning on his boots and stalking out the door. It slammed shut with a thud that made me sick to my stomach again, and those tears finally won the battle, falling over my cheeks.

*　*　*

It was times like this one that made me grateful to have a friend like Ava. While Bridget Jones had taken a back seat the previous night, Ava had made a good dent in the rosé while being my literal shoulder to cry on well into the wee hours of the morning. I'd cried for the mess I'd made of the Food and Wine Festival, for the good friend whose life was about to be thrown into upheaval, and for the man I'd sworn had shown real feelings for me but was now taking away one of the people dearest to me. Not to mention locking up an innocent man for a crime he did not commit.

While I knew Grant was just doing his job, I also knew he must believe Jean Luc was guilty if he was willing to arrest him. Grant's history was not one of someone who blindly followed orders.

While I was still hazy on the details, I knew the reason he'd been transferred to Sonoma County from the SFPD last year had not been that he was looking for a slower pace of life in Wine County than he'd led in the crime-riddled city but that he'd been the subject of an internal affairs investigation. There'd been an incident, and Grant had ended up killing a man. Whether it had been an accident, self-defense, or a moment of weakness on the part of an officer who was seeking immediate justice, I didn't know. Media details were sparse, and Grant's version of events did little to fill in the blanks, glossing over more than felt comfortable to me. All I knew was that when the investigation was over, Grant had been reassigned, ostensibly for a "change of scenery." There were days when I wanted to know what had prompted Grant to take the law into his own hands…and there were other days that I didn't.

Mostly I just wished he'd stop playing Bad Cop and realize that in the current case, he had the wrong man. Despite what the DA thought the evidence said, Jean Luc was innocent.

As the sun woke me the next morning like a freight train slamming into my corneas, that was the first thought that greeted me. An innocent man was going to be arrested. And so far I'd been able to do zero to stop it.

I blinked against the bright onslaught, my body feeling every second of sleep I hadn't gotten the night before. While Ava had popped into my bedroom to wake me every few hours as she'd promised, half the time I hadn't been asleep anyway, too many mixed emotions keeping rest at bay.

I slowly dragged myself out of bed and shoved my jellying limbs into a hot shower. While no amount of makeup was going to cover the bruise on my cheek, I did at least find a way to style my hair off to one side that mostly covered the goose egg at my temple. I added a swipe of cherry red lipstick to try to detract from it and did a smoky eye thing to compensate for the bags hanging under my eyes as a testament to my tossing and turning. I slipped into a pair of cropped jeans and a red cold-shoulder top with ruffled sleeves and was just strapping a pair of high heeled sandals onto my feet when I heard Ava at the bedroom door.

"Knock, knock," she said, pushing it open. "How you doin'?"

"Better," I told her, forcing a smile.

"You would have been more convincing without the grimace."

"Was it that bad?"

She grinned. "Actually, you look pretty good, all things considered." She sat down on the bed beside me, eyes going to my hair. "Good fix." Then her gaze landed on the purple and green bruise, and her smile froze.

"I know it's not pretty," I admitted.

"I've seen worse."

"Now who's the liar?" I said.

She let out a laugh on a puff of air. "Well, it's not for me to decide what sort of shape you're in. You promised Grant you were going to the doctor this morning, remember?"

I groaned. "Fine, but just don't say that name again."

"Grant?" she asked.

"Traitor feels better."

"You know he's only doing his job, Em," she said softly.

"Well his job sucks."

"He cares about you." I felt my heart squeeze as Ava nodded. "He does. I could see it in his eyes last night."

I took a long, slow breath, brushing thoughts of Grant's bedroom eyes aside. "It doesn't matter right now. All that matters today is being there for Jean Luc."

Ava nodded resolutely. "Right." She paused. "But first—coffee."

"You are a wise woman."

* * *

While Ava stopped at the Half Calf downtown for two extra-large lattes, I put in a call to my accountant, Schultz, to get a lawyer lined up for Jean Luc. While I had no idea how we'd pay for it, it was clear he was going to need one.

Once caffeinated, Ava did, as promised, escort me to the walk-in clinic. As we sat in the waiting room, I tried calling Jean Luc, but his phone went straight to voice mail. I couldn't help the bundle of nerves in my stomach at the thought that I might be calling a phone that was now in an evidence locker somewhere. I itched to contact Grant to see if he'd gotten that arrest warrant yet, but instead I docilely submitted to all the tests, poking, and prodding the clinic doctor had before being deemed to have a lump on the head and bruised cheek. I internally winced at how much I'd paid for that brilliant diagnosis as I handed the receptionist my credit card.

Having been medically cleared, I prompted Ava to stop by Jean Luc's apartment next. Unfortunately, it appeared no one was home. The lights were out, the windows covered, and no one answered our knocking on the front door.

"Maybe he's at the winery already?" Ava suggested, ever the optimist.

"Or maybe he's been dragged away in handcuffs already."

Ava shot me a look. "Don't do that to yourself. If Grant had arrested Jean Luc, he'd let you know."

I shook my head. I wasn't sure after the way I'd thrown him out last night. But I tried to follow Ava's bright-side lead and let her drive me back to the winery, where the first thing I did was check the tasting room.

Empty.

If my sommelier had come in early, he hadn't made it behind the bar yet.

Trepidation about what was to come followed me as I wound through the hallways to the kitchen where, thankfully, the scents of French Roast and cinnamon greeted me. I found Conchita at the stove, frying up French toast, and Eddie sitting on a stool at the counter, a mug of steaming coffee in one hand as he adjusted his bow tie with the other. Lime green today, to match the lime-and-fuchsia-checked blazer he was wearing over a pair of pink slacks. I marveled at where on earth one might even buy men's pink slacks as I joined him.

"Good morning, Eddie."

"Good morning, sunshine—oh my word, what happened to you?" Eddie stared at my cheek, his eyes wide in his pudgy red face.

Conchita whipped around at his question, sucking in a breath as she saw me.

"*Ay, mía*, your face!" Suddenly she was at my side, attacking me with hugs and a clucking tongue.

"I'm fine. It looks worse than it is," I assured them both.

"Well, thank goodness for small favors, because *that* looks awful," Eddie pointed out.

"Thanks," I told him sarcastically.

"Please. You own a mirror, dahling."

"What happened?" Conchita asked, loading a plate with three pieces of French toast and pushing it along the countertop toward me.

Even if I were counting carbs, I couldn't resist such an offer. Which I wasn't. Mostly because I wasn't sure I could count high enough to get them all in. As I dug into the cinnamony, buttery breakfast, I filled them in on my ordeal the night before, both of my audience gasping and *oh*ing with such drama that they could audition for a telenovela.

"Did you see who did it?" Eddie asked when I'd finished.

I shook my head. "No. It was too dark. I didn't get a chance to see much of anything before…before I fell," I finished lamely.

Conchita did the sign of the cross and clucked some more.

"Have either of you seen Jean Luc yet this morning?" I asked, looking out the kitchen window as if he might appear any moment.

But both Conchita and Eddie shook their heads.

"He hasn't come in yet," Eddie informed me. "Why?"

I bit my lip. The anticipation of the inevitable was steadily gnawing at my insides, and the last thing I wanted to do was share that burden if I didn't have to.

"No reason," I finally lied. "Just, uh, send him my way if you see him, okay?"

Eddie nodded. "Sure thing, boss."

For fear I'd give away more of that anticipatory dread than I intended, I took the rest of my French toast into my office and finished it at my desk as I checked the emails that had come in via our website. While a couple were from potential clients wanting to know our regular tasting hours, most were written by reporters, looking for sordid details to flesh out their stories about Tyler's demise. Bradley Wu sat in my inbox among them, reminding me of my promise of an exclusive and asking exactly what time tomorrow he could come by to interview me. Ugh. Add one more item to my list of future events I was dreading.

I dragged my fork along my plate, scraping up the last bits of cinnamon syrup as guilt set in that I was enjoying a home cooked meal and Jean Luc was about to be in a cell. While I'd been dancing around Tyler's death for the last three days, I didn't feel like I was any closer to knowing who killed him or helping Jean Luc prove his innocence. I thought back over all of the conversations I'd had in the last few days, trying to find the one phrase or tidbit of information that I might have missed—some small kernel of truth I might have overlooked. Only, unfortunately, I came up with bupkis. While everyone who had known Tyler seemed to have at least one great reason to want the star dead, nothing I'd uncovered so far felt like concrete enough proof to say one of them had acted on those reasons.

Let's face it—as a Charlie's Angel, I was sucking big time.

I licked my fork as I tried not to dwell on that particularly pessimistic thought. I opened my top desk drawer to pull out a notepad and pen that might help me organize my thoughts. Only, as I pulled it open, something else shone up at me.

Tyler's keys.

Alec had seemed desperate to get his hands on these yesterday—desperate enough to risk riffling through my office. Was that because he knew something incriminating was in the trailer? Maybe because Alec himself had stashed it there?

I bit my lip, trying to think what it could be. Jean Luc's stolen gun? Proof of Tyler's embezzling? Or proof that Alec had created some of Tyler's famous recipes? Alec knew as well as anyone who had been at the festival that the police had already gone through Tyler's things. So whatever Alec was after had to be something that the police wouldn't automatically pick up—something that didn't seem incriminating at first. Or that Alec had hidden well.

On instinct, I grabbed the keys and quickly made my way outside and around to the back of the kitchen where the giant trailer was parked. Tyler's large smile greeted me, feeling almost sad now that his fame was inevitably going to fade into obscurity. I glanced around for any other signs of life, but the vendors were just starting to arrive at their booths, festival guests not yet on the premises. There was no sign of Gabby or her newly acquired glam squad. The only other person I saw was Hector, watering the flowers in some of the planters we'd set up around the festival grounds.

I took a deep breath and climbed the three steps to the trailer door, inserting the keys with shaky hands. Why I was shaking, I wasn't really sure. I mean, Grant *had* given me the keys. It wasn't as if I was breaking and entering. Just…opening and entering. There, that only sounded like half a crime now.

I pulled the door open and quickly slipped inside, closing it behind me. I stood there frozen for a three count, expecting someone to come shouting at me to get out. But the only sound I heard was my own ragged in and out as I tried to get my breathing under control.

I slowly glanced around the trailer. A small sofa sat on one side and a bathroom and bedroom at the back. Instead of a traditional kitchen, the RV had been gutted out in the middle and a makeup and hair station put in its place. A large mirror with globe lights surrounding it covered one wall, and an adjustable chair like they used in beauty salons sat in front of it. A counter beneath the mirror was littered with makeup in various skin tones, tubes of hair products, and a blow dryer and several brushes. Either Tyler's glam squad were unorganized or the police hadn't been very careful in their search of the trailer.

I opened a couple of drawers, but all I saw was more cosmetics—nothing that felt incrementing toward either the star or his killer. Unless you counted the fact that Tyler had copious amounts of wrinkle cream and hair dye in his possession.

I moved on to the bathroom. It was barely larger than one of those airplane bathrooms, just enough to turn around in and do one's business. I opened the small cupboards, but the only things in them were a few over-the-counter pain medications and a prescription stool softener. Hmm. Constipated, going gray, and wrinkled. Maybe the larger-than-life Tyler Daniels had been human after all.

I left the bathroom and checked the rest of the main cabin. The sofa yielded nothing, though I wasn't really sure what I expected to find in the cushions. Which only left the bedroom. I glanced out the side window at the festival grounds, now filling with the rest of our remaining vendors. I was starting to get antsy that someone might find me. I quickly made the few steps to the bedroom and opened the door.

Though, as I did, I realized Tyler hadn't so much used it as a place to nap but as a small office. A built-in desk took up one side of the room, and a club chair and a wall of cabinets covered the other. I started with the cabinet, opening cupboard doors to find cookbooks, folders, binders, and notebooks. I pulled a folder out at random, discovering handwritten recipes inside with notes scribbled in the margins like "crisp on high for five minutes first" or "add oregano not thyme." While Tyler may have borrowed some of Alec's techniques—and allegedly personal stories—at least some of his recipes appeared to be his own creations.

I put the folder back, not feeling like it contained any smoking gun, and moved on to the next cupboard. This one contained a variety of offices supplies—stapler, tape dispenser, paper clips. The next one held similar items, and the third was empty except for a couple of power cords. I realized with a sinking feeling it could have been where Tyler had kept his laptop—now the property of the Sonoma County Sheriff's Office, no doubt.

I was about to give up, deciding that the trailer didn't hold anything more exciting than recipe notebooks, when I tried the final cupboard at the bottom of the cabinet and found the door locked.

Now that was interesting.

I pulled the keys from my pocket on the off chance they might be *one size fits all* locks, but they were both a no-go. I quickly retraced my steps, opening every drawer and cabinet in the entire trailer a second time, searching for a key that might fit the lock. Unfortunately, as I felt time tick by, I came up empty. The nerves I'd initially had at entering the trailer had multiplied with each passing moment, the more time I spent in the trailer upping the chance someone would find me. I was nearly in panic mode by the time I'd torn apart the makeup area, office, and bathroom again. No keys.

I was just contemplating the jar of paperclips as the means to a lock picking miracle when I heard a sound outside the door.

Footsteps on the metal stairs.

I froze, even my breath stopping for a split second.

Then I instinctively ducked down, crouching behind the club chair as I heard someone jiggling the locked door handle from the outside. Then a scraping sound, like metal coming up against metal. It took me a moment to realize what I was hearing, but when I did, I felt my pulse pick up to somewhere in the vicinity of a hundred times its normal rate.

Someone else was trying to break into Tyler's trailer.

CHAPTER FIFTEEN

―――――

My breath came out hard and fast as I whipped my gaze around the small trailer for anywhere to hide. Unfortunately, everything in it was built to be tiny, slim, and utilitarian. Nothing bulky to hide behind that wouldn't give me away faster than a two-year-old playing hide and seek with her eyes covered. If whoever was scraping away at the trailer lock made it inside, I'd be totally exposed.

Which meant I had to keep them outside.

If they were anything like me, they were probably afraid of getting caught right now. I had to bank on that. I took a deep breath, taking a gamble, and called out in a loud voice.

"Okay, Grant! Thanks for checking the trailer with me!"

The scraping stopped. I listened in the silence, my heart pounding.

Nothing for a second. Then I heard two quick, pounding steps on the metal stairs and the soft thud of footsteps quickly retreating from the trailer.

I made a beeline for the door, unlocking it and throwing it open in hopes of getting a glimpse of whoever was attempting the break-in.

I caught sight of the back of a figure rounding the building toward the parking lot. They were booking it, and all I could tell in that split second was that they were wearing a cap and jeans. Male, female, age—I had no idea.

On instinct, I took off running after them. And I might have caught up too, if I hadn't dressed that morning for fashion and not running after bad guys. My heel caught on a stray tree root jutting up from the earth, causing me to stumble forward as I caught my balance. Luckily, I did without face planting into the dirt, but by the time I made it around the corner of the building, my mystery figure was nowhere to be seen.

My eyes pinged from one person to the next as the first of our festival guests exited their cars. Several wore jeans. A couple of hats. None were running away in a guilty fashion.

As I stood there, breathing hard, I realized it was too late.

Whoever had tried to break in had faded into the crowd.

* * *

I couldn't help scrutinizing every person I passed as I made my way back to the trailer to lock it up, hoping to somehow recognize the would-be breaker-and-enterer. What had they been after in Tyler's trailer? Had it been Alec, taking matters into his own hands after I refused to give him the keys? Or was it someone else—someone who maybe knew what was in the locked cupboard in Tyler's trailer? My mind immediately went to the embezzled funds, but that felt too easy. Would Tyler really just hide a stack of cash in his trailer? He'd gone through a lot of trouble to cover his tracks on the company books, and using this as a hiding place just felt sloppy.

I itched to ask Grant if the police had opened the cupboard, but no way was I crawling back to him with my tail between my legs after my stand the previous evening. Instead, I tried to tell myself that it probably held nothing—the locked cupboard was just home to Tyler's checkbooks or Rolex. Just a convenient place to store his valuables that had nothing to do with his death.

Still, the fact that I was not the only person looking through Tyler's things was unnerving.

Once I'd locked the trailer and was confident it was as secure as it could be, I made my way to the tasting room, hoping Jean Luc had come in. Only, as I approached the bar, it was my erstwhile winery manager Eddie in his pink slacks pouring our brunch special, Champagne Mules, for the first guests of the day. I cringed as he over poured the vodka and under poured the champagne, hoping the guests weren't as finicky about proportions as Jean Luc usually was.

I watched Eddie serve the two drinks to the couple as I approached.

"Has Jean Luc been in yet?" I asked.

Eddie shrugged. "Still haven't seen him. Late, I guess."

Or incarcerated.

He sent me a big smile that reminded me of Dopey in the Seven Dwarfs as he added, "But don't worry. I've got the bar covered!"

"That's what I'm worried about," I mumbled.

"What was that?"

"Nothing. I'll ask Hector to come in and help you pour," I promised, my eyes cutting to where the couple was sipping at the cocktails. No one spit theirs back out. So far so good.

Eddie nodded. "Maybe a good idea. I mean, if you think Jean Luc might be taking a sick day or something."

It was the *or something* that had my stomach knotting over itself.

I left Eddie as another couple came in looking for a sample of our brunch specials.

Once back outside, I could see that guests were still filtering into the festival grounds. If I had to guess, there were a few more than the previous day, which I took as a good omen. I found an out-of-the-way spot on the low stone wall under an oak tree and dialed Jean Luc's number again. Six rings in, it went to voice mail again. I left a brief message, just letting him know that I had Schultz tracking down a lawyer for him—you know, if he needed one—and to call me when he got this.

I hung up, feeling useless and unsatisfied. I contemplated calling the sheriff's office and just asking if he'd been arrested yet, but that was only stirring the pot. I was trying to talk myself out of jumping into my Jeep and checking Jean Luc's place for any sign of the Frenchman again when I spotted something a few paces away in the brush—a flash of red.

I put my phone in my pocket and took a couple of steps off the pathway. Then it flashed again, and I realized it was a red dress I was seeing—specifically one worn by Gabriela Genova. She was pacing back and forth in the shade of another oak tree with what I assumed was a glass of wine in one hand, as she stopped to sip every few paces.

Wait—scratch that. It was a *bottle* of wine, I realized as she gave a half turn to the left and I spotted our label on the dark green bottle being lifted by the neck to her lips. I glanced at my watch. Just past noon. Wow. Must have had a heck of a morning.

While the wise thing to do might have been to leave the ill-tempered woman sucking down Chardonnay alone, the fact that she had a cooking demonstration to give in half an hour prompted me to approach her. As I did, I noticed she was not only pacing but also cursing and crying. Even the glam squad's mascara was no match for the sobbing tears that streaked down her face in dark, sad lines.

"Gabby?" I said.

She spun on me as if caught with a hand in the cookie jar. Or in a bottle, as the case may be.

"Are you okay?" I asked.

"Do I look okay?" she responded, throwing her hands wide to encompass the mascara streaking, the wine going down her throat like water, and—I now noticed up close—the broken heel of her right shoe she was hobbling back and forth on.

"No," I told her honestly. "You look like you could use a friend."

She scoffed. "Great. Let me know when you find one." She paused, focusing on me for the first time. "Whoa. What happened to *you*?"

I put a hand to my cheek. "Nothing. I, uh, had a rough night."

"Well, that makes two of us," she said, choking back a sob on the last word and turning to her bottle again.

"Oh?" I took a step closer to her. "Do you want to talk about it?"

"What are you, my therapist?" she shot back.

"Is it Alec again?" I pressed.

She pursed her lips together, eyes leaking more mascara-stained tears. But instead of sending another snide remark my way, she nodded.

"What happened?" I asked softly, honestly feeling sorry for her.

"He left me!" She did a hiccup-sob, putting the back of her hand to her mouth. "Can you believe it? *Me!*"

"I'm so sorry," I told her.

She shook her head. "He said he knew everything."

"Everything?" I clarified.

"About Tyler. That I'd been s-s-sleeping with him," she wailed. "And you!" she added, turning to me, her grief suddenly morphing into anger as she trained her eyes on me. "It's all your fault!"

"Me?" I took one giant step back at the crazed look in her eyes.

"Yes, you! You had to go asking questions, had to go nosing into everyone's business. Dragging our lives through the mud!"

Oops. I thought back to my conversation with Alec. "I-I thought he already knew. Didn't you say you thought he knew?"

"No!" She paused, nose scrunching up as if she was thinking back. "I mean, I don't know. I thought maybe he guessed." She paused again, and I wondered just how much of that bottle she'd ingested already. "But it was your big fat stupid mouth that confirmed it for him!"

"I'm so sorry, Gabby," I said, meaning it. While she wasn't exactly on my list of top ten people who gave me warm fuzzies, I hadn't meant to put a wrench in her relationship either.

"You should be!" she yelled, shaking the bottle at me.

The flash in her eyes, the venomous tone to her voice—in that moment I could easily see her being angry enough to want to hurt someone who had been, say, dragging her life through the mud. I suddenly wondered where Gabby had been last night around midnight when I'd been laid out in The Cave.

"Gabby, I honestly think Alec already knew," I told her.

"Well, he certainly knows now!" She let out more Italian curses to the treetops.

I bit my lip. "Gabby, is it possible Alec found out from Tyler?"

She spun toward me, almost toppling over from the uneven height of her broken heel. "What? How? When?"

"Well, maybe Alec suspected something. And confronted Tyler before he died."

Gabby took another fortifying sip from the bottle in her hands before shaking her head. "No. No, we've been over this before, remember?" She stabbed a manicured nail at me, though I could see it had a jagged edge where it had recently been broken. When Gabby went on a bender, apparently she didn't mess around. "Alec didn't know then. He couldn't. H-he just came to me about it last night." She hiccup-sobbed again and slid down to the ground, landing hard on her backside in the dirt as she took another swig.

While I feared what the dirt would do to my jeans, I sat down beside her, feeling her hard demeanor cracking.

"What happened last night?" I asked.

"Alec was angry. He said…he said I ruined everything. That I didn't deserve love. That I was a leech."

"Ouch."

"Yeah, no kidding," she said sarcastically before sipping again. "Me, the leech? No, I did *everything* for that man. I planned everything, I prepared everything, I was the backbone. He was the leech!"

"Alec?"

"No, Tyler! Aren't you paying attention?" she asked. Which might have had more punch if she hadn't slurred the last few words. "And then what does he do to me? He takes away my Alec." She turned to me, tears falling again. "I love Alec."

While she was the biggest pain Hollywood could have sent me, I couldn't help feeling sympathy for her. "Did you tell him that?"

She nodded. "He didn't care. He just said Tyler and I deserved each other, and he left."

"When was this?"

"Last night." She sniffed. "Right after we got back from the festival."

"And what time did he come back?" I asked, wondering if Alec had had enough time to come back to the winery and bash me on the head before returning to the hotel.

But Gabby shook her head. "He didn't. I waited all night, but he never came back. I think he's really gone." She hiccup-sobbed again.

While I felt for her, that also left Alec's evening wide open for attacking yours truly. After the threat in my office, it wasn't a stretch to picture him sneaking around the winery after dark.

"Have you tried calling him?" I asked Gabby.

She nodded. "He won't pick up. I know he has a webcast he's doing from the festival today. I was hoping I'd see him here this morning. But I think he's avoiding me."

"Maybe he just needs some time to cool off," I suggested.

She sniffed loudly again, turning to look at me through her wet lashes. "You think?"

I nodded. "What do you say we get you back to your glam squad and ready for the demo?"

"God, the demo!" She kicked at a rock as if it was its fault she had to go on stage in fifteen minutes. "I can't wait for this wreck of a festival to be over."

That made two of us.

I stood, attempting to haul Gabby up with me. She wasn't very cooperative—or coordinated—so it took a couple of attempts to get her to her feet. I did my best to brush the majority of the dirt off her skirt and intercepted her when she went to take another swig from her bottle.

"Uh, maybe let's just wait until after the demo for this, okay?" I asked cheerily.

She scowled at me but didn't protest as I tried to lead her around the back of the building to the kitchen. Once we'd hobbled our way there, I ushered her into Conchita's care with instructions to get as much coffee into her system as humanly possible. Then I went in search of the bleached blonds to go work their glam magic on her.

Crisis #1 of the day averted, I made my way toward my office for a little privacy to call Schultz and see where we were on that lawyer for Jean Luc.

Only, I never got the chance, as the second I walked into my office, I spotted Crisis #2 leaning against my desk in faded jeans, black boots, and a button down shirt that strained against a pair of impressive biceps as arms crossed unhappily over a broad chest.

Detective Grant.

CHAPTER SIXTEEN

———

I cleared my throat awkwardly, remembering where we'd left things last night. While I still thought I'd been in the right, in hindsight my temper might have taken over my mouth just a little.

"Grant," I said, greeting him in what I hoped sounded like a cool, professional, adult manner.

However, the response that came back to me was anything but professional, laced with an edge and an undercurrent of anger just waiting to explode. "Where is he?" Grant demanded.

"Wh-where… What do you mean?"

"Jean Luc. Where is he?"

I blinked at him. "I-I don't know. He's not here."

"I know. We've looked."

Of course he had. I opened my mouth to say more, but Grant ran right over me.

"He's also not at his home," Grant said, the edge growing with each word. "Or his neighbors' or friends' places."

I swallowed. "I-I'm sure he's somewhere."

"Me too." He leveled me with a stony look. "So, where is he?"

"Wait," I said, a bad feeling taking hold in my gut. "What are you implying?"

"I came here last night as a friend, Emmy," he said, the flecks in his eyes dancing in angry circles.

"Yeah, some friend you are! Just what exactly are you accusing me of?"

His jaw clenched so tightly I could see the veins in his neck straining. "It is a crime to harbor a fugitive."

There it was. I felt the breath rush out of me. "You think I've hidden Jean Luc somewhere?"

"I warned you last night that we're getting a warrant, and this morning he's vanished."

Vanished. I thought a dirty word. While I'd had no hand in tipping Jean Luc off, the fact that the police couldn't find him was unnerving. Either he'd stupidly run out of fear, which only served to make him look guilty, or something had happened to him. I thought of my attack last night. What if I hadn't been the only person the killer had visited last night?

"I don't know where he is," I said, hearing fear edge into my voice. "But the real killer might have hurt him."

"The real killer?"

I bit my lip, realizing how OJ that sounded. "Jean Luc did not hurt anyone."

"Innocent people don't flee," Grant challenged. "Especially without reason." He pinned me with that accusatory look again.

"I didn't say anything to him! Yes, I was angry you were being so irrational and wouldn't listen to reason—"

Grant opened his mouth to protest, but I had no interest in hearing it and continued right on.

"—but I have not talked to Jean Luc since he left the winery yesterday evening. I have no idea where he is. In fact, I've been trying to get hold of him all morning." I tossed my phone onto the desk. "Check my call logs if you don't believe me," I challenged him.

His eyes went to the phone before rising again to meet mine, a dark, flat expression in them.

I could feel angry tears pricking the back of my throat again, that Grant really thought me capable of this, but I refused to let them get any farther than that, straightening my spine and matching his cold gaze with as much indignation as I could muster up.

Finally Grant broke our staring contest, letting out a long sigh as his arms uncrossed and a hand went through his hair. "I don't need to check your phone, Emmy," he said, his voice losing some of the edge.

A small bubble of relief welled up inside me that he hadn't lost *total* faith in me.

"And what about Jean Luc?" I asked. "What if he's hurt?"

"Believe me, we're doing everything we can to find him." He paused, and I could tell he was holding back voicing that he was still looking for him as a missing fugitive and not a victim.

"His car?" I asked. "Is it still in his garage?"

Grant nodded. "But there are lots of other ways out of Sonoma. Train. Bus. Uber."

He was right. And as worried as I was for my friend, part of me could easily see Jean Luc being scared enough to use any one of those as means of running, despite his innocence. Especially if he could feel the police closing in.

"You'll let me know if you hear from him?" Grant asked, moving toward the door.

I nodded, though I wasn't 100% sure I was being honest even with myself in that moment. If Jean Luc really did contact me, I'd have a moral dilemma on my hands.

But Grant must have realized it was the best assurance he was going to get, as he nodded and turned to the door.

"Grant?" I called after him.

He paused, spinning back to face me.

"Uh, did the police open every cupboard in Tyler's trailer?"

He frowned, the question clearly not one he'd been ready for. "I'd have to ask the CSI unit. Why?"

I hesitated to tell him I'd been inside of it, not sure what sort of trespassing charge that could bring. "The, uh, makeup team told me there was one locked cupboard. I, uh, just wondered if the police had gotten a look at the contents."

The frown deepened. "You just wondered." Then he shook his head, his eyes going to the bruise on my cheek. "Emmy, leave this alone, okay?"

I bit my bottom lip, not quite ready to make that promise. "But you'll keep me posted, right?" I asked.

Unfortunately, he was a lot more honest than I was, as he just sent me a vague, "I'll do what I can."

And then he left.

* * *

My conversation with Grant left me unnerved in more ways than one. As I forced myself back out onto the festival grounds with what I was sure was a fake looking smile, all I could think of was Jean Luc, alone and afraid somewhere—at best, thinking he was being hunted down for a crime he didn't commit. At worst—I didn't even want to think of at worst. If whoever had attacked me last night hadn't stopped there, Jean Luc could be in serious trouble.

While everyone connected with Tyler seemed to have a reason to hate him, I couldn't help my mind replaying Alec Post's threat in my office. I'd seen Alec's temper firsthand. And he'd been angry last night, fighting with Gabby. Then he'd disappeared. He had no alibi for when Tyler died and none for when I was attacked. And the last time I'd seen him, he'd been caught going through my things. All of which added up to Alec being my prime suspect. And if there was even a chance he'd done something with Jean Luc, I had to find him.

After doing a quick round of the booths, it was clear Alec was not among them. I stopped briefly at Ava's Silver Girl spot to fill her in, and she promised she'd text me the second she saw him. I thanked her for being my eyes outside and then ducked into the tasting room.

Though, instead of Alec Post, the first familiar face I saw at the bar was Mark Black. Which took me aback, as he hadn't attended any previous days at the festival. He was sipping a glass of Zinfandel and was deep in conversation with a woman in a peacock blue dress who had her back to me. He must have felt my eyes on him, as his intent gaze moved from his companion's face to mine. Then he leaned in and whispered something to the woman, who spun in her seat, giving me a clear look at her face. Ashley Daniels.

"Emmy!" she hailed me, waving one of her bangled arms my way. Though as I crossed the room to greet her, her expression went from congenial to concerned.

"Good heavens, girl, what happened to you?"

My hand went instinctively to my cheek, and I ducked my head, hoping my hair would fall forward to cover the bruising. At least a little. "I, uh, was attacked. Last night."

"Are you okay?" Ashley asked, frowning.

I nodded. "I'll be fine. It's worse than it looks," I said, watching for any reaction from Mark Black. But if he felt any trace of guilt, he hid it beneath a poker face that gave no hint of his thoughts.

"I'm surprised to see you here, Mr. Black," I told him. "I'm hoping this means you enjoyed the wine samples I left you yesterday?"

He nodded, though his bushy eyebrows were drawn down in a scowl that made me wonder what the pair had been discussing when I'd walked in. "Yes. I, uh, tried the Pinot Blanc last night."

"Well, I hope you paired it with something light and full of citrus," Ashley said with a wink. "It's the only way to truly enjoy a top-notch Pinot Blanc."

Mark made a noncommittal grunt and sipped his wine.

"I told Mark he simply must come up here for the last day of the Food and Wine Festival," Ashley told me. "You've done such a lovely job of pulling together some very talented local chefs."

"Th-Thank you," I said, trying not to sound as surprised as I felt. While I agreed that the vendors who'd stayed on had put out some incredible culinary creations, it seemed all that the other press I'd encountered had wanted to talk about was murder. Though, it was very possible Ashley was dealing with her ex-husband's death in the ostrich fashion—if we didn't talk about it, it didn't hurt as much.

"We just had a delightful seared scallop at the seafood booth for lunch, didn't we, Mark?" Ashley added.

Mark did more grunting and sipping.

"Uh, neither of you have seen Alec Post today, have you?" I asked.

Mark shook his head.

Ashley pursed her lips together, causing her deep red lipstick to settle into the subtle lines around her mouth. "No, I can't say I have. But I did see Gabby earlier." She paused. "She seemed kind of a wreck."

"She's…having a bad day," I hedged.

"Poor kid." Ashley clucked her tongue. "She's taking it hard, isn't she?"

I blinked at her, wondering if Ashley knew about the diva's fight with Alec too.

"Tyler's death?" Ashley supplied.

"Oh. Right. Yes." I cleared my throat. "I-I think she is."

"We all are," Mark added before sipping from his glass again.

I bit my lip. So far no one had seemed to be terribly broken up about it, but if they were all going to pretend at grief today, who was I to stop them?

"By the way, the police released Tyler's trailer to me yesterday," I told Mark. "I have the keys to it, but I wasn't sure who to give them to now."

"Well, I'm sure the trailer was company property, wasn't it, Mark?" Ashley answered for him. "And everything in the company belongs to Mark now."

Mark's eyes went up to meet mine, a clear warning in them to keep quiet about just what assets the company did or did *not* have at current.

"Is that right?" I asked him slowly. "Did Tyler buy the trailer with company funds?"

The warning look didn't let up any, but he shook his head. "Let the lawyers figure it out."

"Oh surely you don't expect poor Emmy to keep that monstrosity here until then?" Ashley countered, her arm waving in the general direction of the trailer in a way that made her bracelets jangle again.

"Emmy's a smart girl," Mark said on a sneer. "She can figure it out."

"Alec told me that Gabby could get it back to the studios," I offered.

Mark shrugged and sipped again. "Whatever."

"I'm curious, how late did you stay at Tyler's Place last night?" I asked, watching Mark's reaction carefully as I wondered just how far I could push him.

Two bushy eyebrows raised my way over the rim of his glass. "Excuse me?"

"Just curious where you were last night."

His jaw clenched, his eyes going to the bruise on my cheek. "Are you trying to accuse me of something?" he ground out, the words laced with menace that had me rethinking my strategy to push.

But I licked my lips and charged forward. "The restaurant closes at ten. Did you stay after hours?"

"That's none of your business," he shot back. I could tell it was taking all he had to keep his temper in check.

"Actually, he was with me," Ashley quickly jumped in.

I looked from her to Black. "He was?"

She nodded, the pair of large gold hoops at her ears bobbing with the movement. "Yes, I stopped by his place after the restaurant closed. You know, catch up with old friends." She turned to Mark. "Isn't that right?"

Mark nodded slowly, though I could see some hesitation there. I had half a notion that Ashley Daniels was covering for him. Though, why, I wasn't sure. Was it just the ties of an old friendship? Or was something more going on there?

Though, either way, I'd be hard pressed to dispute the alibi she was providing him.

I was about to press further, when I spotted a figure outside the window, trekking from the main winery building to the festival grounds.

Alec Post.

I felt my heart rate pick up at the sight of my query.

"Well, I hope you two enjoy the rest of the festival," I told Ashley and Mark as I quickly excused myself, threading through the growing crowd in the tasting room to the back doors.

By the time I got outside, I'd lost sight of him and had a small moment of panic that he'd vanished again. Luckily, he was tall and blond, which tended to stand out in a crowd, and I spotted him at the edge of the grounds, quickly walking with his head down, as if on a mission.

I followed, half walking half jogging to keep pace with him. I'd almost caught up when he changed directions abruptly, ducking around the corner of the building, behind the kitchen.

In the direction of Tyler's trailer.

I hurried to catch up, though as soon as I rounded the corner after him, I paused. My initial intention had been to corner him and demand an alibi for last night. But as I saw him look over both shoulders to make sure no one was watching him—good instincts on his part—I hung back. People out for an innocent stroll weren't usually concerned with being watched.

A thought I held on to as Alec approached the trailer. Though, instead of going to the locked door, he quickly stepped around the back of it, the side that was sheltered from view by a couple of large oak trees.

I bit my lip, dying to know what he was up to. I tiptoed forward, trying not to make any sound as I went around the opposite side of the trailer than the one Alec had approached. I did a two count to muster courage and peeked around the back of the trailer.

Just in time to see Alec grab a large rock, weighing it in his hands for a beat before smashing it into the side window of the trailer.

I bit back a gasp of surprise at the destruction, but above the din of the festival, no one would have heard the noise. I watched Alec take off his jacket, using it to push out the remaining few shards of glass in the window, before he put his foot on the front tire, using it as leverage to boost himself up and into the broken window. It all took a matter of seconds, and he was inside.

I felt my breath coming fast, my mind whirling with what I should do. I could call Grant, but by the time he got there, Alec could be long gone. With whatever it was from Tyler's trailer that he was so keen to get his hands on.

I made a quick decision and quietly stepped toward the nearest unbroken window. I crouched next to the large tires a moment, sure my breath was coming out so fast and hard that it could be heard for miles. Then I slowly stretched upward, just enough to peek over the sill into Tyler's makeshift office.

Where Alec Post was crouched down next to the locked cupboard.

He had a screwdriver in hand, seemingly having come prepared, and was digging at the lock with it. I bit my lip, my heart rate kicking up a notch as I watched, waiting to see what he came away with. The anticipation coupled with the fear of being caught spying on the would-be burglar caused a fluttering sensation in my belly.

I was so focused on the scene in front of me that I almost didn't even hear the sound.

Footsteps on dry leaves. Behind me.

Moving closer.

I was slow to register them, and by the time I did, I moved to spin around and see who was spying on me spying.

But I was too late.

Before I could catch even a glimpse of the intruder, a dark object came hurtling toward my vision.

And then nothing.

CHAPTER SEVENTEEN

———

My eyes were closed, my body still, and my head hurt like an elephant was sitting on it. I felt something hard and cold beneath it. I tried to shift to the right, to a more comfortable position, but the pain exploded at my temple as the previous night's goose egg scraped against the hard surface. I shifted left instead, but had much the same result as I realized I had a new injury on the other side. Then I decided it best to stop moving at all. Instead, I lay in the stillness, and listened, waiting for the roaring pain to subside.

I could hear voices from somewhere far off—lots of them. The faint sounds of music wafted toward me as well, a soft, jazzy song.

The festival.

I blinked my eyes open slowly, each flutter of my lashes causing me effort. I was somewhere dark, and it took me a few second for my eyes to adjust to it. But when they did, I realized I knew exactly where I was, the dark rafters of The Cave's ceiling coming into focus above me. How I had gotten here with a heck of a headache, I still wasn't sure. My brain felt fuzzy, like it was thinking through molasses.

I lay there, listening to the far off sounds of the festival for a few seconds, trying to get my bearings. Two larger oak barrels sat to my right, which meant the door to the cellar was on the other side of them. I took a couple of deep breaths, trying to break through the fog in my head, and attempted to sit up.

That's when I realized I was not only on the cold stone floor, but my hands were also bound.

I wiggled my arms, and something tight and plastic bit into my wrists behind my back. Panic bloomed in my chest as I wiggled my legs and found much the same situation—both ankles bound tightly together. I rolled over onto my right side, ignoring the pain in my cheek as the bruise hit the floor, and looked down, my feet coming into focus. Somewhere along my journey I'd lost my sandals and acquired a zip tie that held my ankles together. I could see my skin turning white at the edges of the tie where it bit into my flesh.

That panic turned into a full-fledged attack.

Playing inchworm, I managed to wriggle myself into a seated position with the aid of the stone wall beside me. The room spun with the added elevation of a couple feet, and I leaned back against the cool stones, taking deep breaths in an attempt to get it to stand still, and tried to remember how I'd gotten here.

Alec.

I'd been watching him break into Tyler's trailer. Had Alec put me here? I strained to conjure up the memory. He couldn't have. He'd been inside the trailer. I'd been watching him try to open the locked cupboard. And someone had hit me.

An accomplice? Gabby? Mark Black, having been pushed just one question too far? I had no idea. I also had no idea how long I'd been in the cellar. Minutes? Hours? I seemed to be alone, no other signs of life making sounds in The Cave.

But that didn't mean my attacker wouldn't be back.

"Help!" I tried to call out.

Tried, because my throat was so dry that I could barely cough out a whisper.

I licked my lips, swallowed, and tried again.

"Help?" This time I was able to eke out a noise, but it sounded weak and useless even to my own ears. "Help! Help me!" I said again, fighting through the pounding in my head at each word.

Even as I ramped up to shouting levels, I knew it was futile. The Cave was built to be temperature controlled and weather tight. Which also meant it was virtually soundproof as well. Even if anyone happened by the cellar at that moment, they'd be unlikely to hear much of anything that wasn't drowned out by the music and merrymaking of the festival.

I felt hot tears of desperation behind my eyes. With the bar well stocked and the festival winding down, it was unlikely anyone would come down here for hours.

I glanced around for something I could use to cut the zip ties, but all that stared back at me were the hulking barrels on one side and the cases of wine bottles back in the shadows.

A wine bottle.

I inchwormed along the floor toward the cases, making slow but steady progress. I felt my breath coming hard from the exertion of moving without the aid of limbs, but I kept going until I got close enough to one to turn around and feel with my hands behind me for the neck of a bottle. It took a few tries, but I finally connected with one, pulling it from its protective shelter. I said a silent prayer this worked and tossed it to the ground as hard as I could.

Which, in a seated position, wasn't nearly hard enough to break it. It kind of bounced off the stones with a thud and rolled a few feet away.

I stifled the whimper that rose in my throat and tried the whole process again, grabbing behind me for another bottle from the case. I tried not to think about what sort of creepy crawling bugs I might be disturbing down here as I felt my fingers connect with another smooth bottle again. I found the neck, and this time instead of tossing it down right away, I awkwardly pulled my knees up, leaning against the wall with my shoulders to help support me as I tried to stand.

It took a couple of failed attempts, but I was finally able to get my bound feet up under me and stood upright. Which caused the room to wobble again, but I fought through it, taking a deep breath and throwing the bottle down on the stone floor.

Where, luckily, this time I heard it shatter. I let out a sigh, feeling triumphant, as I crouched back down and gingerly searched for a jagged piece of glass.

A nearly impossible task without cutting oneself. Which, I promptly did, wincing at the sting, but it was nothing compared to what my imagination was conjuring up for when whoever had put me here returned.

I held the glass in my hand, ignoring the way it bit into my palm, and maneuvered my hands so that the jagged edge was touching the zip tie. Only a touch was all I could manage. Actual movement was pretty nearly impossible. I leaned against the wall again, trying to use the gap between the stones to hold the glass and create some leverage.

I heard a tiny scrape of the glass on the plastic and said a silent thank-you.

I'm not sure how long I sat there, wiggling up and down in minuscule movements, chipping away at my bonds one tiny millimeter at a time. Honestly, I had no idea if it was even working or not, as I couldn't see behind me to gauge for progress, but I could feel the bite against my wrists lessening.

Or maybe my hands were just going numb.

I was just about to decide this whole thing was a waste of time, when I heard a sound.

The cellar door opening.

I froze, fear washing over me as a physical wave of nausea. Light erupted in the room as the intruder flipped on the switch, the sudden onslaught blinding me for a second. Footsteps echoed off the walls as the person moved across the room.

My fingers involuntarily tightened around the small piece of glass in my right hand, holding on to it as the last shard of hope I had as I listened to the footsteps stop just on the other side of the oak barrel.

"I see you're awake, Emmy," a voice said.

My mental hamster stopped in his tracks on his wheel as I realized I recognized that voice.

I also recognized the person it belonged to as she stepped from the shadows, a small black gun in her left hand.

"Ashley Daniels," I breathed out.

She arched one dark eyebrow at me. "What? You didn't expect to see me so soon?"

I hadn't expected to see her at all, and the confusion at doing so must have been clear on my face as she threw her head back and laughed.

"And here I thought you'd put it all together by now, Nancy Drew."

All? Not by a long shot. But one thing seemed clear as I stared at the gun in her hand. "You killed Tyler."

The smile on her face faded, and her eyes went flat. "Best thing I ever did for our relationship."

I licked my lips. The admission being said out loud made this all seem way too real. "The alibi you gave me earlier for Mark. It wasn't really for Mark at all, was it?"

She shook her head, earrings swaying from side to side, catching the light.

"It was for you," I concluded.

Ashley shrugged. "I had a feeling Mark wasn't going to dispute it if it helped him. And it sure as heck helped me." She smiled widely again, but I noticed this one never made it to her eyes, which remained dark, flat, and emotionless.

She took a step forward, moving the gun that much closer to me.

I swallowed, my throat suddenly drier than the best Sauvignon Blanc. "Wh-why?" I croaked out.

"Why?" Ashley parroted in a mocking tone. "You want to know *why* I killed Tyler?"

I nodded.

"Well, haven't you figured it out yet, you nosey little thing?"

Trust me, considering my current state, I really wished I had figured it out earlier.

Ashley put a hand on her hip, her bracelets clanking together loudly in the enclosed space. "Money, darling. Isn't it always money?"

"The alimony he paid you?" I asked.

She shrugged. "In part. But I realized that was just the tip of the iceberg."

"How so?" I asked. While part of me was honestly curious, the bigger part of me—the one currently bound and being held at gunpoint—needed to take every opportunity to keep her talking. As soon as I'd seen the gun, I'd started to move that little piece of glass against the zip tie again, in short, tiny movements so as not to attract her attention. And the longer I could keep her talking, the better chance I had of actually breaking through the bonds before she got trigger happy.

"I told you Tyler's lawyer wanted to lower my alimony payments. But did I tell you how low he wanted to go?" Ashley asked.

I shook my head.

"Ten grand. Just ten!"

I'd kill for ten grand a month, but I kept my mouth shut. I had a strict policy never to argue with people holding guns.

"And do you know how much that buffoon was making?" Ashley went on.

I licked my lips. "A hundred grand an episode on *Eat Up*."

Ashley raised an eyebrow my way again and nodded in appreciation. "See, I knew you were doing your homework."

Yeah, if only I'd done it a little better and figured out who had really killed Tyler. You know, before she'd hit me over the head.

Twice.

"But you said your divorce decree was ironclad. You shut down his request," I said, wiggling my jagged little piece of glass behind my back.

"I did!" she yelled. "I'm telling you, I worked hard for that money. I put up with him!" She threw her hands in the air, jangling the bracelets in the echoing chamber again.

"So why kill him now?" I asked. "I mean, you said yourself that you refused to let him lower your alimony. That he had no grounds. And as long as he was alive, at least you'd be getting those payments. Now you're getting nothing."

"Au contraire, my nosey one," she said with a grin. "Now I'm getting it all."

I frowned, not understanding. "Are you saying Tyler willed his estate to you?"

Ashley busted out a hacking laugh again. "Oh, please. He wouldn't put me in his will at gunpoint." She nodded at the weapon in her own hand, clearly enjoying the irony.

"So how did you benefit financially from his death?" I could feel the plastic starting to give a little more. It might be slow, but I was making progress.

"Well how do *you* think, my dear?" she asked, pointing a finger at me. "Now, don't play coy. I could tell from your little exchange with Mark today that you know all about Tyler's self-fulfilling access to the company's funds."

"His embezzling, you mean?"

She pointed to her nose. "There it is."

"Did Tyler tell you?" I asked, thinking back to the way she'd insinuated the pair didn't talk. Then again, she'd also left out the part where she'd killed him, so nothing she said could really be taken at face value now.

But Ashley shook her head. "Tyler didn't have time for the likes of me. Let's face it, I'm much too close to his own age for him to be seen with." She threw her head back and laughed again, though this time there was an edge to it that was bordering on mania.

I wiggled my wrists. I was getting close. I could feel the plastic stretching. Something warm and sticky coated my hands, making them slippery, and it took me a moment to realize it was my own blood. I was clutching the glass so hard it was cutting into me. But I didn't care. I just needed a little more time...

"So how did you find out Tyler had embezzled the money?" I asked. I had to keep her talking.

"Mark told me," she said, grinning as if she felt very clever about that. "He realized Tyler was cooking their books, confronted him, and Tyler told him to stuff it. Typical. His ego was always way bigger than his common sense."

"How so?"

"Well, I mean, how long did he think he could go on stealing like that? He was bound to get caught. And the IRS was not going to look kindly on that sort of thing."

"Mark said he told Tyler to stop."

Ashley nodded. "He did. But Mark was smart enough to know Tyler did whatever Tyler wanted. So, he came to me for advice." She paused and shrugged. "Honestly, I think he might have been digging around for any sort of leverage I could provide against Tyler. You know, some dirty little secret to hold over him to keep him in line."

"Did you give him any?"

Ashley let out a long sigh. "Sadly, I used all the leverage I had years ago. But, if there's one thing I know, it's Tyler."

I could feel I just had the slightest little pieces of plastic still holding the tie together. I tried to pull my arms apart without looking like I was straining. It gave a little but held firm. I tamped down disappointment, continuing to work at it even though I knew I could only stall for so long. "You mean, you knew how Tyler thought?"

"And acted. And where he would keep a nice little cache of stolen funds for his personal use."

Now she had my attention. "Where?" I asked, actually wanting to know this time. "In his trailer?"

"His trailer?" She pulled a frown at me and scoffed. "God, why would you think that? Even Tyler wasn't that stupid."

So much for that theory. I floated another. "Cryptocurrency, then?"

She blinked at me, surprised for a second, then narrowed her eyes. "So you did find it, then. I knew it."

Actually, I hadn't. But I did mentally score one for David Allen. I only hoped I could get out of this situation to tell him one day.

Tears suddenly sprang to the back of my throat, and I quickly shut that line of thinking down. Instead, I focused on the task at hand—or at wrists, as the case may be—slowly sawing away at the last bit of zip tie. "You knew Tyler had a cryptocurrency account," I said, trying to keep her talking.

"Well, I knew he was a whiz at hiding money. Let's say that. I learned that much during my divorce. Swiss bank account—check! Offshore account in the Cayman Islands—check! Shell company—check! He'd managed to squirrel money away in all of them, and I was just fortunate enough that I had a shark of a divorce attorney who found it all."

"So Tyler knew all of those other places to hide his money had already been found. He needed to find a new place to keep his ill-gotten gains," I said, working it out.

She nodded. "Actually, it wasn't even that hard to find it. There are tons of companies out there who have software that follows block chains to track down users associated with any given crypto wallet addresses."

I'll admit, I only understood half of what she'd just said there. "You mean, you hired someone to track down his account?"

"Basically, yes. All I had to give them was an IP address, easy enough to find through his custom domain, and their software did all the rest." She grinned, showing off two rows of perfectly white teeth. "Turns out, Tyler bought quite a lot of those imaginary coins."

"Which you now have access to."

"Look, he was going to get caught embezzling and evading taxes. His assets would have been seized. Which would have meant no more alimony for me. I *earned* that money. It was *mine*. So, I had to get to it first."

"Which meant killing Tyler."

"That was a nice bonus." She shot me the wolfish grin again, and suddenly I had the thought that she'd actually enjoyed killing her ex-husband.

I licked my lips, eyes going to the gun. I knew she wasn't stupid. She wasn't planning to let me leave here alive.

"How did you lure Tyler to the vineyard?" I asked, not really wanting to know the details of the crime but needing to buy time.

"Oh, that part was easy. I just told him I'd reconsidered about having the alimony payments lowered. I wanted to discuss it with him in private. He followed me like a puppy, the stupid fool."

"And Jean Luc?" I asked. "Was he just a stupid fool in your plan too?"

Ashley sighed, showing the first signs of exasperation at my game of twenty questions. "Yes, well, somebody had to take the fall for it, didn't they? I mean, Tyler was a celebrity. It's not like the police could just sweep his murder under the rug."

"But why Jean Luc?"

"Well, it was *his* idea that Tyler come work your little festival. He and Tyler had a long history of altercations. And, I knew Jean Luc certainly didn't have the means to hire a fancy attorney to get him off. He really was quite the perfect scapegoat."

I felt anger rising on his behalf, despite the precarious nature of my situation. "So you framed him."

Ashley simply nodded, as if we were discussing her taste in perfume and not the life of a man who I considered near to family. "It wasn't hard. I mean, everyone knew that Jean Luc owned a gun that he kept under his bed. He used to talk incessantly about how unsafe Los Angeles was compared to gay *Paris*!" she said, using the French pronunciation for effect.

"So it *was* Jean Luc's gun that killed Tyler after all?"

She nodded. "Of course."

"You stole it from Jean Luc's house?"

"That bit was trickier," she admitted. "But I knew when Jean Luc worked for Tyler, he was always particular about how the bar was kept clean."

That sounded like Jean Luc.

"He used to keep his keys and wallet behind a stack of dish towels. I guess he figured no one would dare attempt to clean his bar. Lucky me, he still did. I guess old habits die hard." She grinned. "No pun intended."

"So you grabbed his keys?" I asked, ignoring the pun in poor taste.

"Yes. It would have been a bit easier to be sneaky about it if the tasting room ever had a *crowd* in it."

I tried to ignore the barb.

"But," she continued, "I managed it. I waited until he was busy with another patron at the other end of bar then quickly slipped them into my purse. I finished my drink, drove down to Jean Luc's place where the gun was, predictably, under his bed, and helped myself to it."

"You helped yourself to something else while you were there, too, didn't you?" I asked, the gears turning as everything started to make sense. "A wineglass. With Jean Luc's fingerprints on it."

She gave me that wide, humorless grin again. "See, I knew you were going to figure it out."

"You planted the glass in Tyler's condo?"

She nodded. "Idiot never changed the locks on the place, so I just let myself in and set a neat little stage that looked like two old friends had been having a drink together." She paused. "Or perhaps two old enemies."

"And then you lied to the police about Jean Luc being fired."

She wagged a finger at me. "You almost caught me on that one."

She had no idea how much I wished it hadn't been *almost*.

"Is that why you hit me over the head last night?"

Ashley clucked her tongue at me. "Really, you shouldn't be surprised when such things happen to you. Didn't your mother ever teach you not to stick your nose into other people's business?"

The murderess was pointing out my bad manners. I bit back a snide retort.

"And what about Jean Luc?" I asked, almost afraid to hear the answer. "Where is he now?"

I could have cried in relief when Ashley shrugged. "Haven't the foggiest. Guess he got chicken and ran." She shrugged. "No matter. The police will catch up to him soon enough. They don't look lightly on double murder, you know?"

"Wait—double murder?"

She took a step toward me, pointing the gun ahead of her. "You didn't think I was going to let you live, did you?"

Honestly? No, I hadn't. But a girl could hope.

"The police will never believe Jean Luc would kill me."

"Oh no?" she asked, shaking her head again, those earrings catching the light with each sway. "I'd say desperate men do desperate things. You found Jean Luc hiding out in the wine cellar, there was struggle, and his gun went off."

She took a step forward, pointing said gun out in front of her.

I felt desperation bubble up inside me again and worked my piece of glass back and forth with a fury, attacking the last little bit of plastic. I pulled the bonds taut, feeling plastic dig into my skin.

"You won't get away with this," I said, the phrase lacking conviction even to my own ears.

Ashley's eyes narrowed, her smile grew into a red slash of lipstick across her face, and her voice was low and menacing. "Oh, but I already have."

She put both hands on the gun, leveling it at my head.

Panic surged through every cell in my body, making time stand still. It was now or never.

Clutching the shard of glass in one hand, I pulled with all my might against the zip tie, not caring if she saw me anymore. Almost at once, I heard a soft pop, my arms flew free, and I launched myself forward.

I dove awkwardly with my legs still bound at the ankles, catching her bare arm above the multitude of bracelets with the glass.

Ashley screamed as it dug into her.

The gun went off, and the sound was deafening in the enclosed space as a bullet embedded in the ceiling.

I dropped the glass and grabbed for the gun with both hands. Unfortunately, Ashley still had it in her grip as well, and we fought for it—her teetering on her heels and me barely balancing with my legs stuck together like a mermaid tail. While I was younger, my hands were cut and slippery, and I could feel her starting to win the wrestling match.

Since my head had already taken a heck of beating over the last two days, I decided one more hit was worth it, and I slammed my forehead into hers with as much force as I could muster, giving her a WrestleMania worthy head butt.

She grunted, stumbling backward.

Unfortunately, without her to lean on for balance, I stumbled right with her, practically falling on top of her as we both hit the ground. She went down butt first, grunting as her tailbone connected with hard stone. I was a split second behind her, slamming into her upper body with a force that knocked her flat.

And must have stunned her, as the gun flew out of her grasp, clattering across the stone floor.

Both of us acted in unison, scrambling toward the gun. Luckily since I was on top of her, I had the upper hand. Unluckily, I had no legs to work with, so belly crawling was all I could do, my back half dragging almost uselessly behind me.

"Oh no you don't..." Ashley yelled, and I felt her fingernails dig into my calf as she grabbed at me, trying to pull me away from the gun.

I kicked upward, catching her jaw with the heels of my feet. I heard her teeth slam together and watched her head jerk back. As her grip loosened, I charged forward again.

The gun was still a few feet away, and Ashley regained her senses before I could reach it, again grabbing at my legs. Only this time she flung her entire body weight on them, immobilizing me so all I could do was wriggle in her grasp.

I strained my arms out in front of me, trying desperately to reach the gun first, but it was no use. Ashley had me totally pinned. Then she grabbed at my hair, yanking me backward, and I heard myself cry out in pain, my scalp feeling like it was on fire. I clawed at her hands, trying to break her grip.

"You stupid little thing," she snarled at me as she switched her grip from my hair to my neck, putting one bangled arm around it and pulling so tightly I felt my breath grow shallow. "You really thought you could outwit me? That you could beat me?"

I couldn't see her face, but I heard the maniacal laughter filling The Cave and knew she'd gone so far off the deep end that she was near drowning. She squeezed tighter, and I felt my vision blurring, my lungs gasping for air.

"No one beats me. Not Tyler, not his pretty little groupies, not his slimy lawyer. I always win. I win, you hear me? I win!"

I heard her, but it sounded like it was far away, my hearing going funny, my eyes blurring, everything starting to fade away as oxygen became a scarce commodity in my body. I felt my fingers instinctively clawing at her arm, my control on them slipping away as the fight or flight response took over.

I forced myself to focus through the fog. This was not the way I was going out.

I felt the world closing in as her arm tightened even farther, and I summoned up the last bit of clear thought I could. I made my hands leave her arm and feel on the floor beside me for anything I could use as a weapon. Any lingering shard of glass, any loose stones, anything that would help bring back the flow of air to my lungs.

Just as the room was fading to a dark nothing, my fingers connected with a smooth round object.

A wine bottle. The one that had rolled away from me.

I strained to reach it, feeling it wiggle back and forth in response to my fingers clumsily grasping for it.

"I win! I win! I win!" Ashley was still shouting, yelling like some unhinged cartoon villain.

My fingers finally got a useful grip, and I pulled the bottle toward me. I wrapped my hand around the neck. I said a silent prayer.

And I swung.

"I win! I win! I wi—"

She stopped mid-word as I wielded the bottle backward like a club, connecting with her head with a sickening crack.

Her arms went slack, and I fell forward, gulping in great breaths of sweet, amazing air. Then I scrambled away on my knees, putting some distance between us, before I dared look back at her.

Ashley was slumped on the floor, eyes closed, body limp, and a large red welt in the center of her forehead next to my broken wine bottle.

CHAPTER EIGHTEEN

———

The next few hours were a total blur. I managed to hop to the cellar door and vaguely remembered yelling, screaming, and generally making such a ruckus that Conchita came running from the kitchen to see what was the matter. I'd never forget her face when she saw me, the color draining out in a way that I almost felt bad for soliciting her help. She'd rushed at me, enveloping me in a motherly hug that had all but reduced me to tears. After that, movements blurred. I know someone called 9-1-1, Hector went to the cellar to make sure Ashley stayed put until authorities could arrive, and Ava and Eddie appeared, the pair along with Conchita practically smothering me with attention and affection until EMTs arrived.

Which didn't take long, as a virtual caravan of emergency vehicles descended upon the winery in a symphony of sirens and flashing lights. Uniformed police officers corralled the remaining few festival guests and the jazz band into the tasting room as witnesses, others made for The Cave, and a few hovered near me in the kitchen, waiting for the medical clearance to hound me for a statement. While I'd clearly had better days, the EMTs decided I'd live—which was a relief, considering how close to not living I'd just been—as they dressed the cuts on my hands and told me to ice the lump on my head, take Motrin for the pain, and stay out of trouble in the future. I took all three pieces of advice to heart, hoping to especially stick to the last one.

I was just recounting my ordeal for the second time to a female uniformed officer who had a distinctly sympathetic manner for a member of law enforcement, clucking and shaking her head every few minutes, when a familiar face caught my attention among the crowd.

He was about an hour past a good five o'clock shadow, broad shoulders tense, muscular frame vibrating with energy as he took in the scene. His eyes scanned the room before finding mine and locking on. Then in a second he was by my side, pulling me up from the chair I'd been shakily seated in and crushing me to him in a warm, strong embrace that I never wanted to end.

"You've got to quit scaring me like that," Grant murmured into my hair.

I nodded, my face pressed against his chest.

"What happened?" he asked, finally pulling me back just enough to see my face. His eyebrows drew down in concern as he took in the new bump and the bruises I felt forming around my neck. I'd yet to see a mirror, but if the way I felt was any indication of how I looked, I imagined it wasn't pretty. Like, *just went six rounds with the champ* not pretty.

I licked my lips, drawing in a deep breath to collect my thoughts and recount the whole thing again. "It was Ashley," I said.

Grant nodded. "I know."

"Wait, you know?" I asked.

"Well, I do *now*." He shot me a wry grin. "Came over the radio on my way here."

"Oh." I let out a long breath. "She attacked me and tied me up in The Cave."

Grant's jaw clenched, but he said nothing, waiting for me to go on.

Which I did, giving him the entire rundown of events, including Ashley's full confession. His stony cop face was in place the entire time, and when I was finished, he just shook his head.

"You could have been killed," he finally said, his voice low, barely more than a whisper.

"Hello, Captain Obvious." I gave him a grin, trying to make light of the whole thing. Truth was, it would take me a while to actually *feel* light about it, but just smiling helped a bit.

He answered it with a small lift to the corner of his mouth. "You're a tough cookie, aren't you, Oak?"

I swallowed, not wanting to admit even to myself how close to crumbling that cookie had been.

Luckily, Grant cleared his throat, changing the subject. "I was actually already on my way here when I got the call."

"You were?"

He nodded. "I wanted to let you know we picked up Jean Luc about an hour ago."

I sucked in a breath. "Is he okay?"

"He's fine. Shaken up by everything, but fine."

"Where was he?"

"A motel in Fremont," Grant answered. "He said when his fingerprints were found in Tyler's place, he panicked. He thought the police were trying to frame him by planting evidence. So, he ran."

"But you found him."

He nodded again. "Truth is, it's pretty hard to actually disappear. An ATM camera got a hit with facial recognition a few blocks from his place last night."

"So much for cash keeping you under the radar."

He shrugged. "We probably would have found him sooner if he'd used his credit cards, but in this day and age, any activity is pretty traceable. Luckily, the camera also caught a glimpse of the Uber car he was in, and from there, we had traffic cams follow the vehicle to the motel."

I shook my head. "Remind me never to try to hide from you."

That corner of his lips quirked up again. "You wouldn't dare," he said, infusing the phrase with meaning.

I cleared my throat, shaking it off. "How is Jean Luc now?" I asked. "Have the police released him?"

Grant sighed, running a hand through his hair. "No."

"No?" I blinked at him, some of the anger I'd been harboring the past week seeping back in. "What do you mean, no?"

"I mean I never arrested him."

"B-but you had a warrant," I said, confusion replacing anger. In my defense, I'd had two near concussions in a row, so I was allowed to be a bit slow on the uptake.

"I did have a warrant. And I should have executed it."

"But you didn't," I said, finishing for him. I tried to read the golden flecks slowly dancing near his irises now, but they were giving nothing away.

He shook his head. "I just couldn't."

I felt a genuine smile take hold of my features, the grin unstoppable even if I'd wanted to try. "Thank you," I told him simply.

He gave me a slow nod. I knew if he'd really thought Jean Luc was a killer, he'd have done his job. But the fact that he'd trusted me, had had faith enough in my judgment to hold off, meant a lot. More than I could properly articulate in that moment.

Luckily, Grant was a man of few words himself, and the warmth in his eyes as he stared down at me radiated with a mutual understanding.

"Grant!" A uniformed officer hailed him from the door.

He turned, giving the officer the universal one-finger wait sign.

"You going to be okay?" he asked me.

I nodded. "Between Ava, Conchita, and Eddie, I'll be lucky to have a second to myself."

He grinned. "Good. I'll call you later, then."

And with that, he turned and joined the hordes of law enforcement that seemed to have taken over Oak Valley Vineyards.

* * *

"There's one thing I don't understand," Eddie said two days later as we gathered around the large wooden table on the back terrace, enjoying a family style dinner of spicy pesto fettuccini as the sun sank into the vine covered hills on the horizon. "Why did Ashley attack you the first time?"

"I think she was scared," I answered, twirling a strand of pasta around my fork. "She knew I'd caught her lying to the police about Tyler having fired Jean Luc."

"So that wasn't a mistake?" Eddie asked.

I shook my head. "No, she'd deliberately been trying to make Jean Luc look guilty. Then after Ava and I," I went on, nodding toward my partner in crime who sat to my right, sipping Pinot Blanc, "visited Mark Black and told him we knew about the embezzling, the first thing he did was call Ashley. Turns out the two were closer than she'd let on, their mutual issues with Tyler making them confidants of a sort."

I'd learned as much from Mark Black when he'd shown up at the winery the day after Ashley's arrest. He said as soon as he'd seen it in the news, all the pieces had fallen into place, and he'd come to apologize for inadvertently keeping Ashley appraised of all my findings, painting a big red target on my back. He said he should have disputed the false alibi she'd given him, but at the time he'd honestly thought the two were just looking out for each other, trying to keep Tyler's secrets under wraps to avoid a financial hit after his death. Only Mark hadn't had a clue that Ashley had her sights set on Tyler's embezzled money. In fact, Mark had honestly thought Tyler had spent it all already.

He'd been more than surprised when, using the credentials the police had found on Ashley Daniels, he'd cashed out of cryptocurrency with enough profits on the transaction to pay for the IRS penalties for owing the back taxes from Tyler's falsely reported expenses. It looked like Tyler's Place would keep its doors open after all. Though, whether it stayed Tyler's Place or became Mark's Place remained to be seen. Either way, Mark had felt so bad about the entire thing that he'd agreed to stock Oak Valley's wines in not only the Sonoma restaurant but all four locations. Those orders alone took our little festival from disaster to profitable. With enough left over than I might even be able to get my oven fixed.

"So Ashley was blowing smoke when she pointed you in Gabby's direction, then," my third dinner guest, David Allen, added, leaning back on his wooden chair. He had one arm splayed across the back of Ava's chair in a casual pose as he swirled the contents of his wineglass in the other hand.

"Mostly," I said, lifting my fork to my mouth. I waited until I'd swallowed the bite before continuing. "I mean, Gabby and Tyler *had* been having an affair. And it *had* ended badly. How much of that Ashley had really known or guessed at, I'm not sure."

"So she's not telling the police much, huh?" Ava asked.

I shook my head. As chatty as she'd been in the cellar when she'd thought I was going to end up six feet under, she'd clammed up the second the police had taken her into custody, refusing to speak to anyone other than her lawyer. At least according to Bradley Wu, who had done a full series of articles on the "Victim in the Vineyard" over the last few days.

True to my word, I'd given the reporter the exclusive interview I'd promised when he'd called me bright and early the following morning. He'd been practically giddy to get what he called the only firsthand account of the confession from the "perilously potential second victim of the crazed critic." I'd just been happy the winery had been painted in a positive light for once…not just the place where a man had been killed, but a place where a killer had been brought to justice. At least by Bradley Wu's column in the *Sonoma Index-Tribune*.

Needless to say, there would be no glowing review of the Sonoma Fall Food and Wine Festival printed in the *LA Times*.

Or the *Sonoma Truth Tellers*, for that matter. Though Ava and I had both felt bad enough about that little white lie that we'd taken Mandy a thank-you gift of a couple bottles of Chardonnay and a silver charm bracelet, letting her know we appreciated her honesty but we'd decided not to print the article after all, feeling it would compromise our sources too much. Whether we came off as believable, I wasn't sure. But at least she'd said the mourners had died down at the restaurant, bringing her work environment back to a normal level of crazy.

"And Jean Luc?" David asked, his eyes roving lazily toward the twinkling fairy lights strung above us. "How is he taking all of this?"

I bit my lip. Honestly, I wasn't sure. I'd invited Jean Luc to join us for dinner that evening, but he'd declined, saying he wasn't quite up to socializing yet. I'd be hard pressed to say if it was more about the embarrassment of having been caught on the run or the betrayal he'd felt from Ashley Daniels singling him out as her scapegoat for murder.

"Oh, Jean Luc's back to his old self," Eddie answered for me. "Yesterday I left a cork foil on the bar, and he about bit my head off over the 'unsanitary conditions.' I mean, it wasn't like I licked it or anything!"

I swallowed a smirk as Eddie shook his head, forking pasta into his mouth with gusto.

"Did he ever tell you what he and Tyler had argued about in the first place?" Ava asked.

I nodded. "I did finally drag it out of him."

The day after Ashley had been arrested, I'd given Bradley my interview over the phone, indulged in a big pancake breakfast—courtesy of Conchita—and then taken a care basket of her famous Mexican Chocolate scones to Jean Luc's place. He'd been grateful enough at the offer of friendship—not only in the form of baked goods, but also the fact I'd been one person he could count on to believe in his innocence throughout—that he'd broken down and told me everything.

"Apparently when Tyler was drinking in the tasting room after the demo, he called Jean Luc a 'wine steward.'"

Eddie gasped in horror.

"Exactly," I said in response. "As we all know, Jean Luc is a *sommelier*."

"Anyone who has ever met Jean Luc knows that. I'm guessing Tyler was trying to get a rise out of him?" Ava said.

"One can assume. Having met Tyler, I think that was a bit of a hobby of his. Anyway, Jean Luc got upset and corrected him, and then Tyler said something about pompous French people—"

Eddie gasped again.

"—and you can imagine how that went over. The whole gist of the argument was Jean Luc defending his national pride."

"Oh, poor Jean Luc," Ava said, laughing into her glass.

"If only he hadn't been too proud to tell the police that in the first place," David pointed out.

I nodded. "I know. But I guess by the time Jean Luc realized the gun was missing and his fingerprints had been planted at Tyler's, he was worried no one would believe him anyway."

"What I want to know," Ava said, leaning forward on her seat so that she was haloed in the pink light glowing from the horizon, "is what was Alec Post after in Tyler's trailer?"

"That," I said, "is actually a sweet story."

David quirked an eyebrow my way. "Oh? Do tell. You know I'm a hopeless romantic."

I rolled my eyes. David might be a bit hopeless sometimes, but romantic was the last word I'd use to describe the brooding artist.

"Well, I guess it turned out that for all his hard edge, Alec Post did have a soft spot—for Gabby. He was breaking into the trailer to steal photos."

Eddie frowned, the look totally foreign on his pudgy round face. "Photos? Of what?"

"Of Tyler and Gabby together!" Ava guessed with gusto.

I raised my wineglass her way. "Correct. Tyler had been planning to leak them to the press as a publicity stunt. Contrary to what Gabby thought, Alec did *not* find out about the affair from me. Tyler had spilled it to him."

"Tyler?" Eddie gasped. "But why?"

"In an effort to get Alec to drop the lawsuit. He'd said he'd essentially sell Alec the photos in exchange for the suit going away. Only Alec had refused, and Tyler had wound up dead."

"But still in possession of the photos," Ava jumped in.

I nodded. "However shady it might have been that he was breaking into the trailer, it had been for a chivalrous cause. He'd intended to find the photos and destroy them to save Gabby's reputation."

"Aww." Eddie's shoulders melted down and his face went dreamy. "He really did love Gabby."

I grinned. Now there was a real hopeless romantic. Some days I was a little envious of Curtis.

"And Alec still does," I told them. "Gabby said they're actually planning to move in together next month." At least, that's what she'd told me when I'd called her the day before to process her payment for her hosting duties. She'd even admitted that some of the tension between her and Alec at the festival had been born of suspicion—Alec had half thought Gabby had killed Tyler to keep the photos from surfacing, and Gabby had suspected Alec had killed Tyler in a fit of anger over Tyler stealing his recipes. They'd both been aware that neither had had alibis, and each one was hiding enough small secrets from the other to look guilty.

Alec had been in the process of retrieving the photos when I'd caught him at the trailer. According to what he'd told Gabby, he'd had no idea I was outside and no idea that apparently Ashley had followed me following him. He'd been fully engrossed in breaking into the locked cupboard. Which he had finally done, pocketing the contents before slipping out the front door and back to the festival, being none the wiser that anything else had transpired behind his back.

Now that everything was out in the open, Gabby said Alec had forgiven her affair with Tyler, and the network was even considering him for the position of Gabby's new co-host for *Eat Up*. Though, of course, Gabby would now be the top billing of the show.

"Well, good for them," Ava said. "They deserve to be happy."

"I give it six months," David said, smirking as he sipped his wine.

"David Allen," I chided. "Don't be such a pessimist."

Ava gave me a raised eyebrow over the rim of her glass. "*You're* calling someone out for being a pessimist?"

"What?" I asked innocently. "I've turned over a new leaf. I'm a born-again optimist."

"Give it time," David told Ava with a wink. "My money says she'll be a latter-day pessimist by the end of the week."

I stuck my tongue out at him but couldn't help a laugh.

In fact, we were all chuckling a little, probably helped along by the fact we'd opened at least three bottles of Pinot that night, when a deep voice sounded at the edge of the patio.

"I, uh, hope I'm not interrupting?"

I swiveled in my seat to find Grant watching our little dinner party. He was in his off-duty look—jeans, casual T-shirt, hands in his pockets. Though, even when he wasn't on the clock, his shoulders never seemed to fully relax, his eyes always assessing, and his posture rigid and ready for anything.

"No," I told him, rising from my seat. "Not at all." I gestured to the empty chair I'd originally reserved for Jean Luc. "Join us?"

But he shook his head. "I don't want to intrude."

I opened my mouth to protest, but he continued with, "I just stopped by for a minute to talk to you, Emmy."

"Oh." I tamped down disappointment that he'd be in such a hurry to leave as I excused myself from the table and led Grant to a spot just around the corner of the building where we had a bit of privacy.

"So, what can I do for you?" I asked.

His mouth turned up into a lazy grin. "Actually, it's what I can do for you."

I swallowed hard, the hidden meaning behind that phrase causing all kinds of ideas to dance through my head.

Or maybe that was just the wine.

"Oh?" I asked. "And what is that?"

"Tyler's trailer," he said.

"Oh, please tell me you found the rightful owner of that monstrosity." I'd spent the last two days since the festival ended staring at Tyler Daniels' larger-than-life face outside the kitchen window. Despite the story Alec had floated me about Gabby taking the thing off the property when he was trying to get the keys, both Gabby and Mark had refused to take ownership, claiming it belonged to Tyler's estate. Whoever that may be. Truth be told, I thought neither of them wanted to see his face ever again—let alone ten feet high.

To my relief, Grant nodded. "Not exactly sure where its permanent home will be, but I got authorization to haul it off your property finally. We'll be sending it to a storage facility while the lawyers straighten out Tyler's estate."

"You are a god."

Grant laughed softly. "You are welcome."

"Though, you know you could have saved yourself a trip and told me that over the phone," I pointed out, sending him a coy smile.

"I could have." He took a step forward, filling the space between us as his voice went low and deep. "But where would the fun have been in that?"

Warmth pooled in my belly at the dark, delicious promise in his eyes. One that he didn't hesitate to make good on, leaning in and gently taking my face in his hands as his lips met mine.

I think the earth might have stood still as he kissed me, my entire body melting into his touch as hormones I didn't even know I had suddenly awoken to attention.

When he finally pulled back, my legs were Jell-O, my heart was beating fast, and my mind was vibrating with fantasies that made my cheeks heat. I fluttered my eyes open to find him grinning at me, the look on his face as dreamy as I felt.

"You know, you still owe me half a date," I told him.

He raised one eyebrow at me. "*Half* a date?"

"Uh-huh. You left early on the first one."

He pursed his lips as he nodded in agreement. "Fair enough. You pick the date and time, and I'll make good on that debt," he said as he turned to go. Though he paused, the gold flecks in his eyes dancing mischievously. "I'll even give you a whole date. With *interest*."

I felt all ten million of my hormones happy dance in unison as he winked at me and walked away. By the wolfish gleam in his eyes, I had a feeling this was going to be one date I did not soon forget.

And I couldn't wait.

RECITES

Easy Mediterranean Chicken

4 (6-8 ounces each) chicken breasts
½ cup olive oil
8 cloves garlic, minced
1 ½ cup fresh basil, chopped
1 jar or can (14.5 ounces) marinated artichoke hearts
1 jar (8 ounces) sundried tomatoes julienne sliced
salt and pepper to taste
¼ teaspoon red pepper flakes
1 cup kalamata olives, chopped
crumbled feta cheese to taste

Make 1 day ahead.
Add chicken breasts, olive oil, garlic, 1 cup basil, artichoke hearts, and sundried tomatoes to a large resealable plastic bag or airtight container. Marinate in the refrigerator overnight.

Preheat oven to 400 degrees.
Place chicken in a baking dish, along with the marinade. Add salt, pepper, red pepper flakes, and olives and bake for 20–25 minutes or until chicken reaches an internal temperature of 165 degrees. Sprinkle top with remaining chopped basil and feta cheese then serve warm.

Makes 4 delicious servings!

Tips!
Cooking in the oven keeps the chicken breasts moist and avoids them drying out, as is common with lean meat. However, if you like a sear on your chicken, place them in a pan of hot olive oil, browning each side for 5–7 minutes before placing in the oven.

Adjust your cooking times down to 35–40 minutes or until the internal temperature of 165 degrees is reached. If it's a sunny day, this is also a great recipe to throw on a grill—like at the Fall Food & Wine Festival demonstration!

Wine Pairings
Best served with lighter reds, like Pinot Noir, or a rich white, like Chardonnay. Some of Emmy's suggestions: Dancing Coyote Pinot Noir, Windy Oaks Terra Narro Estate Pinot Noir, Chateau Ste Michelle Chardonnay Indian Wells

Fettuccini Pomodoro

1 cup "00" flour
1 cup semolina flour
3 large eggs
4 tablespoons olive oil
sea salt
3 cloves garlic, minced
½ yellow onion, chopped
1 can (28 oz) San Marzano tomatoes, peeled
1 tablespoon fresh oregano, chopped
¼ teaspoon red pepper flakes
fresh basil to taste
pepper to taste
grated Parmesan cheese

Mix the flour using a sifter onto a clean work surface or large cutting board. Make a well in the center (using your measuring cup works well!). Add the eggs into the well, along with the 2 Tbsp olive oil and 1 tsp sea salt. Using your fingers, mix the ingredients together until you have smooth, firm dough. If the dough is too dry, add a little water. If it's too wet or sticky, add a little more semolina flour. You will want to mix until you have an elastic consistency.
Wrap the dough in plastic or set in a covered bowl for at least 30 min. to rest.

Once rested, divide the dough into small balls (roughly 6–8), and run each ball through the pasta machine. Then fold the pasta into thirds and run it through the machine again. Continue this process until you reach the desired thickness. (See the Tips for rolling without a machine!) Once you have achieved the desired thickness, run the pasta through the fettuccine cutter. Dredge the pasta lightly in flour to prevent sticking and set aside on a baking sheet or drying rack.

In a large pot, boil roughly 3 quarts of water, well salted. Add pasta and cook just until tender and al dente, about 3–5 minutes.

In the meantime, make the pomodoro sauce by adding 2 Tbsp olive oil to a pan, and over medium heat sauté the onion, garlic, and oregano until onion is translucent. Chop or crush the tomatoes and add to pan, along with red pepper flakes, torn or chopped basil leaves, and salt and pepper to taste. Allow to cook 8–10 minutes.

Drain pasta and add directly to the pomodoro saucepan, mixing well before serving. Add Parmesan cheese and enjoy!

Makes 4 servings!

Tips!
You can substitute all-purpose flour for the "00" flour and still use semolina or substitute all-purpose flour for both! You may just a need to add a bit more oil or water to keep it from getting dry. "00" flour is finer and gives pasta the more silky quality. Semolina flour is a coarser, high-protein flour that helps the dough achieve the elasticity. However, you can still make delicious pasta with all-purpose flour, if that's what is in your cupboard!
Don't have a pasta machine? You can roll the dough out by hand on a floured surface. Try to roll as thin as possible without breaking it. Then cut the dough to desired pasta length and roll it up like a jellyroll. Cut the roll into thin pieces. Unroll each strand and cook as above.

Wine Pairings
Best served with red wines that are aromatic and high enough in acidity to compete with the acidic tomatoes, like a Merlot or Zinfandel. Some of Emmy's suggestions: Zinfandelic Sierra Foothills Old Vine Zinfandel, 7 Deadly Zins, Provenance Vineyards Napa Valley Merlot

Tyler's Place "Turn Up the Heat" Burger
1 ½ lbs lean ground beef
1 lb bacon, cooked and crumbled
½ tsp hot sauce
2 tablespoons onion, finely minced
salt and pepper to taste
¼ cup cream cheese
2 ounces sharp cheddar cheese, shredded
1 fresh jalapeño pepper, diced
2 tablespoons olive oil
4 hamburger buns or rolls

Preheat grill to medium-high heat.
In a small bowl, combine the beef, crumbled bacon, hot sauce, onion, and salt and pepper.
In another bowl combine cream cheese, cheddar cheese, and jalapeno.
Divide the cream cheese mixture into fourths. Ball ¼ of the cream cheese mixture and take ¼ of the beef mixture and wrap the beef around the cheese so that no cheese is showing. Lightly brush the outside of the burger with olive oil. Grill for 5–6 minutes on each side. Serve on toasted buns with your favorite toppings or the spicy sriracha aioli recipe below.

Sriracha Aioli

½ cup mayonnaise
2 tablespoons sriracha hot sauce
1 lime juiced
salt to taste

Whisk together the mayonnaise, sriracha, lime juice, and salt. Best served cold, and keeps well, so can be made well ahead of time.

Tips!
If you like your heat turned all the way up, be liberal with the hot sauce in the burger and keep the jalapeño seeds in. You can garnish with more fresh jalapeño as well! If you prefer just a hint

of heat, seed the jalapeños first and use only half. Go light on the hot sauce or substitute Worcestershire sauce—which packs a lot of flavor but less heat. When handling jalapeños, be sure to wash your hands thoroughly after touching them—fresh jalapeño juice can be very irritating to skin and eyes. If you're not a beef fan, this recipe is also wonderful with ground turkey!

Wine Pairings
Best served with red wines that are low in tannins—as tannins accentuate heat!—like a Pinot Noir, or a crisp citrusy white, like a Pinot Grigio. Some of Emmy's suggestions: Lola Wines Pinot Noir, Bargetto Monterey Pinot Grigio, Santa Margherita Pinot Grigio

Summer Fruit Flambé

3 fresh peaches
½ cup fresh raspberries
½ cup fresh blackberries
2 tablespoons butter
2 tablespoons brown sugar
1 teaspoon cinnamon
¼ cup dark rum
vanilla ice cream (optional)

Slice the fresh peaches into wedges.
In a large saucepan, melt butter and brown sugar over medium
heat. Add peaches and cook just until they start to soften, about 2
minutes. Then add the cinnamon and berries and stir to coat.
Remove from heat and add rum, swirling the pan to make sure it
coats evenly. Ignite the rum, and carefully allow flames to
extinguish themselves as the alcohol burns off, usually in about a
minute. Serve immediately—either on its own or over ice cream!

Tips!
Be sure to remove the pan from the flame before igniting! Using
a barbeque lighter or long stick lighter is best for safety, and be
sure to have a lid handy, just in case the flames get out of control
and you need to extinguish them. Try to let the flames extinguish
themselves, as the fruit will have a strong alcohol flavor if it isn't
all burnt off. If you're not an ice cream fan, this is also a great
topping for pound cake or shortcake!

Wine Pairings
Best served with slightly sweet wines with mild acidity that
aren't too sweet to overpower the dessert, like a Moscato or
Riesling. Some of Emmy's suggestions: Brooks Ara Riesling,
Willamette Valley Vineyards Riesling, Bellafina Pink Moscato

Caprese Panzanella Salad

3 cups crusty or stale bread, cubed
½ cup melted butter
3 large heirloom tomatoes (varying colors)
1 cup grape or cherry tomatoes
8 ounces fresh mozzarella in small balls or cut into small pieces
1 cup of basil leaves
¼ cup olive oil
¼ cup balsamic vinegar
1 clove garlic, finely minced
½ teaspoon dried oregano
salt and pepper to taste

Preheat oven to 400 degrees.
Put the bread cubes on a baking sheet and drizzle the melted butter over them. Mix well to coat the bread then arrange in a single layer. Bake in the oven for 10 minutes, flipping over halfway through, and let cool.
Chop the tomatoes into bite-sized pieces and add to a large salad bowl. Tear or chop the basil leaves and add those to the bowl along with the mozzarella. Add cooled breadcrumbs to the bowl. In a small bowl whisk together the olive oil, vinegar, garlic, oregano, and salt and pepper. Pour the vinaigrette over the salad in the large bowl and toss to coat. Let it sit for a few minutes so the bread can absorb the liquid, roughly 15–20 minutes.

Serves 4 hungry guests.

Shortcuts!
You can buy croutons premade or skip the oven step by using more stale or crustier bread—3-day-old baguettes are perfect! If you're in a hurry, you can also buy a balsamic vinaigrette dressing premade. Newman's Own Lite Balsamic Dressing is a very good quick substitute.

Wine Pairings

Best served with crisp, fruity white wines, like a Pinot Grigio or a Sauvignon Blanc. Some of Emmy's suggestions: Michael David Winery Sauvignon Blanc, Heitz Cellar Sauvignon Blanc, Ecco Domani Pinot Grigio

Champagne Mule

6 mint leaves
2 ounces lime juice
2 ounces vodka
4 ounces ginger ale
4 ounces champagne
lime wedges

Muddle together the mint leaves and lime juice. Mix in the
vodka then strain evenly amounts into two champagne glasses.
Add into each glass 2 ounces of ginger ale and roughly 2 ounces
of champagne to top off the glass. Garnish each with a mint leaf
and lime wedge.

ABOUT THE AUTHOR

Gemma Halliday is the #1 Amazon, *New York Times & USA Today* bestselling author of several mystery and suspense series. Gemma's books have received numerous awards, including a Golden Heart, two National Reader's Choice awards, a RONE Award for best mystery, and three RITA nominations. She currently lives in the San Francisco Bay Area with her large, loud, and loving family.

To learn more about Gemma, visit her online at
www.GemmaHalliday.com

The Wine & Dine Mysteries

www.GemmaHalliday.com

Made in the USA
Middletown, DE
30 January 2021